What People Are Saying
About *Come to Me*

"I believe this book should be in the home of every Christian, and they should share it with as many non-Christians as possible. It speaks to us in places in our hearts we may have forgotten about. It speaks to us of a Jesus who was real, a mother who loved Him more than His disciples could know, and how we, who have become His children, are His living legacy. I love this book."

—DAVID BROLLIER
Author of *The 3rd Covenant*

"At first, I admit I was a bit skeptical, because biblically-based historical fiction is one of my favorite genres to read and I've read so many versions of Christ's story as told by other authors. Then, there is Laura Davis. She wrote about the life of Christ through Mary's eyes, and it was simply amazing! When I finished it, I couldn't help but think to myself, 'This book would be such a great witnessing tool. If I knew someone who was lost, I would just hand them this book.' There is so much Scripture packed into this book, but it is not preachy. It is just told as a story from Mary's point of view, and as you are reading, it almost feels like you're there.

"I highly recommend this book, and I look forward to reading more from Laura Davis in the future!"

—CHRISTY JANES
Christian Fiction Reviews

"Kudos to this author for creating a compelling and rich account which builds on Biblical truth in a format that is friendly to any reader, while presenting the truth of the Gospel in a clear and enticing narrative without the limitations of the scriptural accounts, which only portray a fraction of the picture."

—MELISSA MEEKS
Bibliophile's Retreat

"*Come to Me* is a skilfully written historical novel that brings to the table many of the events of the life of Jesus from Mary's perspective. From the time I started it, I simply could not put it down. I love the entire book, but the part of the passion of Jesus was gut-wrenching yet inspiring. How much we must matter to the Creator of the universe to endure the brutality of the cross!

"The final days of Jesus' life after his resurrection made me wish I were there to live the glory of the risen Christ. As I read this book, I found myself immersed in the story just as the disciples were a part of Jesus' life. In a sense, I was there through the pages of this book. A must-read if you are a Christian or a seeker."

—GINO SANTA MARIA
Photographer

LAURA J. DAVIS

COME TO ME

Printed in Canada.

Word Alive Press
131 Cordite Road, Winnipeg, MB R3W 1S1
www.wordalivepress.ca

Mixed Sources
Cert no. SW-COC-001271
© 1996 FSC

Library and Archives Canada Cataloguing in Publication

Davis, Laura J., 1958-
    Come to me / Laura J. Davis.

ISBN 978-1-77069-120-9

    1. Mary, Blessed Virgin, Saint--Fiction.
2. Jesus Christ--Fiction. I. Title.

PS8607.A9554C65 2010   C813'.6   C2010-906640-5

FOREWORD

Dear Reader,

This book is the story of the birth, death, and resurrection of our Lord as told by the one who knew him best—his mother. While it is historical in nature, it is also fictional, as I had to use my imagination in certain parts (e.g. Jesus' childhood, conversations not recorded in the Bible, etc.). With some works of fiction, a writer is free to do whatever he or she pleases. However, when it is about the Son of God, that freedom is somewhat limited. Nevertheless, I have taken some liberties where Scripture was not clear about the order of events.

For example, where were Joseph and Mary living when the Magi came—in Nazareth or Bethlehem? The Gospel of Matthew implies it was Bethlehem, and at least two years after Jesus' birth. Yet the Gospel of Luke says that the young couple went home to Nazareth eight days after giving birth to Jesus. I also asked myself the question, did Mary's parents have to go to Bethlehem to register for the census? If Mary's father was from the line of David, we have to assume they had to travel to Bethlehem as well. Scripture does not mention her parents at all in this regard, so I invented a "what-if" scenario. If you are familiar with the Bible at all, you will recognize my "what-if" scenarios throughout the book.

In the grand scheme of things, what is most important is that the Gospel Message remains the same, which I believe it does. I have included scripture references throughout, so that you can verify for yourself the truth behind the fiction. I would encourage you to read not only the Gospel of Luke, but all four Gospels to get an accurate representation of our Lord.

Ultimately, it is my hope that you will have a better grasp of who Jesus was and still is, and that through this book you will draw near to Him as He longs to draw near to you.

In Christ,
—LAURA J. DAVIS

Part One

"Therefore the Lord Himself will give you a sign: The virgin will be with child and will give birth to a son, and will call him Immanuel."

(Isaiah 7:14)

CHAPTER
— 1 —

S he sat outside for over an hour meditating, praying, and remembering. The rising sun wrapped her in a warm cocoon that threatened to lull her back to sleep. Mary arched her back and stretched. She ran her hands over the cream-coloured pillow covering her precious bench and yawned. Joseph had surprised her with the bench the first year they were married. They would often sit together in the early morning hours, when the rest of the world was still asleep and the sun was waking up.

How she longed for those times again, when Joseph would take her hand and they would begin the day in prayer and dedication to Yahweh. *My sweet Joseph, how I long to hear your voice and feel your embrace once more.*

She had known Joseph for most of her life. In a village as small as Nazareth, it would have been unusual if their paths had never crossed. Older than her by twelve years, Joseph had watched Mary grow from a child into a beautiful young woman. With careful planning, he had placed himself in her life with the purpose of marrying her when she came of age. He had called her "Little Mary" and she had called him her "Gentle Giant," names said with an affection that had grown into a deep and lasting love.

"You're such a long way up, Joseph!" she would laugh. "I get a sore neck just looking at you, much less kissing you."

Then one day he had come into the house and said, "Little Mary, I have a surprise for you, but first you must close your eyes!" Mary obeyed and felt Joseph sweep her up in his muscular arms and place her on something soft and luxurious.

"Open your eyes now," Joseph said, his brown eyes twinkling with excitement.

"Oh, Joseph!" For the first time in their marriage, she was able to look straight into his eyes.

"What is this?" She looked at her bare feet and wiggled her toes into the cream-coloured pillow that stretched across a new oak bench. A small gasp of surprise escaped her lips. "It is beautiful." She sighed as she ran her hands along the back of the bench. "Hear O Israel… Oh, Joseph! You have carved the Shema into it. Oh, how precious." She clasped her hands together and turned toward her husband. "You made me a prayer bench." Her almond-shaped eyes shone with delight.

"Ah, well… my motives are not that pure, I am afraid."

She tilted her head. "Oh?"

"Yes, I was thinking we could use it so you wouldn't get a sore neck kissing me." He wrapped his arms around her tiny waist, pulling her close. "Or you could use it for praying." He shrugged and smiled. "Your choice."

4

She laughed and wrapped her arms around his neck. "I think for now I shall use it for kissing you and later I will use it for prayer."

Mary sighed, a sleepy smile lingering on her face. They had dubbed it the kissing bench. They had thought it was something their children would laugh and giggle over in the years to come. *What a wonderful life we made together!*

It was a good marriage, despite its uncertain beginnings. So many events had happened in those early days that Mary could not imagine which memory she cherished most—the angelic visitation, the birth of Jesus, or his resurrection. The enormity of what had transpired in her life had humbled her more than she realized.

Of course, she would never cherish the memories of what they had done to her firstborn son. Forgiving them was easier than forgetting. She could never forget. How long had it been since that horrible day? She could still smell the blood and hear Jesus' screams mingled with her own. Her chest grew tight with grief as she closed her eyes to dispel the images that had haunted her for the last eleven years.

She was fifty-eight years old and until six months ago had been with her nephew, the Apostle John, on a brief visit to Rome to strengthen the churches there. When the Emperor Claudius began expelling Jews from Rome, John had decided that she should return to his home in Jerusalem for her own safety.

"Poor John," she muttered as she recalled the argument she had had with him over returning.

"It's too dangerous for you in Rome now, woman!" He had pleaded with her all day and finally in anger and frustration gathered up her belongings and started stuffing them into a satchel. "As the mother of our Lord and a Jew, your life is in more danger than mine right now. This discussion is over. You will leave without any more arguments."

Mary remembered folding her arms across her chest and swallowing the angry words that had threatened to spill from her lips. No one had ever talked to her in such a manner.

"John, if it is dangerous, why are you staying? Should I, the mother of the Messiah, become a coward and run to save my life when others are dying? It is not right. Your brother James was beheaded for proclaiming Jesus as the Messiah. I should do no less."

"Jesus charged me with your safety, Aunt Mary. Would you have me dishonour my Lord by shirking my responsibilities?"

That was when she had seen the pain and anguish on his weathered face. She had finally understood. He could not bear losing her as he had his brother, and so she submitted to his wishes.

He took her to Jerusalem, stayed for a while to help her adjust, and then returned to Rome to minister to the churches there. She now spent her days with the other believers in Jerusalem, meeting together regularly for prayer and fellowship. Today she was expecting Luke, a Greek physician led to salvation through the Apostle Paul.

As she waited for his arrival, she kicked off her sandals and wiggled her toes. Although it had rained the night before, it was now a beautiful spring day. Mary loved the earthy smell in the air after a rainfall. It was a combination of mud, water, and worms that oddly reminded her of the seaside. Breathing deeply, she leaned her head against the rough stone of John's home, stretched out her bare feet, and plopped them in the nearest puddle.

From the time she was a child, she had often gone barefoot through the hills of Galilee after it rained, for she loved to squish her toes in the mud and feel the cool blades of grass on her feet. In Jerusalem a plot of grass was hard to come by, which made her miss her home in Nazareth all the more. Joseph had always worried that she might cut her feet on the sharp rocks, or sting them on the nettles hidden throughout the Galilean countryside.

She sighed and closed her eyes. *Oh Joseph, my darling, there is no fear of that here.*

"He is risen!"

Startled, Mary shielded her eyes from the sun and looked up to see a blond, blue-eyed man with a clean-shaven face and strong jawline.

"He is risen indeed! You must be Luke. John has told me so much about you. Come to check up on me, have you?" She smiled, grabbed the bowl of olives that sat beside her, and put it on her lap.

Luke chuckled, his dimples showing off his chiselled features. "Actually, I just wanted the chance to meet my Lord's mother—but don't tell John. He thinks I'm here to inquire after your health."

She laughed, her brown eyes sparkling. "You don't fool me—either of you. John sends so many different people to *check* on my welfare that it's a wonder I can remember all their names."

She patted the bench, inviting Luke to sit. Taking some olives from the bowl, Mary proceeded to pit them. Luke watched in fascination at how quickly her slender fingers worked.

"May I help?" he asked.

Raising her eyebrows, Mary stared at Luke for a moment, then nodded and placed the bowl between them. "Jesus used to like pitting olives, too. He said he found it calming." She giggled. "Unfortunately, he ate more than he pitted."

Luke chuckled as he popped an olive into his mouth.

"I'll tell you what I told Jesus," she said, shaking her finger at him. "If you eat more than you pit, then you've just had your supper."

"Well then, I'd best stop eating them, as I'm used to eating more than olives at my meals."

"Get to work then and I might feed you more than olives!"

Content in an affable silence, they settled into their work. Luke immediately felt welcome, as if he had known Mary his whole life, and he told her so. Mary blushed and thanked him.

"Oh, my goodness!" She suddenly jumped up from the bench and ran into the house.

Luke, perplexed at her sudden disappearance, continued pitting olives. He was about to follow her into the house when she returned with a basin of water to wash the dust off his feet. She knelt on the ground and removed his sandals. Embarrassed that the mother of the Lord was washing his feet, Luke swallowed his discomfort and allowed her to minister to him, remembering the lesson Jesus had taught his disciples the last night they had been together.

When she finished, she proceeded to wash her own feet and then put her sandals back on. This led her to tell him about Joseph and his fear of her running barefoot.

"He was such a wonderful man," she said. "He was a man who feared the Almighty, a good man—especially when I found myself with child." She poured the dirty water from the basin onto the ground and then sat beside him. "You cannot begin to imagine what it was like during those days! I was fourteen years old, betrothed to a man much older than I and with child—but not his child."

She grew still and stared off into the distance. Luke gazed at her in silence, revelling in the fact that he was with the woman who had given birth to the Saviour of the world. He wondered how she had handled that night. Where had she been when the labour began? Who had delivered the baby? Had there been any complications? Luke had so many questions, he hardly knew where to begin.

Mary's eyelids dropped as she let her mind wander back to the night of Jesus' birth. She had been surprised at the pain. In fact, she had never realized it would hurt so badly. Afterwards, oh afterwards, the reward of her son was so great that she had thought her heart would split wide open with love. The King of the world had been born to her!

"Happy thoughts?"

Mary's eyes flew open. Blushing, she smiled and said, "His birth—it amazes me still."

"If you don't mind my asking, what was it like back then? When you found out you were … um … with child?"

"It's been forty-four years since Jesus' birth." She shrugged. "Aside from my immediate family, I've never really talked to anyone about it before." Mary sighed and pitted more olives as she contemplated how much she should tell the young doctor.

CHAPTER
— 2 —

L uke was anxious. Mary had been silent since he had asked about Jesus' conception. *How could I have been so bold?* He cast a worried look at Mary and sighed. *True, I have my reasons for coming, but not just to check on her as John requested. I need an accounting of the events leading up to Jesus' death and resurrection.* He chewed absently on his lower lip, his brow furrowed in deep concentration. *If I am to write anything about my Lord, it has to be accurate. I need to know more about Jesus' childhood. Only Mary can give me those details.* He continued pitting olives, all the while trying to determine how best to approach her. *How many times through the years have I wanted to speak to her about her son? Who better to talk about Jesus' life than his mother?* He glanced briefly at her and could see she was still deep in thought. *What about her? How does she feel with so many people clamouring after her for the same thing? People wanting to touch her because she is the mother of Jesus. She is a servant of the Lord, just as I am. She has suffered through persecutions, sorrows, and afflictions like the rest of us—and yet somehow she has endured everything with grace and dignity. She is an example to us all, of godliness and faith. It is a thrill just to be in her presence.*

Luke checked his thoughts. He realized how easy it would be to turn his respect and admiration for Mary into misled adoration and worship. This was the problem with the recent converts in Antioch—especially the women. They wanted to emulate Mary, to follow her example of obedience, faith, and purity of heart. Their intentions were commendable, but what began as imitation quickly escalated to god-like worship. He knew from John that the believers who put her on such a high pedestal distressed Mary and he hoped she would not think he was like that, especially when he made his intentions clear.

They both started speaking at once.

"I'm so sorry..." he stammered.

"It was frightening and... what?"

"I don't want to offend you, Mary. I'm just curious."

"I'm not offended, Luke," she said, patting his arm. "It's time I told someone about those days. I might not remember everything when I get older."

"That was the next thing I was going to ask you."

"What? How old I was?" She placed her hand to her cheek in mock surprise.

"No," he answered, his blue eyes crinkling in delight. "I was wondering if you would mind if I write down what you tell me. I believe it's important to keep a record of what has happened to you, from Jesus' conception, to his death and resurrection and—"

"Of course!" She stood abruptly, almost knocking her bowl of olives off the bench and hurried into the house. Within minutes, she came back outside with a writing tablet.

"I should have thought of that myself." She handed the tablet to Luke, retrieved the bowl of olives, and turned back toward the door. "We will break our fast and you can transcribe my words." She turned at the door, concern on her face. "You will be as accurate as possible—won't you, Luke?"

"Of course!" He breathed a sigh of relief. "I am honoured you would trust me with this task."

Mary smiled, nodded, and walked into the house. This was the right thing to do. She could feel it deep inside her, as if Jesus himself were urging her to talk.

Sometime later, the smell of fresh baked bread wafted through the air, igniting Luke's taste buds. He seated himself on the cushions that lined the carpeted floor surrounding the low table which held a simple meal of fish, bread, fruit, cheese, and olives. As he made himself comfortable, he listened to Mary begin her story with the birth of John the Baptist.

"A voice crying in the wilderness," Luke observed.

"Yes, preparing the way for Jesus, just as the prophets foretold." Mary nodded as she handed Luke a cup of water and then poured one for herself. Luke offered up a prayer of thanksgiving and they began to eat.

"He was a beautiful baby." Mary took the bread, broke off a piece, and handed the rest to Luke. "John, I mean. I was present at his birth, you know."

"You were?" he asked as he reached for some grapes that sat in a bowl in front of him.

"Yes, his mother Elisabeth was my cousin. She was somewhat advanced in age when she discovered she was with child. Her story is united with mine. I think I shall start there, if that's all right with you." Mary took a sip of water and without waiting for Luke's reply, began her story.

———

The stone floor was cold as she rose from her pallet to help her mother prepare the morning meal. Her father would be shearing the sheep today and he needed a hearty meal to sustain him. Her bare feet padded across the bedroom floor to a table which held a pitcher of water and a basin for bathing. She washed her face and then dressed in a gown suitable for her daily chores.

As she brushed her hair, Mary's thoughts turned to her impending nuptials to Joseph ben Jacob. It would not be long before she would wed her beloved, and he would take her to live in the home he had built for her. He had assured her it would be ready in time.

Mary was both excited and afraid of her impending marriage. She was excited because she would have her own home to run and, one day, children to rear, and afraid because she was not ready to be intimate with Joseph.

"Don't fret so, Mary!" her mother Rebekah had scolded after Mary revealed her concerns to her. "Joseph is a good man. He is also very wise and sees your turmoil. He loves you very much, dear one, and you have nothing to fear from him."

"I know, I know. I am foolish to worry when I love Joseph so much. I am very blessed to be marrying a man I love." She thought about her childhood friend Rachel, who had married the previous year to a righteous and devout man named Levi, son of Jonah. Rachel had met him while visiting relatives in Bethlehem. It had been love at first sight, and before the year was out they were betrothed.

Mary remembered how happy Rachel had been, and how scared she was before her wedding. Like Mary, she had no idea what to expect on her wedding night and, unfortunately for Mary, after Rachel wed she would not divulge any secrets that might ease Mary's jitters. Whenever Mary attempted to question her, Rachel's face turned bright red and then she started to giggle. Mary was not sure if her wedding night would be funny, embarrassing, or terrifying. She supposed, like every other maiden in the village, she would have to wait to find out. She determined to trust God to calm her fears, and so she kept her concerns for the Lord of Hosts alone. After a time, the worries about what might happen turned into looking for ways to make Joseph happy.

She was very adept at using a loom and enjoyed it just as much as she loved to cook, and so each day when her chores were finished she made gifts of handmade robes, tunics, or blankets for her beloved. She listened to her mother's instructions on everything from dying cloth to making oil. She also heard numerous words of advice from her relatives on how best to keep her husband happy and her household running smoothly.

Mary was sure that no maiden had ever received so much advice on marriage. She had been helping her mother with the cooking and cleaning ever since she was a young girl. *Does everyone as-*

sume that just because I am betrothed I have suddenly forgotten every-thing I have learned? Do they think that being in love has made me empty-headed?

"Mary! Are you up yet?" her mother called from the kitchen below.

Mary jumped, quickly covered her head with a shawl and de-scended the ladder from her room to the kitchen.

"Good morning, Ima!"[1] she said, giving Rebekah a peck on the cheek.

"Good morning! I was just about to milk the goat. I meant to do it last night but my back was hurting again. My fingers are not doing much better either." She shook her head as Mary clasped her mother's hands and began to massage her gnarled fingers. "Your father said he would do it, but he came to bed rather late and I for-got to ask if he had remembered."

"I'm sorry you are in so much pain, Ima, but Abba was very tired last night," Mary remarked. With mischief in her eyes, she added, "He had a rather long night with Anna."

Rebekah raised her eyebrows. "I beg your pardon? Who is this Anna?"

Mary giggled and replied, "You remember Anna, Ima—she has curly white hair and is very fat."

"Humph! White hair and fat? Who is this woman? I think your father has forgotten himself." Rebekah stood up and walked to-ward the milk bucket, stealing herself from laughing aloud—oh how her girl loved to tease.

---

[1] Hebrew for "Mama" or "Mother."

Mary's eyes twinkled. "Oh no, Ima, she's not a woman. She is one of our sheep. You remember, don't you? She was in labour last night and Abba stayed with her. We now have a beautiful little lamb named Treasure."

Rebekah grabbed Mary's face and kissed her on the cheek. "Such a joker, you are!"

Mary laughed as she snatched the bucket from Rebekah's hands. "I'll run and get the milk, Ima. Don't worry, I'll be quick."

CHAPTER
— 3 —

Mary greeted the animals as she opened the gate to the pen behind their home. The sheep bleated a response and she drew closer to have a look at the new baby.

"How are you doing, Treasure?" She reached a tentative hand toward the new lamb and was greeted with a wet nose. She giggled in delight at the new lamb's curiosity. "You're friendly." She scratched behind his ears and slowly withdrew her hand when his mother grunted her disapproval. "Come now, Anna! It's just me. You know I wouldn't hurt your baby for the world."

A nudge from behind her almost caused Mary to topple forward. When she turned to scold the animal responsible, she was filled with regret.

"Oh, Olive, I'm so sorry we did not milk you last night." She grabbed a stool and a bucket, sat down, and began kneading the swollen udders of the disgruntled goat. "Here I was playing with the new baby and you are about ready to burst." Soon, the steady rhythm of the milk squirting into the bucket soothed both her guilt and the goat's discomfort. As Mary cooed comforting words, she gradually began to feel that she was not alone. "I'm almost finished, Ima. I'll be right in," she said, turning her head slightly.

"Greetings, you who are highly favoured! The Lord is with you."

Mary scrambled off her stool and fell hard on her bottom, almost knocking over the bucket of milk. Her mouth hung open in a silent scream as she stared at the man before her. He had an aura about him that was ethereal. She knew at once that this was no ordinary man but a heavenly being.

He extended his hand toward her and pulled her to her feet.

"Who... who are you?"

"I am the angel Gabriel. Do not be afraid, Mary. You have found favour with God." Gabriel smiled at the young girl before him. He motioned for her to sit on her stool, concern for her evident on his face. Grateful to be off her feet, Mary obeyed, her knees almost buckling beneath her. Minutes passed in silence as Mary tried to process what was happening.

"Why have you come to me?" She lifted her gaze to the angel before her and Gabriel smiled with compassion.

He drew himself up to an enormous height and with a resounding voice announced, "You will be with child and give birth to a son, and you are to give him the name Jesus. He will be great and will be called the Son of the Most High. The Lord God will give him the throne of his father David, and he will reign over the house of Jacob forever. His kingdom will never end."

"How will this be, since I am a virgin?"

"The Holy Spirit will come upon you, and the power of the Most High will overshadow you, so the holy one to be born will be called the Son of God. Even Elisabeth, your relative, is going to have a child in her old age, and she who was said to be barren is in her sixth month. For nothing is impossible with God."

"I am the Lord's servant." Mary bowed her head and folded her hands in her lap. "May it be to me as you have said." Shaky limbs kept her rooted to her stool. When the angel did not say anything else, she dared to look up and discovered he was gone.

For a short time, she sat in stunned silence, unsure if she had been dreaming or if it had been real. *I am to have a child? A holy child of the Most High God?*

"I wonder how it will happen," she muttered as she resumed milking Olive. "What did the angel say, Olive? The power of the Most High would overshadow me. What does that mean? Will I know when it happens? Will it hurt?"

Olive bleated, turned, and nudged Mary with her nose. "I'm sorry, Olive. I will try to be gentle. It's just that I'm a little overwhelmed right now," she explained as she lessened her grip on Olive's udders.

"How will I explain this to Joseph?" She gasped. "Joseph!" She stopped milking and placed her hand on her abdomen. "Do you think he will believe me, Olive? Or will he think I have been unfaithful to him?"

Olive bleated again and began to move away. Mary snatched the full bucket away from the errant goat's hooves and slowly walked back to the house.

Will he think I am crazy if I tell him the truth? she wondered. *What am I to do? How will I explain it to everyone?*

Keeping her virginity was something her parents had taught her was special and important. They had warned her that if she ever lost it before marriage not only could she be stoned, but she could also lose her chance to be used by God.

Therefore the Lord himself will give you a sign: The virgin will be with child and will give birth to a son, and will call him Immanuel. [2]

The scripture all but shouted at her. *Why me? Why am I highly favoured? Does that mean the prophecies are being fulfilled in me this very day?*

"Elisabeth! Gabriel said Elisabeth was with child—in her sixth month. I must see her at once, for surely the Lord has favoured her as well."

"Mary, what took you so long? I was just about to come and find you," her mother said as she took the bucket from her.

"I'm sorry, Ima. I had not meant to take so long, but something happened."

Rebekah poured the milk into a jar and set the bucket down. Concerned, she looked at Mary and noticed she was trembling. She guided her to a chair. "Sit down, child, and tell me what has happened to you." Rebekah sat in a chair across from her daughter.

"I don't know where to start. I… I'm not sure if you will believe me."

---

[2] Isaiah 7:14.

"Mary, you have never caused me grief. You have always been faithful to God and to us. I have never known you to lie. Therefore, I would have no reason not to believe you. Now come... tell me, Dear One... what has happened?" Rebekah grasped Mary's hands and, feeling they were cold, began to rub them. The concern and love in her mother's eyes gave Mary the courage she needed.

"Is father up yet?" she whispered.

"Does he need to be?"

"I'm not sure."

Rebekah felt the hairs rise on her neck. A growing concern centered itself in the pit of her stomach.

"Mary, just tell me and then I will decide if it is something for your father's ears."

Mary nodded and told her mother everything. Rebekah tried to keep her face from showing any emotion as she listened to her daughter's tale. Her main thought was that Mary had become emotionally unstable due to her anxieties over her impending wedding to Joseph. She knew that Mary had been afraid of the marriage bed, but she did not think she would go to such lengths to avoid it.

However, as Rebekah listened, her heart quickened. Hope stirred within her, making her think that Mary's incredible tale might have actually happened. *Did Mary have a dream, a vision, or an actual encounter with an angel? My daughter is to be the chosen one? No! Such foolishness! It is every Jewish mother's dream, to be sure, but not Mary, not in this day and age.*

Rebekah's mind swam with the possibilities. If ever there was a time the world needed a Messiah, it was now. She shook her head and snapped out of her reverie, focusing on what Mary was saying.

"…and was now six months with child," Mary said, finishing her story.

"Who is?"

"Cousin Elisabeth. Didn't you hear me, Ima? Gabriel said she was even now in her sixth month."

"Elisabeth? That is impossible. Elisabeth is very old, Mary." Rebekah shook her head. "No… she cannot be with child."

"But she is, Ima," Mary insisted. "The angel said so."

Rebekah stood and began to gather food for breakfast. She had to think and keep herself busy while she reasoned this through. *Is this really happening? Is Mary well?* She glanced at her daughter and wondered if she should call for a priest. She tried to determine what to do as she poured some oil in a pan. As she considered the consequences of Mary's story, she grew more agitated and before she realized what she was doing she began to refry flat-cakes she had already made. She rolled her eyes in frustration then wiped away the beads of sweat that had begun to form along her hairline. Removing the frying pan from the fire, she then turned and faced her daughter.

"I don't know what to think, but I do know one thing—your father will not understand. He will think Joseph has had his way with you and he will be furious."

"Joseph has not touched me, nor has any man." Mary's face turned red with indignation. "You know how frightened I have been." She looked up at her mother with tears in her eyes. "Don't you believe me?"

Rebekah sighed. "I want to… and yet… I am hoping you are mistaken somehow."

Mary frowned. "Mistaken? No, it was real. How can I prove it to you?"

"I suppose we'll just have to wait and see, won't we?" Rebekah moved closer to Mary and placed a comforting hand on her shoulder.

"You will have to wait, Ima. I already know." Mary leaned over and placed her head in her hands while Rebekah rubbed her back. "I only wish there was some way I could make you believe also." Mary heaved a sigh. "It's too bad Elisabeth is not nearby. If you saw her, you would have no doubts about what has happened to me. For if she is with child, then I did see an angel. How else could I know such a thing?"

Rebekah's eyes widened at the realization of what Mary had said. "That's it, Mary! You will go see Elisabeth and find out how she is. She is old and she will need help if she is with child, as you say." Rebekah paced the floor as a plan formed in her mind. "You can stay until she gives birth, so by the time you return you will be about three months with child yourself—if what you say is true. If Elisabeth is expecting, you have nothing to fear from your father, as he will accept everything you have said as a sign from God. However, if she is not with child, and you are … " She swallowed hard as fear for her daughter overwhelmed her. "Then you must never return."

CHAPTER
— 4 —

Luke ate some fish and took a sip of water. From time to time, he had interrupted Mary to clarify points, but for the most part he had eaten his breakfast with one hand and written with the other.

After their meal, the servants cleared away the dishes and brought fresh fruit and fig cakes. It was at times like these when Mary was grateful John had insisted that she have servants. She had always loved to cook and through the years had never needed assistance. As she aged, however, she found the extra help a blessing.

"How did your father react when he heard the news?" Luke asked as he bit into a chewy fig cake.

"The news about me or Elisabeth?"

"Both."

"Actually, my mother did not tell my father about me until sometime after I left."

Luke frowned. "She deceived him? But what was her excuse? How did she explain your reasons for leaving?"

"Oh, please don't misunderstand. She did not deceive him, not really. She just felt it would be better to let me leave without upsetting him with the news that I might be expecting. She told my father that I had a vision of Elisabeth being with child. It wasn't until I was well on my way that she revealed the rest of my 'vision,' as she called it. Her only deception, if indeed there was a deception, was in not telling my father about the angel. Since she did not believe it herself, she refused to admit I had actually seen one." Mary shrugged. "Elisabeth was my mother's dearest cousin. She was anxious for her and that is what she told my father."

"But why send you alone?" Luke asked. "Why wouldn't she go with you?"

"Well, that's simple. My mother had suffered back pain for many years. It would have been too long a journey for her to make. Elisabeth lived in the hill country of Judea, way past Jerusalem, and we were in Galilee. Therefore, my father did not think it strange that my mother would send me alone. Concerned for my safety, he arranged for me to travel with friends who were also going to Judea. Actually, it was remarkable how everything worked out. God had definitely planned that journey for me." She shook her head and sighed. "A difficult time, to be sure, and one which, when I think about it, prepared me for another journey I would have to make with Joseph." Mary thought to herself for a few minutes on the events that followed. "It took a long time to get there. I remember traveling on foot most days and sometimes on the back of a donkey when I got too tired."

"What did you think you would find when you arrived?"

25

"I had no doubt that I would find Elisabeth with child, if that's what you mean."

"And what did you tell Joseph?"

"I told him my mother was sending me to see her cousin, as she was with child and needed help. Naturally, he was worried that I would be so far away and I would be gone for some time, but he did not question why I was going. He trusted me."

Luke nodded and took another fig cake from the plate before him. Mary reached for one as well and nibbled on it, giving Luke time to write. As he did, she thought about what she would tell him next.

———

It was a tragedy and a miracle at the same time. Six months ago, he had lost the ability to speak. Six months ago, she, a woman well advanced in years, had conceived a child. Elisabeth closed her eyes as she remembered the day Zechariah had come home from serving at the temple in Jerusalem. She had been so happy to see him, as he had been gone six weeks. Her happiness soon vanished, however, when she realized Zechariah could no longer talk. Through hand gestures and using a writing tablet, she began to understand that he had seen a vision while he was serving in the temple. Unable to speak, he had completed his time of service and returned home.

After trying to explain to her what had happened, he wanted nothing more than to hold her in his arms. She had been surprised at that, as it had been some time since they had come together as man and wife. But oh, what a blessing it had been. She smiled as she remembered the day she discovered she was no longer barren. The Lord had finally bestowed His favour on her.

"The Lord has done this for me," she had said. "He has shown his favour to me and taken away my disgrace among the people."

How blessed she was to finally have the privilege of motherhood. No longer did her neighbours look at her with pity. How surprised they were when, after being in seclusion for five months, she had made her first public appearance. The looks of astonishment. The gasps of surprise. Then her dear friends had all rushed to her at once and showered her with glad tidings.

She suppressed a giggle. Never in her life had she felt so happy, and may the good Lord forgive her, she was swollen not only with child, but also with pride. Which is why, lately, she had begun to worry. She was six months along and had still not felt her baby move. *Surely, it should have moved by now,* she thought. She knew in her heart that God had special plans for this little one. Zechariah's experience in the temple had confirmed that for her. *I am being silly! God would not punish me for my pride by taking my little one away from me. He is an understanding God and a forgiving one. He knows my pride comes only from being so happy that He has blessed me. What a foolish thought to have.*

Zechariah tossed and turned in his sleep as the memory of his vision in the temple played itself out in his head. He remembered being chosen by lot, according to the custom of the priesthood, to go into the temple of the Lord and burn incense. When the time for the burning of incense came, all the assembled worshipers were praying outside.

Then an angel of the Lord had appeared to him, standing at the right side of the altar of incense. When Zechariah saw him, he was startled and had backed away in fear. But the angel had said to him, "Do not be afraid, Zechariah. Your prayer has been heard. Your wife Elisabeth will bear you a son, and you are to give him the name John. He will be a joy and delight to you, and many will rejoice because of his birth, for he will be great in the sight of the Lord. He is never to take wine or other fermented drink, and he will be filled with the Holy Spirit even from birth. Many of the people of Israel will he bring back to the Lord their God. And he will go on before the Lord, in the spirit and power of Elijah, to turn the hearts of the fathers to their children and the disobedient to the wisdom of the righteous—to make ready a people prepared for the Lord."

Zechariah had asked the angel, "How can I be sure of this? I am an old man and my wife is well along in years."

The angel had answered in a voice that shook Zechariah to his core. "I am Gabriel," the angel had said with fire in his eyes. "I stand in the presence of God, and I have been sent to speak to you and tell you this good news." Gabriel had then pointed at Zechariah and declared, "And now you will be silent and not able to speak until the day this happens, because you did not believe my words, which will come true at their proper time."[3]

Elisabeth placed two freshly baked loaves of bread on the table, covered them with a linen cloth, and then left the kitchen to rouse

[3] Luke 1:13–20.

Zechariah from his night's sleep. She did not see through her window the caravan that was coming up the road to her home. Nor did she see the young Galilean girl jump off the donkey she was riding and run up to her door. The knock brought her back into the kitchen. Peeking out the window, she was surprised to see strangers gathered outside her home.

Cautiously, she opened the door.

CHAPTER
— 5 —

"ary!" she exclaimed as she drew her cousin close. "Dear Mary! What are you doing here?"

"Elisabeth!" Mary hugged her and at the sound of Mary's greeting Elisabeth gasped and clutched her stomach.

In a loud voice, she exclaimed, "Blessed are you among women, and blessed is the child you will bear."

Mary's eyes widened in shock. *Elisabeth knows? How could she know?*

"But why am I so favoured, that the mother of my Lord should come to me?" Elisabeth asked, cupping Mary's cheek with her hand. "As soon as the sound of your greeting reached my ears, the baby in my womb leaped for joy. You are blessed, my child, because you have believed everything the Lord has told you."

The realization that the Holy Spirit was even now speaking through Elisabeth brought tears of joy to Mary's eyes. God had confirmed Elisabeth's pregnancy to her by letting her see Elisabeth with her own eyes. Today He was telling her that she, too, was with child. Mary did not know how or when it had happened. She only knew that she could feel the Holy Spirit working within her as well.

"My soul glorifies the Lord," Mary said, raising her hands in worship, "and my spirit rejoices in God my Saviour, for He has been mindful of the humble state of His servant." She closed her eyes and lifted her hands to the heavens. "From now on, all generations will call me blessed, for the Mighty One has done great things for me. Holy is His name."

She joined hands with Elisabeth and they worshipped together, exalting God and praising Him for His mercy and love. As the two women embraced again, Elisabeth silently chastised herself for not seeing to the needs of those who had brought Mary to her. She offered them bread and water for the rest of their journey, but they declined. They quickly retrieved Mary's belongings and, after placing them beside her, assured her they would send a messenger to let her father know she had arrived safely.

Mary's face grew hot with embarrassment as she watched her traveling companions depart. They had just witnessed her very private greeting with Elisabeth. She could tell by their stunned looks and quick departure that her revelations had made them uncomfortable. What would these friends of her father—her neighbours in Nazareth—report to Joseph? Could they begin to understand that she carried the Promise of Israel? She thanked them for their kindness and noticed as she spoke that those who only moments before had been unafraid to speak with her now would not even look at her. With sudden clarity, Mary knew that the road ahead was going to be very rough indeed.

Zechariah woke at the sound of Elisabeth's shout and ran into the kitchen. Hearing Mary's words of praise, he fell to his knees in worship. *The Messiah! My wife's cousin is to bear the Messiah? Everything is happening as it should. My son is going to prepare the way for the Lord.* Zechariah could not contain the tears that streamed down his face. His soul rejoiced and he ached to voice his praise.

Elisabeth, sensing Mary's discomfort after bidding the others farewell, drew her in and closed the door. As she turned, she noticed Zechariah prostrate on the floor, weeping.

"Zechariah! My darling, what is it?" She ran and knelt beside him.

"Zechariah!" Mary exclaimed as she touched his heaving shoulders. No sound came from his mouth and Mary thought she had never seen anything so pitiful.

"What has happened to him?" she asked as she helped Elisabeth lead Zechariah to a chair.

"He has not been able to speak for some time." Elisabeth poured a cup of water for her husband. "He was serving in the temple and from what I can tell he saw an angel or a vision of some kind, and when he came out he could not speak." She wiped her husband's tears with her shawl and handed him the water. He took the cup and sipped as he tried to catch his breath.

Mary looked at him with a mixture of awe and love. "I also had a vision, Cousin," she uttered. "An angel came to me."

Zechariah's hand began to shake as he listened to her. She told him of the angel's appearance and of the child she now carried. Zechariah motioned for his writing tablet and after Elisabeth retrieved it he wrote the name Gabriel and showed it to Mary with a questioning look.

Mary nodded. "Yes, an angel named Gabriel. He came to me. That is why I'm here. He told me Elisabeth was with child. Did he come to you as well?"

Zechariah nodded, his heart burdened with all the things he wanted to say. But he knew mere words could not express the wonder of what was yet to come.

CHAPTER
— 6 —

The months passed and as Elisabeth neared her time of delivery, Mary began an intense period of morning sickness. She thought it humorous that she had come to help her cousin in her time of need, when instead it was Elisabeth who was helping her.

A routine developed each morning before Mary rose from bed. Servants would bring her hot water with mint in it and dry wafers to help ease her nausea. Although it did not prevent her from vomiting, it did help ease her stomach afterwards. When she had bathed and dressed, she would join Elisabeth and Zechariah in their morning prayers. In the afternoons, she found herself napping during the day at the same time as Elisabeth.

"This is very strange indeed!" she yawned one afternoon on her way back to bed.

"What is?" Elisabeth asked as she gathered up some clothes to wash.

"Going back to bed in the middle of the day. Why, my parents would be appalled!"

Elisabeth laughed and patted her bulging stomach. "It may feel strange at first, but with the way we are being doted on by Zechariah and the servants, what else have we to do? Besides, our bodies and our babies need us to rest."

"I suppose so." Mary shrugged. "Still, it feels very strange to be so tired."

"It will pass. In fact, today I feel as if I could bake a hundred loaves of bread and still have energy left over." She dropped the soiled linen into a reed basket.

Mary smiled and reached out to pat Elisabeth's stomach. "You must be getting close to your time then. My sister Salome was very energetic right before her baby arrived."

"Really? Perhaps I should run around the yard to see if anything happens." She laughed and headed out the door with the basket of linen perched on her hip. Mary chuckled and started toward her room when Elisabeth's raised voice caused her to turn around. Zechariah was trying to grab the basket out of his wife's hands. But she was having none of it. Mary laughed silently as she watched her cousin make it clear through a series of frantic gestures that these chores were to be done by the servants only.

Zechariah's face turned red with frustration and, much to Mary's surprise, his balding head reddened as well. She felt sorry for her cousin as he tried to get his independent wife to do as she was told. Clearly, he was annoyed with Elisabeth, not only for her insistence that she was well enough to work but because he could not yell at her for attempting to do so.

How she loved them both! They had been married for well over fifty years and seemed, at least to Mary, to be very much in love. Elisabeth was quite tall, her long brown hair, which she kept braided and wrapped around her head, streaked grey. Nevertheless, she looked radiant. Being with child definitely seemed to agree with her.

As Zechariah succeeded in taking the basket from Elisabeth's hands, a sudden startled look came over her face. A loud pop was heard and as she looked down at her feet a pool of water began to collect. Mary's tiredness quickly vanished and was suddenly replaced with dread. She knew the basics of childbirth, but she had never actually delivered a child. She only hoped she knew enough if the midwife did not arrive in time.

But Zechariah was way ahead of her. He rang a bell which summoned Elisabeth's handmaid. Upon seeing her mistress in distress, she ushered her to bed and ordered another servant in the household to run for the midwife.

Mary quickly gathered the swaddling cloths she and Elisabeth had prepared for the baby and took them into her cousin's bedroom to have them close by. Ordering the other servants to boil water and bring fresh linens, Mary gathered the other items she knew they would need. As Elisabeth's handmaid helped her lady into the birthing chair, Mary surveyed the room to make sure everything was ready—blankets, water, towels, salt to rub over the baby, a sharp knife to cut the cord, a cradle in which to place the babe.

Everything seems to be here, she observed. *Now all we have to do is wait.*

The screams, which had been increasing in intensity over the last five hours, suddenly stopped. Zechariah, who had been pacing before his wife's chamber door, came to a halt. He turned to Mary, who had been running back and forth from him to Elisabeth for the last few hours. She was just about to go into the bedroom when a new voice made its presence known.

Mary's face lit up. "Wait here, Zechariah. I'll go and see how she's doing."

Zechariah looked anxious, but nodded and then waved his hands as if to say, "Hurry up. Go find out how my wife is."

Some time passed before Mary returned with Zechariah's son, freshly bathed and swaddled. She carefully placed the baby in the crook of Zechariah's arm, then stepped back to watch father and son bond.

"He is beautiful, is he not?" Mary said with wonder, thinking ahead to her own baby growing inside her.

Zechariah nodded and kissed the sleeping babe's forehead. He looked toward the bedroom with questioning eyes.

"She's doing very well. Her handmaid is cleaning her up and getting her into a fresh gown. She'll call you when you can see her." Mary smiled. "Congratulations, Zechariah. Praise God for His goodness to you and Elisabeth!"

Zechariah nodded, handed the baby back to Mary, then fell on his knees in praise to God.

Eight days later, Elisabeth and Zechariah welcomed their neighbours and relatives into their home for the baby's circumcision. A Hebrew surgeon named Lemuel was called to perform the ceremony.

"This is a wonderful day!" Lemuel rejoiced, clapping his hands together. "We have gathered together to celebrate with Zechariah and his wife Elisabeth in the birth of their son. I am sure that this little one, who came to them so late in life, will bring them great joy!" He took the baby from Elisabeth and cradled him in his arms. "This ceremony of circumcision was instituted by Yahweh as the sign of the covenant between Him and the Jewish people. It reminds us that we are to belong to God, worshipping and obeying Him. On this day it is also tradition to name the baby." He looked to Zechariah and asked, "Will this child be named after you?"

"No! His name is to be John," Elisabeth spoke up.

"John?" Lemuel asked, his bushy eyebrows rising up to meet his hairline. "But there is no one among your relatives with that name."

Each person present started talking at once, thinking Elisabeth must be mistaken.

Lemuel turned to Zechariah and asked, "What is the child to be named?"

Zechariah asked for a writing tablet and wrote, "His name is John."

"John? Are you sure?" Lemuel asked again.

"His name is John!" Gasps of surprise came from all corners of the house as Zechariah's voice returned to him. Laughing and crying, he began to dance around praising God and prophesying.

"My love!" Elisabeth reached toward her husband, who grasped her in a firm embrace. She cupped his face in her hands and wept. "I have missed your voice."

Zechariah threw caution to the wind and kissed his wife firmly on the mouth. "Praise be to the Lord, the God of Israel, because He has come and redeemed His people!" Zechariah lifted his hands toward the heavens and cried with joy as he praised God. The people around him felt the glory of the moment and one by one began to kneel in prayer.

Zechariah took John from Lemuel and, lifting him high in his arms, proclaimed, "And you, my child, will be called a prophet of the Most High, for you will go on before the Lord to prepare the way for Him. You will give God's people the knowledge of salvation through the forgiveness of their sins."[4]

Elisabeth and Mary hugged each other and sobbed as Zechariah continued to prophesy. The wonder of it all took their breath away. Zechariah could speak again! What other great things would happen? Their neighbours were filled with awe and, as the weeks passed throughout the hill country of Judea, people began talking about the new baby born to Elisabeth and Zechariah. All who heard the story wondered about it, asking, "What then, is this child going to be?"

For the Lord's hand was with him.

---

[4] Luke 1:67–69.

CHAPTER
— 7 —

I left about one week later," Mary said as she stood up to stretch. "Some of Zechariah's relatives were traveling to Cana, which is beyond Nazareth as you know, and they brought me safely home."

There was a knock at the door and Mary excused herself from the table to go see who it was.

"Matthew!" She opened the door wider, inviting him in. "What a pleasant surprise." Matthew kissed her cheek and she returned the greeting.

"How do you fare Mary?" he asked, as she directed him to a chair and took off his sandals.

"Wonderful! Luke is with me. Are you hungry?" she asked as one of the servants came with a sponge and water to wash the dirt off Matthew's feet.

"Luke is here? How fortunate. Yes, I'm famished." Matthew smiled, rubbing his stomach.

"Good, for we were just eating. Come, we have plenty."

He followed Mary into the main room of the house, which held the long table at which Luke was reclining. The two men exchanged greetings and news on the other disciples while Mary attended to Matthew's meal.

She listened to them both, marvelling that the Lord had brought both disciples to her door on the same day.

"Matthew," she said, turning toward him. His black curly hair framed his face, making his beard appear fuller than it was. "Do not be offended, but may I ask what brings you this way?"

"No offense taken." He waved his hand in dismissal. "Truly, I do not know. I awoke yesterday morning intending to visit Peter, but I felt compelled to visit you instead. I prayed about it and felt the Lord was speaking to me. Being concerned for you, I decided to come immediately." Matthew looked at them both. "I do not see you ill or hurt. So, do you have any idea why I'm here?"

Mary looked at Luke, who raised his eyebrows and shrugged. She grinned and said, "By any chance, do you like to write?"

"And what did your parents say when you told them of Elisabeth's news?" Luke asked as he passed some bread to Matthew.

"I brought a letter from both Elisabeth and Zechariah, confirming the birth of John and they—well, let's just say they were happy and excited for Elisabeth and disturbed and worried about me."

"So, your parents—did they believe you were carrying the Messiah?" Matthew asked. He had been delighted when Mary suggested he join Luke in keeping a record of the events of Jesus' life, for he had been considering the importance of doing so for some time.

Mary sank into a cushion and made herself comfortable once again. "They did believe, especially after reading Zechariah's letter. But amazingly, that isn't what they struggled with."

"You had remarkable parents, if they did not even question your purity," Luke interrupted, shaking his head. "Forgive me, Mary, but if my sister had told me a story like yours, I'm not sure I would have been supportive at all. What was it they struggled with?"

Mary smiled and once more remembered with fondness the protection she received from her parents, from Joseph, and most of all from her Heavenly Father.

———

"She's home! She's home! Heli, come quickly, Mary's home!" Rebekah ran outside to help Mary with her belongings and to thank those who had brought her safely home again. She hugged Mary, then said to her escorts, "Please, won't you stay and sup with us tonight? We'd be honoured to have you in our humble home."

Grateful to have a place to rest and eat, Zechariah's relatives stayed the night, enjoying the company of Mary and her family and bringing news of all that was happening in and around Jerusalem. They rejoiced together over Zechariah and Elisabeth's good fortune and confirmed for Heli and Rebekah that Elisabeth had indeed brought forth a son. In the morning, they said their goodbyes and thanked the family of Heli for their hospitality.

After everyone had left, Heli turned to Mary and asked the question that had been on his mind since she had arrived. "My daughter, is it true? Are you now with child?"

Mary eyes darted between her father and mother, not knowing how either would react to her news. She took a deep breath, straightened her shoulders, and said, "Yes, Father... I carry the Son of God."

The groan that emitted from Heli was wrought with despair. He fell to his knees and began sobbing. Mary was alarmed and looked to her mother for reassurance. *Does Abba think I am a harlot, or does he believe my story?*

Rebekah put her hand on Heli's shoulder and smiled at Mary. "Your father and I have been deeply distraught these few months Mary, wanting to know the truth. The letters you brought with you from Elisabeth and Zechariah have confirmed what you said. They both expressed a deep belief that you do indeed carry the Messiah." Rebekah hesitated. "What we have been struggling with, however, is how Joseph will react—what he will do? I know it is ridiculous, but we have also feared the talk of our neighbours. There was some talk... while you were away..." She frowned as she tried to forget the gossip of her neighbours, who had heard of Mary's situation from those who had taken her to Elisabeth's home. The looks of scorn in the marketplace had been unbearable, the looks of pity even worse. Conversations that came to a halt whenever she was near only fed her belief that the whole village was talking about her daughter. Through it all, she had kept a smile on her face and her head held high with the secret knowledge that maybe, just maybe, her daughter was the one God had chosen to bring forth the Messiah.

"We have learned one thing throughout all of this—God has everything in control. We are both in awe of our Saviour, who has bestowed this honour on our daughter. Blessed be the name of the Lord!" Rebekah fell to her knees and wept with her husband. Mary could not believe her good fortune. Her wonderful, understanding parents had not reacted rashly, but had waited instead on the Lord to answer their cries. Weeping, she knelt with them and together they praised the Lord for His goodness.

When Joseph heard of Mary's return, he prepared to go and see her at once. He had missed her dearly and couldn't wait to hold her in his arms once again. She would be surprised when she saw their home completed. He had worked on it daily while she had been away.

In the beginning, he had been angry with Rebekah and Heli for sending Mary on such a long journey, angrier still when he started hearing the filthy rumours about his Beloved. It took every ounce of control he had not to react harshly toward his neighbours, who were declaring that Mary had claimed she was with child. Ridiculous! Not only that, but they said she believed she carried the Messiah. After a time, Joseph began avoiding his neighbours, for the more he saw them, the more enraged he became. These people had known Mary all her life, yet they had spouted horrible lies about her. He had thought it best to keep away from them until Mary returned.

He shook off his anger and picked up his pace. Soon they would be married and all this evil talk of Mary's infidelity would be put to rest. He brought her face and form to mind. Oh, how he loved her. While she *was* beautiful, with dimples on both cheeks, long ebony hair, and a slender figure, he was more impressed with her personality and spirit. She was a hard worker, helping her father with the sheep and her mother with the household chores. She was kind and gentle to anyone who met her and her devotion to Yahweh convinced Joseph that all the lies spouted about her were false. Yes, Mary would make a wonderful wife and in just two months their marriage would finally take place.

Coming upon the home of Heli, Joseph stopped short when he heard loud cries coming from inside the house. He quickened his pace, concerned that something had happened to Mary. He was about to rush in when he heard Rebekah speak, and the words she spoke knocked the wind right out of him.

CHAPTER
— 8 —

There was a loud buzzing noise coming from somewhere, but he couldn't tell what it was or where it was coming from. It felt like it was inside his head. Joseph felt hot and cold at the same time. He had not heard anything else Rebekah had said except those six impossible words: "You do indeed carry the Messiah." Breathing hard, he had turned and ran back home.

"Mary? My Mary, with child? How could this be? How could my little Mary do this to me? Who is the father? Surely, Rebekah and Heli do not believe she carries the Messiah! Could it be true? Were my neighbours right all along?" He mumbled to himself all the way home, attracting curious stares from his neighbours and friends. Mary loved him—he knew that. *She would not have been unfaithful to me… would she?* Tears filled his eyes and his body shook with emotion. He did not want to believe such things about Mary. He could not!

I must be mistaken. But no, it is clear what Rebekah said—what she believed. Perhaps the whole family of Heli is going mad. The Mes-

siah? What are they thinking? He shook his head. *No! She does not carry the Messiah. That is too foolish even to contemplate.*

The realization that she had committed the act of adultery, punishable by stoning, poured over him. He trembled as he thought of what awaited her. "NO!" he sobbed aloud as he opened the door to his home.

"Joseph!" His father Jacob rushed toward him. "What is it, my son?"

"Oh, Abba!" he cried as he fell to his knees.

He hated what she had done, but he could not bear the thought of seeing her stoned. Somehow, someway he would protect her. As Joseph considered what to do, he wept for all he had lost and resolved to break his betrothal to Mary in the morning.

It was decided that both Heli and Rebekah would go with Mary to inform Joseph of all that had taken place in their lives. The three of them had spent the night in prayer, beseeching God on how best to break the news to Joseph. They all knew the dangers—he could divorce Mary if he suspected she had committed adultery. They had been betrothed for almost a year. The betrothal was a binding, legal contract for their forthcoming marriage. It effectively said that Mary belonged to Joseph, and the punishment for any man who violated her sexually was death by stoning. How could they make Joseph understand that there was no other man?

Heli glanced at his daughter as she walked serenely beside him. *How can she be so calm?* He looked at Rebekah and saw her worried frown. *Well, at least I'm not the only one concerned.*

Mary looked up at her father, smiled, took his hand, and patted it. "Don't worry, Abba, all will be well. God has not abandoned me."

Heli felt his eyes tear. He nodded his head, unable to speak as they came to the door of Joseph ben Jacob. He knocked twice and announced himself.

"Joseph, it's Heli. Mary is here with her mother. We wish to speak with you."

They could hear rustling inside and some moments passed before Joseph opened the door. Mary gasped when she saw his red, swollen eyes.

"Joseph!" she cried as she moved toward him. "What is the matter? Is all well with you and your family?" She reached up to caress his face, but he grabbed her hand and pulled it down.

Mary stepped back, her brown eyes confused at Joseph's behaviour. "Joseph?"

He did not reach to embrace her, nor did he invite her family into his home. Instead, he drew himself up and, without looking at Mary, addressed Heli in a sombre voice.

"Heli, I was at your home yesterday. I know why you are here. I did not intend to eavesdrop on your conversation, it just happened. But there have been rumours and what I heard has taken me by surprise. Before I do anything at all, I must know one thing."

Heli nodded. "Ask whatever you wish, Joseph."

Without looking at Mary, Joseph kept his eyes focused on Heli and asked, "Is Mary with child?"

The startled looks on their faces confirmed what Joseph feared. Heli nodded and answered, "She is."

Joseph stumbled back into the house and, anxious for him, they followed him in. His legs were shaking and he knew he needed to sit down. Mary could see his struggle and brought a stool for him.

"Oh, Joseph! Dear Joseph!" She tried to comfort him, but he pulled away from her. "Do not despair, my Beloved, for I carry the Messiah."

He looked at her sadly, shaking his head in disbelief. "Oh Mary, you don't really believe that, do you?"

She placed a tentative hand on his arm, breathing a sigh of relief when he did not brush it away. "Joseph—I am still a virgin. I have not been with any man, and though I cannot prove this, I have no doubt that God will be faithful and reveal His plan to you in time." Tears pooled in her eyes as she felt the weight of his sorrow. "Please, trust me, Joseph. I would never be unfaithful to you."

"I don't know what to believe, Mary! It's unthinkable either way."

"Would you put her out, Joseph?" Rebekah asked, fearing for her daughter's future. "She is with child. If you divorce her, people will assume it's not your child and she will be stoned."

Joseph stood up quickly, knocking over the stool he had been sitting on. Mary jumped back, startled at this side of her betrothed. His eyes were wild with grief, his voice filled with rage and disbelief. "It isn't my child, woman!"

Heli stepped forward to protect his wife and daughter, afraid for the first time of what Joseph might do in his anger. Joseph shook his head, shocked at the rage that filled him. He loved Mary, but her betrayal cut him deeply. She stood there, her face showing nothing but love and compassion for him and he wondered for a brief second if she was telling the truth. However, he knew what she was proposing was unthinkable and he turned away, disgusted at himself for loving one who had betrayed him.

"Leave me! My soul is in agony and I do not know what to do."

"Joseph, please ... " Mary wept as she moved toward him.

"No! Please, Mary—I will let you know in the morning what I decide. I cannot bear to see you right now. I beg of you ... leave me alone!"

Heli nodded and hurried Mary and Rebekah out the door, already deciding that he would send Mary back to Elisabeth until her baby came. *Surely*, he reasoned, *the Messiah would be better off with Zechariah, a temple priest. Perhaps that has been God's intention all along.*

In the morning, he would take Mary there himself.

CHAPTER
— 9 —

Joseph spent that day and half the night contemplating his choices. Jewish and Roman law both demanded that a man divorce his wife if she was found guilty of adultery. Roman law actually treated a husband who failed to divorce an unfaithful wife as a panderer, exploiting his wife as a prostitute. Although he followed God's laws, Joseph shuddered to think what his Gentile neighbours would say. Not to mention his Jewish neighbours. His reputation was at stake for the rest of his life.

"However," Joseph reasoned aloud to his father as he paced the cold floor of his home, "if I do not divorce her, my friends and neighbours will all assume I compromised Mary." He believed himself to be a righteous man and he could not stand the thought of being gossiped about in such a way.

"On the other hand, you could always profit by divorcing Mary publicly," Jacob suggested. "If you take her to court, you can impound her dowry and perhaps recoup the bride price I paid at your betrothal."

Joseph looked around the home he had worked so hard to build. "Yes, that would pay for this house." He shook his head. "No! Abba, that won't work either. It will bring shame to Heli's family. It's not their fault Mary has been unfaithful." Joseph's shoulders slumped forward. "Maybe I should just provide her with a certificate of divorce in front of two or three witnesses. Get it over with quickly and quietly."

Jacob nodded, his lips drawing into a thin line. "If that is what you wish. We would have to forfeit any economic reimbursement, but it would minimize her public dishonour."

Joseph knew suffering already awaited Mary. Her condition would ruin any chance of her ever marrying again. He growled in frustration. "I am such a fool, Abba. How can I risk her possibly being stoned to death? I still love her. How can I avoid sending Mary to such a fate?"

Jacob shook his head and frowned. "My son, how can you not?"

Joseph groaned and rubbed his temples.

"It is late. You have much to think about." Jacob patted Joseph on the back. "I will leave you to your ponderings. Good night."

"Thank you, Abba. Good night. I will let you know what I decide in the morning." Jacob nodded and disappeared into his bedroom.

Joseph sighed, frustrated at the many scenarios that played themselves out in his mind. His father was right. There was only one option for him—he had to divorce her. To fail to do so would violate both the law and custom and bring enduring reproach on his household. He crawled into bed with a profound sense of loss.

Somehow, he would get through this and forget that Mary, daughter of Heli, ever existed.

She was laughing, her eyes a bright twinkle that outshone the stars in the sky. They mesmerized him. *Are her eyes always this bright?* As he watched her, she began to glow. *Mary? What is happening to you? Wait—it isn't Mary—what is happening? Why is everything getting so bright?*

"Joseph!"

That was not Mary's voice. It was unlike any voice he had ever heard before—magnificent and reverberating.

"Joseph, do not be afraid!"

As the light began to grow brighter, Joseph found himself unable to move. His chest tightened in fear. His eyes, although closed, were blinded by the light shining around him.

"Joseph, son of David, do not be afraid to take Mary home as your wife, because what is conceived in her is from the Holy Spirit. She will give birth to a son, and you are to give him the name Jesus, because he will save his people from their sins."

Joseph sat up in bed, his chest heaving. He searched his room for the source of light, but found only darkness. *A dream?* No, it was much more than that. He knew with all his heart that he had just experienced something wonderful. He could still feel the presence of holiness, could still hear the angel's voice:

"… what is conceived in her is from the Holy Spirit."

"Mary told the truth!" Joseph was at once giddy with relief and remorseful that he had not believed her.

"… she will give birth to a son."

She is to have a son? But not just any son… the Son of God. The Messiah! And I am to be this child's father? I will have the privilege of raising him as my own? I am not worthy of such a responsibility. The thought of it sent his heart racing once again. Mary was the one who this was directly affecting and yet she seemed to be at peace with it. *Of course, she has had at least three months to accept it,* he reasoned. He had only just heard yesterday. He groaned as he remembered his outburst. *Will she accept my apology now? Will she understand why I was so upset? Will Heli welcome me again at their door after the way I treated them?* Joseph jumped up from his cot and threw on a fresh tunic. A sense of urgency propelled him to hurry to the home of Heli. He would go to Mary at once. Before the day ended, he would make sure they were officially man and wife.

"Joseph brought me home to be his wife that very day," Mary said to Luke and Matthew, her face a myriad of emotions. "Although he had no union with me until some time after Jesus was born." Mary blushed and stared at her hands. "It would not have been right, you see, since I carried a Holy Child. We simply couldn't bring ourselves to… to… "

Matthew coughed and, trying to ease her embarrassment, he decided to change the topic. "It is wonderful the way our Heavenly Father worked in your life and in the life of Joseph. Were there any other instances of angels appearing? Or dreams?"

"Yes," Luke chimed in. "I'd be very interested to know about Jesus' birth and his life as a child growing up. What was that like?"

Mary relaxed as Luke and Matthew steered the topic back to safer ground. "Oh, Jesus was a very bright child. He was unusually gifted in his ability to meet someone and make him or her feel immediately at ease—as if he already knew them. He was very endearing and loved to laugh. I can remember my father taking Jesus into the fields with him to tend the sheep. Of course, most of the time Jesus spent with Joseph learning the trade of carpentry, but my father knew how much Jesus loved animals, and whenever the shearing had to be done Jesus was right there, always lending a hand.

"I remember one time, when he was very little—about the age of seven—his grandfather gave him his shepherd's staff and together they walked into the hills to find a green pasture for the sheep to feed on. He was so tiny and that staff so big." She sighed and closed her eyes as they began to tear. Embarrassed, she wiped her face and said, "How silly of me! Weeping over memories I cannot get back. Forgive me, there are times when I just long to see him again."

"It's all right, Mary. We understand," Matthew said as he stood up. "Why don't we go outside?"

He offered his hand to Mary and she nodded in agreement as he helped her up.

Luke stood and gathered up the writing tablets. "You know, that sounds like a wonderful idea, Matthew. Why don't we adjourn to the roof?"

They followed stone steps up the side of the house that led to a flat rooftop. A canopy held aloft by tall cedar beams provided shade from the blazing midday sun. Underneath the canopy, col-

55

ourful pillows lay scattered atop a rug Mary had woven from goat hair.

Luke gave Matthew his writing tablet and they settled themselves down into the plush cushions.

"This was a good idea! I love it up here," Mary said, smiling and breathing in the fresh air.

"Would you tell us now, Mary... of his birth?" Luke asked after everyone was settled.

She nodded and began again.

———

He came storming up the hill toward his home with an edict from Caesar Augustus in his hand. A decree had been issued that a census should be taken of the entire Roman world and everyone was to go to their own town to register. It was the Jewish custom to enroll by tribes and families. Joseph was of the family of David and would have to be enrolled where that family had its landed inheritance—Bethlehem, at least a week's journey from Nazareth. Mary was also from the line of David and she, too, had to be registered.

"This so-called 'census' is nothing more than another grab for more tax money," Joseph muttered to himself. "Why Caesar thinks anyone has any assets left with his greedy hands always reaching for it, I have no idea!"

At first, he had been frustrated that he would be forced to leave his wife for such a ridiculous reason. Then his frustration had turned to outrage when a Roman official told him that his wife had to go with him—no excuses.

"How could she possibly stand the journey? She is with child and is approaching her final month," he had argued. "Surely Caesar Augustus would not expect her to endure such a trip!"

The official had smirked and said, "Caesar expects only one thing, and that is obedience from his subjects. If you fail to comply, you will suffer the consequences." Joseph had not bothered to find out what those consequences would be. Instead he had turned and stomped away.

As he neared his home, he saw Mary talking animatedly to her mother and father. All three seemed upset and Joseph knew at once that they had heard about the edict. Heli's and Rebekah's concern for their daughter's welfare was evident.

"I see you've heard about Caesar's plans?" Joseph asked as he waved the edict in his hands.

Heli turned to him and with a sad shake of his head said, "This is ridiculous, Joseph. To force a woman with child to take such a journey…" He trailed off, overcome with worry for his daughter and unborn grandchild.

Rebekah reached out to comfort him and asked, "What if she just doesn't go? How would they know? So many people will be there, after all. Would it really matter if one girl is missing from the crowd?"

"Perhaps not," Joseph said. "But I would never be able to leave Mary alone while I go to Bethlehem. She could have the baby and there would be no one here to help her."

"I suppose if they wouldn't miss one girl, they probably wouldn't miss her mother either, would they Heli?" Rebekah asked.

Heli smiled and shook his head. "We will all go to Bethlehem. I myself must register. There is no other way."

Mary nodded. "It must be this way, Ima. Do you not see how Yahweh has arranged this census? For it is written: *'But you, Bethlehem Ephrathah, though you are small among the clans of Judah, out of you will come for me one who will be ruler over Israel, whose origins are from of old, from ancient times.'*[5] Everything is as it should be," Mary said with confidence.

Heli nodded slowly, his weary eyes dawning with understanding. "She is right. Everything is unfolding as it should. I forget sometimes, my daughter, the miracle of whose child you carry."

"You know, I recall the Rabbi speaking those very verses last Sabbath," Joseph added, "and I have been pondering them ever since—about what it meant, concerning the babe Mary carries. God's Son, if He is to be the ruler over Israel, must come out of Bethlehem to fulfill the Scriptures." He shook his head in amazement. "I was wondering how we were going to end up in Bethlehem. God is using Caesar's evil census to get us there." He laughed. "God is great! We need not worry for Mary, for He does indeed have everything in control."

---

[5] Micah 5:2.

CHAPTER
— 10 —

They made plans to leave at once, for the larger Mary got the more uncomfortable she became. Heli and Rebekah would travel with them, as they, too, needed to register in Bethlehem. This was a great comfort to Mary, as she did not want to be away from her mother at this time in her life.

Joseph had built a sturdy wagon to carry their provisions and made a place for Mary to sleep should she become too weary; two of his finest oxen pulled it. Heli brought two oxen and a wagon of his own with their belongings, as well as a goat for fresh milk along the way. Mary and Rebekah gathered up the necessary food, water, clothing, and other supplies needed for themselves and the coming baby.

As the weeks progressed, huge caravans were seen passing through Galilee into Judea. People from far and wide were returning to their own towns to register. Nazareth itself was starting to fill up with so many people that Joseph feared if they did not leave soon, they would be unable to find a room once they arrived in

Bethlehem. Realizing how anxious his son was, Jacob, Joseph's widowed father, had left the previous week for Bethlehem and promised to reserve a room for them as soon as he arrived. By the middle of the second week of the last month of Mary's pregnancy, they were ready to leave. So, with joy and trepidation as to what lay ahead, they began their long journey to Bethlehem.

Mary was confident the pains she had been experiencing for the last half hour were not signs that the baby was coming. She was certain she had at least another week before the baby was due. *I could, of course, be wrong about that,* she thought as she rubbed her stomach. *But either way we still have at least another day before we will even be close to Bethlehem, so if the baby is thinking of coming… well… it just can't!* Her back was hurting terribly, even though she had been lying down in the wagon for quite some time. She decided that perhaps it would be better to walk, that maybe she needed to stretch her legs.

"Joseph!" she called out. "I would like to walk now, please."

For the past week and a half, this was how it had gone—a little time in the wagon, a little time walking. It was certainly easier for her, but she knew the many stops they made were causing the trip to take much longer. Every time Joseph stopped the wagon for her, Heli would stop his wagon, which caused Rebekah to run ahead to see if Mary was all right. She fussed over Mary and made such a commotion that a simple stop to change from lying down in the wagon to walking could take at least twenty minutes. This happened several times before Heli put his foot down and insisted Rebekah let Joseph take care of his wife. "If you are needed, Joseph will certainly let you know," Heli assured her. Rebekah frowned in frustration, folded her arms, and watched silently as Joseph stopped his wagon once again.

As Joseph helped Mary down from the wagon, he noticed that she was grimacing. He began to worry once again about the toll this trek was taking on her. Normally, it would take about a week for this journey, but everyone agreed the slower the pace, the better for Mary. However, Joseph was starting to worry that the baby might come before they even reached Bethlehem. He had never thought the trip would take this long!

"Are you feeling well, Mary?" he asked once again.

She looked up at him, patted his face, and smiled reassuringly. "Do not worry, my Gentle Giant. God will not let this baby be born until we reach Bethlehem."

He grabbed her hands and kissed them. "Are you in much pain? Do you need your mother?"

She looked back at her mother, who was starting to get out of her wagon again, but Mary waved her off. She turned to Joseph and stammered, "Oh Joseph, I love my mother so, but she is starting to… how I can say this nicely? She is starting to…" Embarrassed, Mary looked at the ground. "… agitate me."

Joseph laughed aloud, trying hard not to look in his mother-in-law's direction. Snorting with merriment, he held Mary's hand as they started walking. Mary joined in the laughter, grateful to be on her feet once more.

"How much longer do you think it will be before we get to Bethlehem?" Mary asked, enjoying the warmth of Joseph's sturdy hand holding hers.

"Let me see … it's late in the day and we need to stop soon to rest and feed the animals. I think we will probably get there by early tomorrow evening. Do you think you can manage that?"

Mary nodded. "I'll be fine. My back just hurts a lot right now. Perhaps when we stop for the night you could rub it for me?"

"I will, and I'll rub your feet as well," Joseph said as he squeezed her hand.

"Joseph, you are so good to me." Mary smiled lovingly at him as they continued on their way.

"You know, I think I'll run up and see how Mary is doing," Rebekah said as she attempted to jump down from the wagon once again.

"Woman, leave them be!" Heli protested as he reached out and grabbed her arm. "Mary is fine with her husband."

Rebekah frowned, disgruntled at being treated like a child. "Heli, her legs are going to swell if she keeps walking. She needs to rest. I only want to make sure she feels well."

"And you think Joseph has not already asked her how she is feeling?" He shook his head and smiled. "I love you, Rebekah, but sometimes you can be very controlling."

"That's a hurtful thing to say!"

"Maybe so, but it's the truth."

"I'm not trying to control anyone or anything, Heli! I just care a great deal about my daughter."

"True enough." Heli nodded. "You do care for Mary. I have no doubt about that. But don't you think, Rebekah, that maybe—just maybe—you might be caring too much?"

62

"What do you mean?"

Heli paused to collect his thoughts, then said, "Do you believe Mary carries the Messiah?"

"Of course I do! Why would you ask me that?"

"Well… if Mary carries the Son of God, don't you think she is being cared for by a greater power than you?"

Rebekah was silent for a moment and then, with a trembling voice, answered, "I know she is cared for and watched over by Yahweh, Heli. I know that. I just cannot get my heart around it. I can't let her go." Rebekah leaned against her husband's shoulder and began to weep. "She is the mother of the Messiah. She is my daughter. She is so young to be given such an honour. I would see her safe and happy, for I fear for her future."

Heli smiled and pulled her close. "As do I, dear one. Nevertheless, you need to start putting your trust in God. Trust in His love for Mary, for Joseph, for the baby, and yes, even for you. He knows what you feel. Your love for Mary is very protective—as a mother bear protects her cubs. I think it is how Yahweh feels for us, His children… very protective. Rest in Him, Rebekah, everything will be fine."

Rebekah sighed and looked into Heli's eyes. "You are a good and patient man, Heli. I love you."

He nodded and said, "I love you, too, dear one. I love you, too."

CHAPTER
— 11 —

The following day, when they were near the outskirts of the city, her water broke. She had been experiencing labour pains with mounting intensity all day long. Joseph had been aware of her discomfort and had increased his pace. Earlier, Heli and Rebekah had gone ahead to see if Jacob had been able to secure rooms for them in Bethlehem. Now, Joseph and Mary were alone. Just the two of them, amidst a sea of people, all crowding to get a room.

"Oh, Joseph!" she whimpered as she clutched her stomach. "How much longer?"

"Mary, it will be all right! Try to stay calm—we are getting closer to the city gates now. We are almost there." Joseph was frantic with worry. He had no idea where Mary's parents were, or even his own father.

"Joseph, do you see your father or my parents?" Mary cried, voicing Joseph's thoughts.

"No, dear one. However, do not worry. We will get a room. No one would turn down a woman about to give birth."

People graciously parted for them as soon as they realized Mary's condition, but unfortunately for Joseph that was the only kindness he would find. Inn after inn turned them away.

"Sorry, we have no rooms available."

"Sorry, no room here!"

"I feel sorry for your wife, sir, but there is nothing available."

Every innkeeper said the same thing. No room. Mary's cries were breaking Joseph's heart. He feared Mary would be delivering the baby right there in the street. Silently, he prayed to God for an answer and His Heavenly Father heard his cry.

"Joseph!"

"Heli!" Joseph hugged his surprised father-in-law with all his might. "Praise the Lord we have found you! Mary is about to bring your grandson into the world and there are no rooms available anywhere. Please tell me you have found a room somewhere."

"There are no rooms available, Joseph, not anywhere. But—"

"Have you seen my father?" Joseph interrupted. "Surely, he would have found something by now."

"I have not seen Jacob at all. But let me tell you—"

"Oh, Joseph, please help me!" Mary cried from the back of the wagon. "It's getting closer!"

"Heli, what are we to do? She can't have the baby in the street!"

"That's what I've been trying to tell you, Joseph. We have a place." Heli grabbed the reigns of the oxen from Joseph and started to drive them through the crowd.

"A room? You have a room? Well, why didn't you say so?" Joseph sighed with relief. "Mary, it's all right, we are going to our room now. Can you hang on?"

"I don't know, Joseph. Please hurry!" she sobbed. They went as quickly as they could to the far end of the street, where Heli directed Joseph to the back of an inn.

"What's this?" Joseph asked as they neared the entrance to the stables.

"Your room," Heli declared as he carefully retrieved Mary from the back of the cart.

"You can't be serious!" Joseph protested as he watched Heli carry Mary to a stall in the back of the stable. "Heli, she cannot give birth in a stable."

Heli laid his daughter on a fresh bed of hay covered with a blanket. He stood, then turned to face his bewildered son-in-law.

"She can and she will. It's clean, it's warm, and it's private." Heli was adamant and Joseph could tell by the look on his face that his father-in-law would not change his mind.

"It's fine, Joseph," Mary whispered, her strength waning. "It's fine."

Joseph, clearly at a loss, looked to Rebekah, who arrived with warm water and fresh cloths. Surely, she would agree with him. Mary could not give birth here—could she?

Rebekah pleaded silently for Heli to take Joseph outside. She placed a comforting arm on her son-in-law and said, "It is as it should be, Joseph. We have cleaned out the stall. We have fresh hay. We are even using the cattle's feeding trough as a little crib for the baby. Go now. Mary will be fine."

Heli took Joseph forcibly by the arm and marched him toward the front door of the inn. Heli had met the innkeeper earlier—an elderly widow by the name of Anna—when he had been looking for rooms. After telling her about Mary, she had been saddened not to be able to offer them a room.

"However," she had added, "if you simply cannot find a room anywhere else, come back here and we'll make room for her in the stable. It's clean, warm, and close enough to the inn that you could still take meals here and get what you need when her time comes. I'll keep it ready for you."

Heli had nodded his thanks but inwardly cringed at the thought of Mary giving birth in a stable. *My daughter—my honoured daughter will not be giving birth to the Messiah in a stable full of animals. Not if I have anything to say about it.*

After he had eaten his noonday meal with Rebekah at the inn, Heli had spent the day searching throughout Bethlehem for a room just for Mary and Joseph, for he knew it would be impossible to find rooms for all of them. By early evening, he had begun to realize that his search was futile and he became resigned to using the stable the innkeeper had offered. It was as he was starting back to the inn that he had run into Joseph. Now, as they waited for the birth of the Messiah, Heli felt at a loss as to what they could do to pass the time.

"Let's sit and have some wine," he suggested to Joseph as they entered the inn. "It will calm us until the babe arrives… besides, you look a little ill."

As Joseph sat down at the table, Heli motioned for the servants to bring them some wine. Anna, the innkeeper, brought them cheese and bread as well.

"I hope this will fill you, as we are past serving the evening meal," she said.

"We are most grateful. Thank you," Heli said as Joseph sat by silently, a worried frown on his face.

Anna looked at Joseph with compassion. "Do not fear for your wife, sir. I will notify you when the baby arrives. Take heart, everything will be all right."

Joseph lifted his weary eyes to hers and smiled. "Thank you. I appreciate your kindness. May Yahweh bless you for all you have done for us this day." Anna nodded and left for the stable to help Rebekah.

All was quiet for a while and Joseph was about to go and see how Mary was faring when the door to the inn flew open and several bedraggled looking men entered.

"Is this the place?" they cried. "Is this where the child lies?"

"Child?" Joseph sat up straight, the rising hairs on the back of his neck signalling his alarm. "He has come!" he whispered to Heli, and then quickly, before Heli could react, he exited through a side door that led to the stables.

Intrigued with the men who entered, Heli asked, "What child?"

One of the men stepped forward and spoke for them all. "We are shepherds. My name is Josiah, and these are my friends. We were watching our sheep tonight and we saw... we saw..." He looked at his friends for support and they nodded their encouragement for him to continue. "We saw an angel!"

"Bah! What good is the word of a shepherd? You are either lying or drunk," one of the patrons said, dismissing him with a wave of his arm.

"We are neither drunkards nor liars. I tell you, we saw an angel of the Lord! I am not lying. He actually appeared to us and it was terrifying. The angel said to us, 'Do not be afraid. I bring you good news of great joy that will be for all the people. Today in the city of David, a Saviour has been born to you—he is Christ the Lord.'

"Then he said, 'This will be a sign to you: You will find a baby wrapped in clothes and lying in a manger.' Then, if that wasn't enough to shock us, all kinds of heavenly beings appeared in the sky with the angel and they were praising God and saying, 'Glory to God in the highest, and on earth peace to men on whom His favour rests.'"

Josiah looked at the faces around him and, seeing he had everyone's interest, he continued. "What I am saying is the truth. When the angels went back into heaven, we decided to come to Bethlehem to see for ourselves this event which the Lord had told us about. So, we have gone to every inn and home around Bethlehem to see if any babies have been born. We ask again... is this where the child lies?"

Heli knew at once that his grandson—God's son—had been born. He turned to the men and said, "Follow me."

Rebekah met Heli at the entrance to the stable. "Heli," she exclaimed, her eyes shining with delight. "You have a grandson!"

"I thought so." Heli pointed to the shepherds who had followed him and now stood at a distance. "These men have been proclaiming our grandson's arrival all over Bethlehem. Come, Rebekah, hear what they have to say. It will give our children time to get acquainted with their little one."

Joseph found Mary resting with the baby lying in the feeding trough beside her. In the stall next to them, a milking cow peered over the railing to inspect her new neighbours. Joseph marvelled at how quiet the animal was—as if it somehow knew the new occupants needed their rest.

How beautiful Mary looks, Joseph thought. Mary's long black hair had come loose and was draped like a blanket over her arms. She was a picture of contentment, her red cheeks the only sign that she had just been through the pain of childbirth. Hesitantly, he walked toward the feeding trough that held Jesus. Realizing that God had humbled Himself by taking human form, in order to redeem humanity, brought Joseph to his knees in prayerful adoration of the infant before him. Quietly, so as not to disturb Mary, he picked up the baby and gazed at him in awe. This was the Son of God! Joseph ran his hand over the tiny head, noting the thick, curly black hair that covered his ears. As Joseph carefully inspected his adopted son, Jesus squirmed, opened his eyes, and stared up at him.

"Hello, Jesus," Joseph whispered, his eyes glistening with tears.

He held in his arms the Promise of Israel. His whole body trembled with joy and relief over the days' events. Fearing he would drop the babe, he kissed his forehead and placed him back in the manger.

Mary stirred. "Joseph."

"My beloved one, you have a beautiful son," he said. "How do you fare? Is all well?"

"Everything is fine, my darling. However, I think I shall sleep a thousand sleeps tonight," she yawned. "Does my father know yet that he has a grandson?"

"Indeed I do!" Heli announced as he and Rebekah re-entered the stable. "In fact, the birth announcement has already been proclaimed."

Puzzled, she looked at him. "Proclaimed?"

"Throughout Bethlehem—in every inn, apparently."

"Abba, how could you have done that so quickly, when I have just given birth?"

"Actually, you already have visitors—or rather, Jesus does. Are you up to seeing them, Mary? I know you are tired, but they have quite a story to tell you."

Mary and Joseph exchanged curious glances. "Visitors… proclamations? I am already intrigued," Mary said as she struggled to sit up. "Tell them they may come in."

Quietly, the shepherds shuffled into the warm, cozy stable. As soon as they saw the baby in the manger, they fell to their knees in worship. Mary watched them in silence, struck numb by the sudden clarity of who the baby in the manger was. *I just gave birth to the Son of God. Blessed be the Lord!*

She looked around the stable. What a contrast! Cows, goats, and sheep surrounded her. She sat in a bed of hay while the king of the world slept in a feeding trough at her side. And wonders of wonders, shepherds were kneeling in the hay worshipping her son. She looked at Joseph, who had also fallen to his knees. What a night. What joy! Her heart overflowed with thanksgiving for Yahweh's provision and she wept with happiness.

Chapter
— 12 —

Sometime later, Jacob heard the shepherd's report of the birth and made his way to the stable where Mary and the baby lay. He was filled with remorse that he had not been able to find Joseph and Mary a room before she had gone into labour. To think that his grandson had been born in a stable tore him apart. However, when he entered the stable and beheld the scene before him, he was struck immediately with the rightness of the situation.

Shepherds knelt in adoration of his grandson. Heli and Rebekah, along with Joseph, knelt with them while Mary looked on. Somehow, the lowly stable took on an aura of sacredness, as if he were standing on holy ground. Jacob had felt it almost immediately when he walked through the door and was reminded once again about the circumstances of this infant's conception.

The Messiah is my grandson? This wee little baby, sitting in a feeding trough? He looks so normal.

"Abba!" Joseph smiled, removed Jesus from his manger, and carried him to his father.

"Would you like to hold him?" he whispered.

Jacob stretched out his arms and soon felt Jesus' warm, tiny body squirming in them. He was surprised the Messiah felt like any other infant.

Tears filled his eyes and he blinked them back. "My heart feels like it's going to burst with joy."

Joseph grinned. "Mine burst three hours ago."

Mary laughed as she watched them and it was then, as Jesus heard her voice, that he started to cry. Jacob, startled at the sound, quickly handed him back to Joseph, who quickly handed him over to Mary.

"You both act as if you'd never heard a baby cry before," she said with amusement as she settled Jesus in her arms. "He needs nourishment, so if you don't mind…" She motioned for her family and the shepherds to give her some privacy.

The men obliged and stepped outside to wait while she fed Jesus. Rebekah showed Mary how to hold him and, as she watched her grandson nurse, they began to hear a commotion outside.

"What is going on out there?" Rebekah frowned. "Surely, those shepherds must realize you need your privacy."

"I'm sure it's not them, Ima. They were very respectful."

"Hmm… just the same… I'm going outside to remind everyone that you and the baby need rest. There will be plenty of time for visits later."

"Ima, I really don't think…" But she was gone before she heard a word. Mary crinkled her nose and smiled at Jesus. "Your

Savta[6] likes to tell people what to do." Jesus stopped feeding and listened to her voice. "Don't worry. I don't think you'll have to worry about her." She chuckled to herself and Jesus resumed his suckling. Soon all was silent and Jesus grew tired and fell asleep at Mary's breast. She lifted him to her shoulder and patted his back, and as she did she heard her mother cry out.

What is going on out there? Is Ima all right? Jesus began to squirm as he sensed her tension. Cooing softly to him, she rocked him in her arms.

Rebekah rushed into the stable. "You won't believe it, Mary," she whispered. "Something extraordinary is happening."

"What is it?"

"Half the inn—nay, half the city—is standing outside this stable."

"Why?"

"Because of the story the shepherds have been spreading, about Jesus' birth and the angels who told them about it. They have come to see the baby for themselves."

"Approximately how many people would you say are out there, Ima?"

"Too many to count! It's overwhelming—the shepherds must have told everyone in the city."

"What do they want?"

"To see Jesus, of course." She saw the look of fear in Mary's eyes and noticed how tightly she was holding him. "Oh, Mary, do not fear. They are not here to hurt him, but to worship him."

---

[6] Hebrew for "grandmother."

"What should I do? I am far too tired to see anyone else tonight. It has been a very full evening for me and Jesus already."

"No need to worry. Your father, Joseph, and Jacob are standing guard over the stable like Roman soldiers." She laughed. "They realize you need your rest they are not letting anyone else in the stable tonight."

"Perhaps tomorrow, if they are still interested, they can see Jesus." Mary sighed as she rubbed Jesus' back. "I am just so incredibly exhausted right now."

"Quite understandable, under the circumstances." She smiled and leaned down to kiss Mary on the head. "Your father and I want to give you and Joseph time alone with Jesus, so we are going to spend the night camping outside the stable with Jacob."

"Ima, are you sure? It will be so cold. There is plenty of room in here for all of us."

Rebekah shook her head. "It's a warm night and they already have a fine fire going. We'll be all right… do not forget, Mary, that once all the animals are brought in for the evening it will be quite crowded in here."

"Oh yes, I did forget about that. You won't mind spending another night in the open?"

"Not at all," Rebekah said, waving her hand. "We have many people to visit with and share our joy."

"I wish I had the strength to receive them." Mary yawned, trying hard to keep her eyes open.

"Don't worry. You just rest." Rebekah took Jesus from Mary's arms and placed him back in the manger. "You won't mind staying in this stable, will you?" Rebekah asked as she placed another blanket over Jesus.

"Actually, I find it quite comforting." Mary yawned again. "You know how much I love animals."

Two weeks later, after the circumcision and naming ceremony and after they had registered with the authorities for the census, Rebekah, Heli, and Jacob prepared to return home.

"I will see you soon, Ima." Mary wept as she hugged her mother goodbye.

"Oh Mary, please don't cry. You know how hard it is for me to leave you." She held Jesus in her arms and was loathe to hand him back to her daughter. "However, your father and Jacob both need to return to Nazareth, for there is much work to be done. I know you will be fine here with Joseph. I only wish you were coming back home." She kissed Jesus on the forehead and reluctantly returned him to Mary.

"We will only be in Bethlehem for a little while, Ima. After my time of purification has ended and we have presented Jesus at the temple in Jerusalem, we will come home to Nazareth. We will see you in about two months," Mary assured her mother, kissing her on the cheek.

"You act as if you will never see each other again," Heli interrupted. "Now give me my grandson, so that I might say goodbye." Mary grinned and handed Jesus to Heli.

"You were most fortunate to secure a room here at the inn in exchange for carpentry services," Jacob mentioned as he waited for his turn to hold the baby.

"Yes, Anna has plenty to keep me occupied," Joseph agreed. "She has already ordered new tables for the inn."

"And a better bargain I have never made!" Anna proclaimed as she came out of the inn to see the threesome off.

"It's only been two weeks, but the news of this baby's birth has made my place very popular. I've even had to hire more servants." She grabbed Jesus' finger and smiled. "Besides, I enjoy having an infant around. It keeps me young." She winked.

Everyone laughed and said their final goodbyes. Joseph drew close to Mary and put a comforting arm around her shoulder as he waved goodbye to his father and in-laws. "Well, I guess I'll go get those tables started!" he said once the trio disappeared from sight.

Anna looked at the sleeping baby in Mary's arms and took comfort in the fact that the little one would be safe at her inn. She, along with all the others who had come to see the baby, had felt something akin to awe at the whole spectacle of his birth. She would miss the young family when it was time for them to go.

"I'd best tend to my other guests. You let me know if you need anything." Anna gave Mary's shoulders an affectionate squeeze and went inside.

Alone, Mary walked around the courtyard of the inn, rocking Jesus in her arms until he was fast asleep. "I love you so much," she whispered as she kissed his tiny nose. "If you are this easy to handle, I shall recuperate quickly."

CHAPTER
— 13 —

When the time of her purification was completed, Joseph and Mary took Jesus to Jerusalem to present him to the Lord. As they approached the Holy City, Joseph quickened his pace and steered the oxen toward the temple stables. Mary walked alongside him, carrying Jesus in her arms.

"I love Jerusalem." She sighed.

Joseph smiled. "Don't we all?"

Mary nodded. "Look at the temple, Joseph. When the sun hits the gold panels on the walls, it's almost blinding to the eye."

"It is magnificent, isn't it? You would think that after coming here year after year, we would not be amazed by its beauty."

"Well, it does change every year, since Herod is still building it. I wonder when he will be done?"

Joseph shrugged and did not answer. Mary shifted Jesus in her arms and walked silently beside Joseph, lost in her own thoughts.

Here was a place the Great God of Heaven had selected for his chosen people to meet and worship Him. Mary had never seen anything so spectacular. Only one thing marred the beauty of the temple for her—the animal sacrifices that took place within its walls. She remembered when her parents had first brought her to Jerusalem. She had been shocked at the brutal way in which the innocent creatures lost their lives. Placed on the altar alive, the animal's neck was slashed, its blood sprinkled around the altar, all to atone for man's sin.

Mary shuddered, trying to banish the memories from her mind. It broke her heart to see innocent animals slaughtered for her sins. Even today, in accordance with Jewish law, she and Joseph would have to make a sacrifice in order to end her time of purification. She looked at Jesus' beautiful face and compared it with the innocence of the lambs offered for sacrifice, both so pure and totally at the mercy of others. *Why does Yahweh require a blood sacrifice to atone for man's evil?* She wished there could be another way, and wondered if her son—God's son—would someday, somehow put a stop to this horrible part of their faith.

Before they entered the temple area, Joseph paid a small fee and left the oxen at the temple stables. He then went to purchase a pair of doves for their offering, while Mary took Jesus ahead to the Women's Court.

Sometime later, as Joseph entered the courtyard, he regretted that Mary had gone ahead of him, for the number of families present made it difficult to find her. After pushing his way through the crowd, Joseph gave his offering to the temple priest, searched for Mary, and soon found her in a secluded corner, quietly nursing Jesus.

"Are you almost finished, Mary?"

"Yes, Joseph. In fact, Jesus has just now gone to sleep." She rearranged her clothing and gently placed Jesus against her left shoulder. Patting his back, she heard a soft belch, a slight cry, and then all was peaceful. "He always falls asleep while he's eating," she said with a grin. "I often wonder if he gets enough to eat."

Joseph reached out and gently stroked his finger down Jesus' nose. "Of course he gets enough to eat," he responded. "Don't you know all men fall asleep after a good meal?"

"Oh, Joseph!" She giggled and they began to walk toward the area of the temple where babies were consecrated to the Lord.

"I am so thankful the consecrations are all done at once," Mary said as she surveyed the crowd of people waiting to dedicate their babies. "Why, if we had to wait in line for this we would be here until tomorrow."

Joseph nodded his agreement. He was glad he was able to get Mary close enough to hear the words of the priest as he blessed the many babies before him.

As they stood and listened to the priest, Joseph noticed an elderly man enter the courts. Although frail in body, he exuded an inner strength that seemed to make him stand out. *A Holy Man?* Joseph wondered as he watched him. He appeared to be questioning each couple as he passed by them. Joseph noticed he would nod, then move on to the next couple.

"I wonder who that is," Mary said as she shifted Jesus in her arms.

"I was just thinking the same thing," Joseph answered. "I wonder what he is asking everybody."

"I suppose we'll find out. He's coming this way."

The old man soon stood before them and introduced himself as Simeon.

"Long ago, the Lord God revealed to me that I would not die before I had seen the Messiah, and today I was moved by the Spirit to enter the temple courts," Simeon recited, his gaze wandering to the baby in Mary's arms.

"Woman," Simeon said, "I have asked several parents here where their babies were born and what line they come from. Might I ask the same of you?"

"Our son was born in Bethlehem and is of the line of David," Mary answered.

Simeon's heart stirred within him. "May I hold him, so that I might give him a blessing?"

"Yes, of course," Mary replied as she placed Jesus in Simeon's outstretched arms. "His name is Jesus."

Simeon's wrinkled face grew bright as he gazed at the baby in his arms. "Jesus?" He nodded and smiled at the name's meaning, "God is with us."

Simeon lifted his eyes to Heaven, blessed the baby, and praised God, saying, "Sovereign Lord, as you have promised, you can now dismiss your servant in peace. For my eyes have seen your salvation, which you have prepared in the sight of all people, a light for revelation to the Gentiles and for glory to your people Israel."

Simeon handed Jesus back to Mary and, blessing the young family, he said to them, "This child is destined to cause the falling and rising of many in Israel, and to be a sign that will be spoken against, so that the thoughts of many hearts will be revealed." He took Mary's hands and with eyes full of concern said to her, "And a sword will pierce your own soul, too."

Mary was speechless. This was the blessing? It sounded like a curse. She looked at Joseph, beseeching him with her eyes to get her out of there before she began to cry.

"I—I don't know what to say, sir," Joseph stammered as he took Mary's hand in his. "I'm sure my wife and I will never forget your words."

Simeon, oblivious to their bewilderment, nodded, touched the baby's head once more, and then disappeared into the crowd. As Mary and Joseph watched him leave, an elderly woman approached them. She had been watching Simeon, and she knew something unusual was happening when she saw the old man make an appearance in the Women's Court. She heard the blessing he gave and knew she had to see the baby.

"Please, my dear. Might I have a word?" She snagged the sleeve of Mary's robe, causing Mary to stop short. Joseph put a protective arm around his wife and was about to rebuke the woman, but stopped when he saw her. Her back was bent at an odd angle and she walked with a cane for support. He felt sore just looking at her. He stilled his rebuke and turned to listen.

"I am a prophetess, and my name is Anna. I never leave the temple, but I worship here night and day—fasting and praying. I heard Simeon's words about your baby. Praise God! For your child has been born as an offering for many—for all those looking forward to the redemption of Jerusalem."

As Anna was speaking, Joseph noticed that a crowd was gathering to listen to Anna. The more animated Anna became, the more the crowds pressed closer, intent on seeing Jesus.

"Mary," Joseph whispered as he eyed the crowd. "I think we should leave. Quickly, give me Jesus."

Without another word, Mary handed Jesus to Joseph and, holding fast to each other, they pushed their way through the people toward the outer courts, through the city gates, and back home to Nazareth.

CHAPTER
— 14 —

We stayed in Nazareth just long enough to visit our family and friends, pack the rest of our belongings, and move back to Bethlehem," Mary said to the two disciples as she continued her story.

"Why did you feel you had to live in Bethlehem, when Joseph had just finished building you a home in Nazareth?" Matthew asked. "Wouldn't you have been more comfortable with your mother close by—less lonely?"

"It would have been wonderful having Ima near. However, I was not lonely. A dear friend of mine, Rachel, had lived in Bethlehem for some time and, of course, we still knew Anna from the inn. Even if we had not known anyone, Joseph would still have moved us to Bethlehem because of Micah's prophecy," Mary explained.

"What prophecy?" Luke asked.

"But as for you, Bethlehem Ephrathah, too little to be among the clans of Judah, from you One will go forth for me to be ruler in Israel," Mary recited. "Joseph felt it was important to stay in Bethlehem. It was close to Jerusalem and Joseph wasn't sure what Yahweh would require of us in raising His son."

"What do you mean?" Luke asked.

"Well—we weren't entirely sure if Jesus was to be raised by us or in the temple, so Joseph wanted to be close to Jerusalem until we had a clear leading from Yahweh."

"A wise decision," Matthew said, writing furiously.

Mary nodded. "When Jesus was born and the shepherds came and told us how the angels had appeared to them, I thought that was astounding. Just to think of how Yahweh was celebrating the birth of His son. Then later, the Magi came, following a star that had appeared in the sky. They believed it proclaimed God's glory, to show that the Messiah had finally come." Mary tilted her head slightly and smiled. "I often think Yahweh created that star as a comfort for me and Joseph."

Luke furrowed his brow and asked, "You and Joseph…?"

"Yes, to let us know in His own loving way that Jesus was His son—our Messiah—and that He was watching out for us." She looked at Luke while brushing a fly away from her face. "It also confirmed to Joseph that I did indeed carry a holy child. Yahweh is such a loving and great God to have considered my fears and concerns about Joseph's doubts. But He began to use Joseph in other ways, and Joseph grew to be a fine father to Jesus."

As the two men silently contemplated all that Mary had told them, she stood up and said, "I need to begin preparations for this evening's meal. You will both join me, of course?"

Clumsily, they both stood and nodded, "Oh, yes. Thank you," Luke said, accepting her invitation for the both of them. "I'm anxious to hear more of your story, if you're not too tired, of course."

Mary laughed, "Ah, well—you should be the ones to worry about being tired, I think."

"Why?" Luke furrowed his brow and tilted his head.

Mary smiled secretively without answering and made her way downstairs.

Luke turned to Matthew and asked, "What was that all about?"

Matthew shrugged his shoulders and grinned, "My best guess is that we are going to be put to work."

"Put to work?" Luke grunted. "You can't be serious."

Matthew laughed and draped his arm around Luke's shoulders. "Did I ever mention that Mary and my mother were the best of friends when they were growing up?"

Luke stared at Matthew as if seeing him for the first time. "Then you must have known Jesus when he was younger!"

Matthew nodded. "Yes, his brothers and my brothers used to play together. In fact, Mary would often put us to work when we became too idle."

"Is that why you think she's going to make us work for our dinner?"

"Indeed I do, and we're going to do everything she asks."

"We are?"

"Of course. She's the mother of the Messiah, Luke. Are you going to say no to her?" Matthew laughed and slapped Luke on the back, then hurried down the stairs after Mary, with Luke following close behind.

As Matthew had suspected, Mary did put them to work. Her servants could have easily done the chores she chose for them, but as she pointed out, "It is a poor man that does not work for his meal." And work they did. They brought water in from the well, collected fuel for the fire and, much to Luke's chagrin, baked bread in the outdoor oven.

"Once you get the dough thin enough, place it on the heated pebbles in the oven." She demonstrated, stretching and pounding the dough to a proper consistency. "As soon as you place it on the pebbles, almost immediately take it out, for it will burn if you leave it in too long."

Luke was stunned and insisted that this was women's work. Matthew laughed as he listened to Luke try to argue with Mary.

"Mary... it is not right for you... a woman... to be telling me what to do," Luke pointed out. "I, of course, do not mind bringing in such heavy things as water for you, although you do have servants to do that, and I certainly don't mind finding fuel for your fire—however, again, your servants could do that as well. But I will not lower myself to baking bread like a... a... "

"Careful, Luke," Matthew quipped. "You just might go hungry tonight."

Mary stood with her hands on her hips, looking at Luke as a mother looks at a disobedient child. "Luke, I am sorry if you think baking bread is a chore that would be too hard for you."

"I did not say it was too hard!"

"No? Then you could bake bread without my supervision?"

"Of course." He stood straight and huffed, offended at her remark.

"Good! I am so glad you see it that way," she said as she made her way back into the house.

"That's not the point," Luke sputtered. "I am a man—"

She turned to him, her eyes twinkling with delight. "Yes, I know, Luke… but I'm sure you will be able to do it anyway." She smiled and disappeared into the house.

Luke stood there, mouth gaping, unsure of what had just happened. Matthew was laughing so hard he thought his sides would split. He handed Luke some dough and began to explain to him once again the fine art of baking bread.

Later, as they sat inside enjoying the bread, Mary remarked, "You did such a good job on this bread, Luke. I'm so proud of you."

Luke turned red, but beamed from the praise. "Thank you very much, not only for the lesson in bread making, but in humility."

Mary and Matthew laughed and Mary, not wanting to embarrass Luke further, asked, "Shall I continue with my story?" Both men nodded and she continued.

"What I am about to tell you I learned from the Magi who paid homage to Jesus. Apparently, they followed the star from the east for some time. Everywhere they stopped, they asked about the birth of the King of the Jews. Eventually, they came to Jerusalem and requested an audience with King Herod."

———

"It has begun. The One we have waited for, who made the stars and planets in the heavens above, has finally arrived," Caspar confirmed. The tall dark man looked again at the strange star that had appeared one month earlier. He knew the constellations in the sky like the back of his hand. He and others like him had been studying the heavens for as long as he could remember. Never before had he seen a star like this one.

For years, they had diligently searched the ancient prophecies and the heavens for a sign that would be for all people. Generation after generation had waited for his coming and now they knew instinctively that he had arrived. The King of Kings—the Messiah—was now among men.

He turned to his companions and asked, "What do our scrolls say? Do they say anything about the God of Israel?"

Melchior unravelled a scroll, scanned it, and then began nodding excitedly. "The God of Israel will someday send a mighty king to rule over all the earth. This king will put an end to all war and will rule righteously over his people."

"It is a sign from God. We must follow it, my brothers." The leader of the ancient tribe of seers urged his fellow astronomers to join with him. "If you have read the prophecies and have followed the alignment of the planets, then surely you must come to the same conclusion."

"Caspar, my young friend, I agree that something significant has occurred," Melchior responded. He was the oldest of the seers that had gathered. Respected by all, he knew the others would listen to him. "This is indeed a new star in the sky, but we must not be hasty. We must wait and see how long the star will remain. We will search the sacred scrolls again, and when we are all in agreement we will look for the Messiah."

"I'm sorry, Melchior, but I agree with Caspar—we must leave immediately." An audible gasp was heard as all heads turned in the direction of Balthasar, the youngest of the seers. To contradict Melchior was a rare thing. However, Balthasar's wisdom was great for one so young, and because of that he had never been afraid to speak his mind. He was a great interpreter of dreams, could read untold things in the stars, and to date had never been wrong in his predictions. If something was going to happen of any significance, Balthasar knew about it before anyone else.

Encouraged by Balthasar's boldness, the other seers who had gathered voiced their agreement, urging Melchior to change his mind, which he did with some reluctance. After much debate, they decided that Balthasar, Caspar, and Melchior would go pay homage to the newborn king as representatives of their country. The only question that remained was how to find him.

"If we follow the star, it will lead us to the King," Balthasar stated.

"Where do the ancient scrolls say we will find him?" asked someone from the group of men that had assembled for this important meeting.

"They do not say where, but I assume that the God of the Jews would likely be in Jerusalem," Caspar observed as he stood waiting for a decision from the others.

"Get supplies together then. Prepare for a long journey. Let us leave within the week and follow this strange star to wherever it leads us," Melchior commanded after a lengthy silence.

"Also, bring gifts of gold, frankincense, and myrrh," Balthasar added, "for I have seen that these particular gifts will be needed for the Holy One."

CHAPTER
— 15 —

Sire, we are most grateful that you would take the time to see us." The Magi bowed low to the ground in respect for Herod, King of Judea, Galilee, and Iturea. They had traveled many miles and many months since the star had first appeared. When they saw that the star was leading them in the direction of Jerusalem, they were overjoyed. It only made sense, they discussed, that the King of the Jews would be born in Jerusalem. So they hurried directly to the temple to question the temple priests.

When Herod had heard about their questions, he summoned all his chief priests and teachers of the law to the palace and asked them where the Messiah was to be born.

"He is to be born in Bethlehem, sire, in Judea," one of the priests had answered.

"Why do you think he is to be born in Bethlehem?" Herod had asked, his heart racing at the threat to his throne.

"It is because of the scriptures that we believe this," a young teacher of the law had responded. He unrolled a parchment containing a particular scripture and began to read aloud: "'But you Bethlehem, in the land of Judah, are by no means least among the rulers of Judah; for out of you will come a ruler who will be the shepherd of my people Israel.'"

Herod sat in stunned silence as he listened. *The King of the Jews? Surely, that story is not true.* His first thought was for the reaction of the Jews should they suspect their Messiah had arrived. They would demand he renounce his throne. He had to do something immediately or else find himself unable to control the people.

"Tell me," Herod swallowed as he tried to control his rising emotions. "Have any of you talked to the Magi who have recently arrived from the east?"

"I have, sire," another priest replied. "They believe the Messiah has been born. But we assured them it was simply not possible."

"Why do you say that?"

"Because, sire, we would have known about such a momentous event. We have served Yahweh all our lives and we know Him better than anyone. We are His priests and teachers. Something of this magnitude—the Messiah appearing—would certainly not escape our attention." The others nodded their agreement, causing Herod to think that perhaps he was alarmed for no reason. *Either that or these priests are becoming full of themselves. Can anyone really know the mind of the living God?* He waved his hand, dismissing the priests, charging them not to repeat what they had discussed with anyone, and then secretly sent for the visiting Magi.

Now those same Magi bowed before him, waiting expectantly for confirmation of the birth of the Messiah.

"Tell me, when did you see this star appear in the heavens?" Herod asked.

"Sire, we observed it almost two years ago as we were surveying the night sky," Caspar answered. "We noticed at once that it was a new constellation of a significant brilliance, never before seen in the heavens. Believing that something of great magnitude had happened, we searched all our ancient scrolls and determined that the Messiah, the King of the Jews, had at last been born."

"Do you know where he has been born?"

"No, sire, we do not. We have only been following the star, hoping that it will lead us to the child, that we may worship him."

"Worship him?" Herod tried hard to mask his anxiety. It was one thing to have foreigners coming into his country to worship a king—it was quite another when that king was not him. "Of course, you may worship whom you please," he said. "However, I am the King of Judea and my people, both Gentile and especially Jew, recognize me as their King. You would do well not to cause my people confusion in this matter."

The Magi bowed low to the ground and Melchior said, "Sire, you are indeed a great King. The reason we came to Jerusalem first is the magnificent temple you have created and are still creating for the God of the Universe. It is because of your belief in the Great and only true God that we know you also wait for the promised Messiah—a king unlike any other."

"That is quite true," Herod lied, "and since I can see you mean the child no harm, I will tell you that I have recently discovered from my chief priests and teachers of the law that you will find the child in Bethlehem." He would send them there, Herod decided.

They would find the child for him, and then—he would kill him. "I urge you to go there. Make a careful search for the child, then report back to me when you find him, that I may go and worship him as well."

Astounded at this good news, the Magi nodded their agreement. Unable to perceive the hatred and jealousy Herod harboured in his heart for the newborn King of the Jews, they thanked him and left.

———

"By the time the Magi arrived in Bethlehem, Jesus was almost two years old," Mary continued as they were finishing their meal. "Apparently the star seemed to move and they followed it until it stopped over our house in Bethlehem."

"How long was it there?" Luke asked.

"It was only there for a short while, just long enough for the Magi to find us."

"What did it look like?" Matthew asked.

Mary tilted her head and pursed her lips as she tried to describe what she saw. "You are both familiar with the brightness of the North Star?" Both men nodded. "Well, it was perhaps more brilliant than that."

"It didn't shine like the sun?"

"Shine like the sun?" Mary giggled. "Matthew, if it shone like the sun, don't you think Herod would have found us a lot sooner?"

Matthew's face reddened and he rolled his eyes. "That was a silly question, wasn't it?" He laughed. "What I meant was this—

was it brighter than all the other stars in the sky? Did it have an unusual brilliance to it?"

"I suppose so, but then again I have never been an astronomer." She shrugged. "It was definitely brighter than the North Star. The Magi seemed to be the only ones who recognized it, though. Not even Herod and his priests recognized that a new star had appeared in the Heavens. Other than that, I don't know what to say."

"What about the people of Bethlehem and the story the shepherds told of Jesus' birth? Did you tell people that Jesus was the promised Messiah?" Luke asked, changing the topic.

"Oh my, no!" Mary's eyes grew wide. "Both Joseph and I felt it was better to let the people think of Jesus as just a normal baby, which he was—except for his extraordinary conception. You know how people are—especially the religious leaders—they would have thought it blasphemous for us to call our son the Messiah. So we kept silent."

Matthew agreed, "A wise choice. It would have been dangerous to reveal something like that."

"Yes, indeed." Mary nodded. "Which leads me to the next part of my story."

———

Their excitement grew as the star they had followed for so long finally brought them to an unassuming house in Bethlehem. Joseph had been sitting outside on Mary's kissing bench enjoying the night air when the men and their contingent of camels, horses, and servants arrived.

"Peace be unto you!" they called as they dismounted.

"Unto you as well," Joseph replied. "May I be of assistance to you gentlemen?"

"We have followed that star," Caspar answered, pointing above him. "We have come from a great distance, sir, and for many months, in search of the King of the Jews." He dismounted from his horse. "It stops here at this house. Is there one within who deserves our worship and praise?"

Joseph felt his chest tighten in fear. He had noticed the unusual star a few nights ago, but thought nothing of it. Now he wondered how many more would follow it, seeking the King of the Jews. He had almost forgotten that Jesus was not his flesh and blood son. Reluctantly, he nodded and motioned for the men to come inside.

When they saw the child with Mary, they bowed down and worshiped him. Then they opened their treasures and presented him with gifts of gold, frankincense, and myrrh. Joseph and Mary were at a loss for words and could only say thank you, which they did repeatedly, overwhelmed that the Magi were bowing before their little boy and worshipping him.

After a while, the men made ready to depart, but as they were about to leave, Balthasar told Joseph and Mary all that Herod had said to them, and that he had wanted to know the exact whereabouts of Jesus. When he mentioned Herod's name, Mary once again felt that familiar stab of fear in her heart.

Balthasar saw the look of concern on Mary's face and told her that they had been warned in a dream the night before not to go back to Herod, and he assured her that they would return to their country by another route.

"But," he cautioned them, "be careful. Herod is a jealous king and he will not let his throne be threatened. Guard the secret of your child carefully."

And with those final words of warning, they left.

That night, while all of Bethlehem slept, the star's bright light dimmed, and an angel of the Lord appeared to Joseph in a dream.

"Get up," he said, "take the child and his mother and escape to Egypt. Stay there until I tell you, for Herod is going to search for the child in order to kill him." Joseph awoke with a start and a feeling of dread spurred him to action.

"Mary," he whispered, as he shook her shoulder gently. "Mary, my love, wake up."

"What is it, Joseph?" Mary yawned. "Is Jesus all right?"

"Jesus is fine. He is asleep. But we must leave at once for Egypt." Joseph found a sack and started throwing their belongings into it.

"What? Joseph, what are you doing? What's going on?" Mary blinked, sat up, and rubbed her eyes.

"An angel of the Lord appeared to me in a dream and said that Herod was going to try to kill Jesus. He told us to leave for Egypt at once."

Mary gasped and quickly jumped out of bed. "We must leave now?"

"Yes. Let Jesus sleep while we get everything ready, but we must leave tonight, before daylight." He ran outside and began hooking the oxen up to the wagon.

"Oh look! The star has gone out," Mary said as she followed him outside.

Joseph looked up at the sky and worked faster. Mary saw his fear and began to tremble as the need to flee overpowered her. Joseph saw her shaking and went to her. He wrapped his arms around her and whispered words of comfort. "Don't worry, Mary. It's better this way, as we can make our escape under cover of darkness. Everything will be all right." He kissed her forehead and she looked up at him and smiled, drawing strength from his embrace.

"We must hurry," he reiterated. Mary nodded and began gathering food and other items they would need, for the journey would be extremely long and dangerous.

When they were ready, Joseph gathered up a sleeping Jesus and laid him gently atop a sheepskin blanket in the back of the wagon.

"Joseph, will we stop and say goodbye to Anna and Rachel?"

"We cannot delay, Mary. We will send word to them once we are safe. But for now we must not waste any time."

Mary was very disappointed but understood Joseph's concern. They had both encountered angels before and they knew enough to obey. So without another word, Mary obediently followed Joseph out of Bethlehem, away from her friends and into an uncertain future.

CHAPTER
— 16 —

We traveled toward the Mediterranean coast and boarded a ship in Joppa, which took us to Egypt." Mary sighed as she remembered the details of the harrowing journey. "We had no idea where we would stay—we only knew we had to go. If not for the gold the Magi had given us, we would not have been able to afford the fare for the ship."

"Were you able to inform your family of your whereabouts?" Luke asked, humbled by the obedience and trust both Mary and Joseph had exhibited in their lives. He could understand why God had chosen this couple to raise His Son.

Mary nodded and replied, "Yes, to our surprise, on the road to Joppa we met an acquaintance of Joseph's who was traveling through to Cana. Joseph asked him if he would mind delivering a message to my parents in Nazareth. He assured us that he would."

"He did not wonder why you would leave your home with all your belongings and not tell anyone?" Matthew questioned.

"If he did, he didn't ask." Mary shrugged. "Joseph was always making journeys away from Bethlehem to purchase cedar and other supplies for his carpentry business. I assume the man simply thought Joseph was taking me with him this time.

"But that was the least of our worries. By the time we neared the port of Joppa, we started hearing horrible stories of what Herod was doing to the children in and around Bethlehem. Hundreds of people with little ones were crowding the docks when we got there. Everyone wanted to get out of Judea." Mary's eyes glazed over as she relived those days. "It was because of Yahweh's provision that we actually got on a ship. The soldiers started arriving like a mass of locusts just as we were putting out to sea. I remember thinking a storm was coming—it sounded like thunder at first, but then I realized it was coming from the ground, so I thought perhaps it was an earthquake. Then I saw them, hundreds of Roman soldiers on horses, bent on destroying all baby boys two years old or younger. They were just babies and they were dying because Herod feared for his throne."

Mary's face grew pensive as the memories flooded over her. Tears pooled in her eyes as she recalled the tragic events. "The screams of the mothers and fathers whose babies were ripped from their arms is something I will never forget. When the soldiers realized that the parents had no place to run but into the sea, they started rounding them up and herding them all toward the dock. Just before Joseph ordered me below deck, I saw one centurion go through the crowd and, if a child looked to be two years old or younger, he would slit its throat while still in its mother's arms. If anyone tried to run, they were chased down and speared through together with their child."

"I heard that whole families died trying to protect their babies," Matthew said, shaking his head. "I cannot understand evil like that. I can see how one man might be consumed with evil—but a legion of men, doing one man's bidding? Did they not have a conscience? Were they all so possessed of the devil that they could carry out such a monstrous act?"

"It is a hard thing to contemplate, Matthew," Mary said. "Man seeks to please man—they are concerned for all the wrong things and never the right things. Until they seek to please Yahweh, study His Word, and live for Him and Him alone, they will never know what goodness really is. Satan has control of their hearts as long as man says no to God." Mary wiped her face of the tears that had fallen.

She abruptly stood. Luke and Matthew started to rise but she said, "No, please sit—I will return shortly. I just need to be alone for a minute. Excuse me, please." She turned and ran down the stairs from the roof where they had taken their evening meal.

Luke rose to go after her, but Matthew grabbed his arm, saying, "Let her go, Luke. Sometimes it is overwhelming for her. She just needs to take a breath, put some water on her face, and she will be fine. Mary is resilient. She will be back shortly with a smile on her face and ready to share again."

"Perhaps we should call it a night, Matthew," Luke suggested. "She has talked all day and I can see she is getting weary. We can finish this tomorrow."

"As you wish. I'll go find her to see where we can sleep to-night." Matthew rose and started to head down the stairs. "Oh… I almost forgot!" he exclaimed, snapping his fingers and turning around.

"What?" Luke asked as he followed him toward the stairs.

"In the morning… before we talk to Mary again… "

"Do you think she will be too upset to continue?"

"No, it's not that." Matthew shook his head, leaned in, and whispered, "Do you think you could… you could…?"

"Could… what? Out with it, man! I will do anything to cheer Mary up! What do you want me to do?"

Matthew nodded and playfully punched Luke on the arm. "Do you think you could make some of that tasty bread again? It was delicious!" he said with a smirk and a laugh as he took off down the stairs, with Luke chasing behind him.

"I can't believe I was tricked not once but twice in one day," Luke chuckled as they gathered to break their fast the next morning.

Mary giggled while she passed some fresh bread and cheese to Luke. "Now you know what it was like for Jesus when he was growing up. We were always laughing, always having fun with each other. Some people think my son went around with a serious frown on his face all the time, never taking time to enjoy the little things. But he enjoyed life feverishly. Each day was a gift to Jesus and if he taught us all anything, it was that we should not let a day go by without making full use of it."

Matthew chewed silently and nodded. He swallowed his food and added, "He was a lot of fun—a real jester."

COME TO ME

Luke's eyebrows arched in surprise. "Jesus?"

"Don't look so surprised, Luke," Mary chided. "He was a child once, you know. He liked to laugh just like everybody else."

"What would he do?"

"Nothing bad, of course—Jesus was always mindful of another's feelings," Mary stated as she passed a plate of figs to Matthew. "Just fun things, like we did with you to get you to make the bread." Mary looked at Matthew and the two started chuckling again.

"Humph! Go ahead and laugh, but if my mother were still living she would be delighted to know that her son, the doctor, had performed the intricate surgery of baking bread."

"We won't tease you anymore, Luke," Mary giggled. "But you should know that whenever Jesus had fun with someone, it was usually with family and he would always have a valuable lesson behind it. That way, the poor victim would not only learn something, but he would also be able to laugh at himself at the same time."

"So who did Jesus get his sense of humour from—you or Joseph?" Luke asked as he recovered his writing tablet from a nearby table.

"A little from both of us, I think," she replied as she rose from the table to retrieve a pitcher of fresh water. "Although spending time with his cousins John and James didn't help matters. Jesus called them the 'Sons of Thunder' for good reason. I never saw two boys who liked to laugh and jest as much as those two. They were always getting into trouble. Fortunately, my son was a good deal wiser and far more intuitive than his cousins were. He knew it was one thing to laugh *with* someone, but quite another to laugh *at* someone." Mary poured them each a cup of water, then sat down at the far end of the table. "Are you ready for me to tell more of my story?"

"I am," Luke said as he took a sip of water. "Matthew, do you have your tablet?" Matthew held his tablet aloft and Mary began again.

CHAPTER
— 17 —

J oseph, Amos has arrived to pick up his chest," Mary announced to her husband as he finished sanding the wood piece before him. "He brought Avi with him and I've asked him to stay for the morning meal."

"Avi?" Joseph muttered as he concentrated on his work. His bronze arms were speckled with wood shavings and sweat from a long morning's work.

"Yes... Amos' son?"

"Amos?" Joseph muttered. Mary rolled her eyes and smiled. She could tell Joseph had not heard a word she said. He was receiving so many orders lately that he barely had time to eat, much less talk to her. She shook her head and grinned. "My love, you work far too hard, so I insist you eat on time today. Especially since we have guests."

Joseph nodded and grunted his agreement, then continued working. He was creating a new design for one of his wealthier patrons—an intricate pattern of olive branches carved into the lid of a cedar chest, inlaid with gold. The chest itself was so deep that once, Jesus had gone into Joseph's workshop and hid in the box while he was playing with his friends. The lid had accidentally slammed shut on him and, had Joseph not been coming in to work on the chest, Jesus would have suffocated. From that point on, Jesus was forbidden to go into the workshop if his father wasn't there. An obedient child, he hadn't entered Joseph's workshop again without finding him first.

A dove carved into each corner of the chest carried a twig from an olive branch in its beak. While Joseph had found the carvings time-consuming, he had also found it very satisfying to have created such a design with his own hands. When he was finished with this piece, Joseph knew his business would increase even more. He ran a keen eye over the chest, rubbing oil into the grooves of the carving. He was pleased with himself. He had never made such an exquisite piece. In Bethlehem, the orders he received were never as fancy as this. Tables, chairs, maybe a chest or two, but never anything so intricately designed. Certainly none of them would have gold. Except for those few citizens who were prosperous, Joseph rarely had the opportunity to let his talent for woodworking stand out.

Since they had come to Alexandria, the Lord had brought more than one wealthy customer to their door. The intellectual and cultural influences in the city were prominent everywhere one turned. The Great School of Alexandria was noted for mathematics, astronomy, medicine, and poetry. The Great Library of Alexandria held more than half a million books and scrolls. Joseph was confident Yahweh had brought Jesus here to grow up so that he could take advantage of everything the city offered. Joseph was determined that Jesus would receive a good education.

Yes, Joseph pondered, *everything is working out according to Yahweh's plan.* It was only because of Yahweh's provision that they had found a home and started a business within the first two weeks of their arrival.

Though no angels had appeared to them again, both Joseph and Mary could, at times, feel their presence surrounding them. After they had arrived in the port of Alexandria, they were at a loss as to where they would live. They knew there was a large Jewish settlement in the eastern part of the city, so they headed there right away. Joseph had no idea if they would find suitable living quarters, or if they would have to stay at an inn, but Mary kept insisting that God would provide, and as usual she was right. Upon entering the settlement, they were greeted by a young child about the age of five who had asked them, quite innocently, who they were.

"I am Joseph and this is my wife Mary and our son Jesus. And who would you be?" Joseph smiled at the inquisitive dark-haired youngster.

"I am Avi. My father is the Rabbi at our synagogue. His name is Amos. I've never seen you before. Are you new here? Do you need a rabbi? My father is a great rabbi! You should come and meet him."

Joseph laughed quietly to himself as he remembered how Avi had peppered them with questions in rapid succession, while taking Mary's hand and leading them directly to the synagogue. When they told Amos about the slaughter of the children in Judea, and that they had barely escaped, he was quick to lend his hand in getting them settled. Before they knew it, they had a home with ample space for the three of them, with room enough to open a carpentry shop.

"Joseph! What bad manners you are having today, my friend," Amos said, entering the shop and plopping his huge body on a nearby stool. "I know Mary came to tell you I was here, so I was expecting you to come into the house. Instead I have to come and find you."

Joseph wiped the sweat off his brow with his forearm and smiled sheepishly at Amos. "Forgive me, my friend. I was just putting the finishing touches on this chest." Joseph stepped back to give Amos a better look.

"Ah, you have outdone yourself this time, my friend." Amos ran his hand over the lid of the chest in admiration. "I'm sorry I did not ask for the same design on mine. Of course, I would never be able to afford it, so I suppose it's just as well." He laughed. "Your work is by far the best in all of Alexandria, Joseph. Perhaps in all of Egypt. The Lord has blessed your hands."

"Thank you, Amos. Your kind words bring joy to my heart." He walked over to a table that held a bowl filled with water and washed his hands. "So, did Mary show you your chest?"

"Yes, indeed! It looks wondrous! Adah will be thrilled when she sees it."

"When will you give it to her?" Joseph dried his hands on a towel, then indicated with a nod for Amos to follow him inside the house.

"Today is the ninth anniversary of our marriage, so I will give it to her as soon as I get home. She has begged me for a chest to put

110

things in since we were first married. I thank Jehovah you came along when you did, for I do not think my wife would have been satisfied with another year passing and she having to put her gowns and robes in sheepskin sacks."

After they finished their meal, Joseph and Amos returned to his wood shop while Jesus and Avi were allowed to go outside and play. Jesus was now four years old. They had been in Egypt two years. Mary prayed daily for a sign that it was safe to go back to Bethlehem, but Joseph insisted that as long as Herod was alive they would remain in Egypt. He assured her that Alexandria had much more to offer Jesus than their little village of Bethlehem and it was probably part of God's plan for them to stay. She began to wonder if she would ever see her family or friends again.

They had developed a regular pattern of communication through friends and acquaintances traveling from Alexandria to Nazareth to Bethlehem, but it wasn't the same. Sometimes it could be months before a letter arrived from anyone, or before she could send one out. She hoped they would be able to return soon, while Jesus was still young. She wanted her family to see the black curly locks of hair that surrounded his face. To see the dimple in his left cheek when he smiled and the sparkle that was ever present in his ebony eyes. Mary sighed. *Someday,* she dreamed.

Looking at Jesus through her kitchen window, she was struck once again by his similarities to Joseph, especially in his manner-isms. When Jesus smiled, he cocked his head at a slight angle, as Joseph did when he was amused at something. When concentrat-ing, he would furrow his brow and purse his lips in the same familiar way of his earthly father. Mary had been so afraid there would be some kind of holy glow around her son that indicated he was not normal, but her fear was short-lived, for Yahweh wanted His Son protected until his appointed time as much as she did. Mary often wondered how and when Jesus would come into his kingdom. He did not seem to understand at this young age who he was. *It's just as well*, she thought, *for it gives me more time to enjoy him.*

She finished washing the dishes and stepped outside to sit on her kissing bench and watch the children play. She was surprised to see them arguing. Jesus had something in his hand and Avi was trying to grab it away from him.

"No!" Jesus shouted. "You will hurt it! Leave it be."

"It's already dead, Jesus. Just give it to me and I will bury it." Avi roughly grabbed Jesus' arm and tried to pry his hands loose, but whatever it was that Jesus held Mary could see he would not give it up for anyone. She ran to his aid, suspecting he had some sort of creature in his hands, as he was always picking up lizards, birds or mice, thinking he could keep them as pets. Mary shook her head. *This boy needs a dog*, she thought.

"Jesus, may I see what you have in your hands?" she asked as she knelt on the ground beside him.

"He has a dead bird and he won't let me have it!" Avi shouted as he stamped his foot. "It's not fair. I found it first."

"It's not dead, Ima." Jesus cradled the bird to his chest. "I can still feel it breathing. Please, can we help it?"

"Let me see." Mary pried Jesus' hands apart to find a baby sparrow, close to death. "Oh dear, this little bird does indeed look beyond our help." She scoured the treetops for the mother bird and saw it perched in a nearby acacia tree. "Jesus, look! The mother wants her baby back."

"See! I told you. Let it go." Avi placed his arms across his chest and waited impatiently for Jesus to obey his mother. "Let me give it to the mother bird."

"You mustn't touch it, Avi," Jesus warned as he walked over to the acacia tree. "It isn't strong enough for rough hands."

"I won't be rough. I promise."

"Jesus, what are you planning to do?" Mary followed him over to the tree.

"I'm taking it close enough so that it may fly up to its mother."

"It's too young to fly, Jesus. The bird must be put back into its nest by hand." Mary stood with Jesus at the base of the tree and held her hand out to him. "Put it in my hand and I will put the sparrow on the first branch. The bird's mother will tend it once she sees it."

"I could climb up and put it back in its nest," Avi offered. Mary could see he was anxious to grab hold of the bird and was glad her son kept the tiny creature cradled in his hands. Although Avi was seven years old, he was not as mature as Jesus was at four and, as Jesus had observed, Avi tended to be too rough when he was excited.

"No one needs to put it anywhere. It will fly away on its own," Jesus said with confidence. He brought the tiny bird closer to his chest and gently stroked its wings. Turning his back on his mother and Avi, Jesus cooed softly to the creature, whispering words into his hands only the bird could hear.

Avi squirmed beneath Mary's restraining hand on his shoulder. She could feel his anxiety mounting and wasn't surprised when he escaped her grasp and bounded toward Jesus. Just as he was about to grab the bird, Jesus lifted his arms towards the tree, opened his hands, and the baby bird flew away.

"Did you see that?" Avi squealed. He watched as the bird flew directly to its mother, who chirped wildly. "That bird was dead! It wasn't breathing! How did you do that, Jesus?"

"Avi, it obviously was not dead, only dazed," Mary said. "Jesus did nothing more than wait until it was ready to leave his hands."

Jesus waved to the bird and its mother and giggled in delight as he watched their reunion.

"See, Avi? It wasn't dead, was it, Ima?" Jesus' innocent smile unnerved Mary, for she was certain the bird had been dead and she knew this little miracle, if indeed a miracle had taken place, was just a sign of things to come.

CHAPTER
— 18 —

The knock was so soft she almost missed it. When she opened the door, the curly haired boy standing before her grinned, waved a chubby hand and said with delight, "It's me, Savta!"

Rebekah's eyes grew wide with excitement and she scooped the child up into her arms and yelled, "Heli! Heli! Come quickly! Hurry!" She peppered the boy with kisses while he giggled and kissed her back.

Heli came running into the room. "Rebekah, what is it? Is everything all right? You sounded…" And then he saw him. "Jesus? Is it Jesus, Rebekah?" He broke into tears. He put his arms around his wife and grandson, rejoicing that Jesus was finally home. Mary and Joseph, who had watched the reunion from a distance, quickened their pace and were soon enveloped in hugs and kisses from Heli and Rebekah.

"When did you get back?"

"Oh my, how Jesus has grown."

"Mary, he looks just like you."

"When did you get back?" Rebekah repeated as she gave Mary another kiss.

Mary laughed. "Early this morning. We went to see Jacob first. Then we unpacked our things and came here."

"It's been so long," Rebekah lamented. "We feared we would never see you again."

"Mother, I'm sorry we left the way we did, but the angel that appeared to Joseph made it clear that we were to leave at once."

"A good thing you obeyed, too," Heli said. "The horror that took place in this country by Herod's hands was unbelievable." He shook his head at the vile memories. "You are safe—that is all that matters."

"We were protected by Yahweh everyday," Joseph assured them. "Why, the gold the Magi brought us kept us living quite comfortably. We had a fine home, I continued my carpentry business, and it was quite profitable. We had wonderful friends— Yahweh took great care of us." Joseph patted Heli on the back reassuringly and continued, "Another angel appeared to me. He told me it was safe to return to Israel. But when I heard that Herod's son Archelaus was reigning in Herod's place, I thought it would be safer to return to Nazareth. So unless we hear from the Lord again, we are here to stay."

"This calls for a celebration." Heli clapped his hands. "Tonight we will have a feast and invite our friends and relatives to celebrate your return."

"A feast?" Jesus squealed, his eyes wide with excitement.

"Yes, Jesus, a feast. A great time to make merry!" Heli said as he took him from Rebekah's arms and twirled with him around the room.

The celebration lasted throughout the evening and into the next day, with many people dropping by to welcome Mary and Joseph home. Several of their friends remarked at how fortunate Mary and Joseph had been in getting away before Herod's massacre against the children. Although the attack was concentrated mainly in Bethlehem, many surrounding cities had not been spared. Several of Mary's friends had lost their babies, and this weighed heavily on her heart. She learned that her good friend Rachel, from Bethlehem, had not escaped the heartache, and her dear little boy, Joshua, had been killed before her very eyes.

"A voice is heard in Ramah, weeping and great mourning, Rachel weeping for her children and refusing to be comforted, because they are no more."[7]

Mary was amazed at the coincidence of this scripture. She knew it was not talking about her Rachel, but it certainly was appropriate, for Rachel still wept for her son. Her husband Levi, after much pleading from his distraught wife, had moved them back to Nazareth from Bethlehem after the attack so that Rachel could be with family while she mourned. Levi feared for his wife's sanity and wondered if she would ever recover. So he was greatly relieved to see Mary back in Nazareth. He knew she would be a big help to Rachel, for they had known each other since childhood.

---

[7] Jeremiah 31:15; Matthew 2:18

"Joshua was everything to me." Rachel rested her head on Mary's shoulder. They had slipped away from the festivities to talk and were now sitting on Mary's kissing bench outside her home. "Now I just feel so empty, Mary, as if my life is over." She started crying and Mary placed an arm around her shoulders and began to cry with her.

"Rachel," she said as she hugged her friend, "Yahweh feels your pain and sorrow. He will not let you down. Do not lose hope, for our God can turn evil plans like Herod's into good."

"How, Mary? How can the death of hundreds of babies be turned into good? You have no idea what it was like!" she snapped. "You weren't there! How did you know it was coming, Mary? How did you know?"

She did not know what to say. Rachel was one of her best friends. Would she understand how Yahweh had been working in her life? That the Messiah had been born to her? That Jesus had been protected from Herod for that very reason?

"Rachel, will you trust me when I say that if I could have warned you, I would have?"

"I'm sorry, Mary. I didn't mean to lash out at you." She patted Mary's hand. "Forgive me. I know it was just a coincidence that you left before the slaughter. You could not have known about Herod's plans." She sniffed and wiped her teary eyes. "I am just jealous that you have a son and I don't."

Guilt overwhelmed Mary once again. She *had* known Herod's plans! Would it have hurt if she had warned her friends in Bethlehem, or somehow gotten a message to Rachel? *This is going to haunt me for the rest of my life,* she thought. The worst part was that she had been suspecting for some time now that she was with child again. She guessed she was at least three months along. She had not told anyone yet, not even Joseph. To reveal something like this to Rachel now seemed almost cruel.

Tears sprang to her eyes as she grasped Rachel's hand. "Rachel, I am so sorry for your loss. If I could bring Joshua back to you, I would. My heart is breaking for you and if my heart weeps just think how much more Yahweh weeps for those dear babies who were lost. They are safe in His hands now and your grief will not be forgotten. You will find hope and comfort again."

"Thank you, Mary," Rachel sighed as she rested her head on Mary's shoulder. "You have been my comfort this day. I have needed your presence in my life desperately."

"And now I am here. Yahweh has heard your cry already." She smiled. "Do not lose hope. Yahweh's plans for you will be made known soon enough."

"How can you be so sure, Mary?"

"Trust me," she said with a smile. "He has ways of getting ones' attention." She patted Rachel's hand. "Let's rejoin the others and get a bite to eat, shall we? You could use some fattening up, you know," Mary teased.

Rachel smiled and together they walked arm in arm back to Heli's house.

CHAPTER
— 19 —

Six months later, I gave birth to a boy we named Joses."

Mary, Luke, and Matthew were once again on the rooftop, both men transcribing Mary's words as she shared her story.

"How did Rachel react to that?" Luke asked, compassion for her friend evident in his eyes.

"She was thrilled for me because she, too, found herself expecting again—which of course delighted me." Mary stood up, walked to the edge of the rooftop, and looked down into the street. "We spent the months of our confinement together making clothes for the infants to come. Rachel gave birth one month after me, to a boy named Matai."

"Doesn't that mean a 'gift from God'?" Matthew interrupted.

Mary turned, smiled, and nodded. "Yes it does, for the Lord heard her cries and blessed her with another son."

"And how did Jesus react to all of this?" Luke inquired.

"He was five years old by then and was thrilled to have babies around. He looked at them as if they were his personal playmates." Mary beamed. She walked back over to the cushions and sat once again with the two men.

"As the years passed, I had three more boys—James, Jude, and Simon—and two girls—Anna and Ruth." She put a pillow behind her back and leaned against the stone wall. "They were a lively bunch," she continued. "Joseph and I found our lives to be very fulfilling. He instructed each boy in the trade of carpentry."

"Did Jesus like carpentry?" Luke asked as he poured a cup of water from the jug he had carried up to the roof.

"Yes, he did. In fact, as he grew he especially loved to help Joseph in the wood shop, where he would carve little dolls for his younger sisters to play with."

"How was he with the other children, and how were they with him?" Matthew took the jug from Luke and poured water for himself and Mary.

"Thank you, Matthew." Mary accepted the cup and drank from it. "He was a very perceptive child and sensitive to those around him. His younger siblings adored him, for he was never harsh and always had time for them. He was wise beyond his years. He could hold a conversation with any adult and would often leave them wondering if this was really Joseph's son. He spoke with the wisdom of one who had been properly schooled. However, he had no formal training, except that which he learned from his father and the teachers at our local synagogue."

"My mother used to tell me about the time you lost Jesus. Can you tell us about that?" Matthew suggested.

"Lost him? What happened?" Luke shifted position to get more comfortable.

Mary took a deep breath and expelled it. "Well, every year we went to Jerusalem for the Feast of the Passover. It is never an easy thing to travel with little ones, but what made it special was that it was not just with our own immediate family but friends and other relatives as well. So we were able to help each other out if any needs arose.

"Now, when Jesus was twelve years old, we went up to the Feast once again. We sang and talked as we traveled. It was a wonderful time to catch up with family and friends. The children would often run from family to family to visit with their friends as they walked." Mary chewed her lower lip in concentration. "At times, it was difficult to know where one's children were over the course of the week, and in order to keep from getting lost in the crowds of travelers, many parents would send word up or down the line to let the other parents know where their children were.

"Every year Elisabeth and Zechariah brought John with them to the temple and Jesus could hardly wait to visit with his cousin," Mary continued.

"John the Baptist?" Luke clarified.

"Yes." Mary nodded. "It was the only time of year when Jesus would see John. John loved the Lord and was always searching the scriptures. He was fortunate in that he was properly schooled. Zechariah was, after all, a temple priest, and they could afford a good education with the finest teachers. Jesus was younger than John by six months, but he loved to sit at John's feet and listen to what he had learned."

———

As the band of weary travelers approached Jerusalem, many decided to make camp on the outskirts of the city, near Bethany, where the crowds were not as large. Those fortunate enough would find room at an inn. Most were prepared to set up tents and camp for the two weeks they would be there.

"Ima," Jesus said as he helped his parents unpack the wagon, "do you think we'll be able to find John in this crowd?"

"Not here—we will find him tomorrow at the temple," Mary responded as Joseph handed her the necessary utensils she would need for making supper. "Zechariah is serving there this year and Elisabeth and John are staying in quarters provided for the temple priests and their families for special events like Passover."

"I wish we could go into the city today," Jesus sighed.

"Time enough for that tomorrow," Joseph said as he handed bedding to Jesus. "We will leave early in the morning. It will give us time to worship at the temple. Then we will join Elisabeth and Zechariah at their home for the Passover meal. You will have plenty of time to visit with John. Don't worry."

"I'm not worried, Abba, just excited."

They laughed and worked together to get their tent up before sunset. When Jesus had finished helping his father, he started a fire for his mother to cook over, then gathered his siblings and kept them occupied with stories and games until the evening meal was ready.

Mary so appreciated her eldest son's ability to keep the children quiet. He always seemed to sense when she was tired and, without being asked, he would gather up the young ones and keep them out from underfoot.

She looked at them now, sitting quietly at Jesus' feet while he told them wonderful stories that always held a hidden meaning. The children loved these stories because after the tale was finished, it was their turn to figure out what it meant. It kept them occupied for hours, and for that Mary was grateful.

"Our son is going to be a fine teacher, I think," Mary said to Joseph as she watched Jesus.

"It's hard to believe he's only twelve," Joseph said. "His wisdom is not of this world."

Mary sighed. "I forget sometimes—do you think he knows, Joseph? Do you think he comprehends his destiny?"

"I'm not sure. When Joses was born, I remember Jesus kept running outside to look up into the sky. I asked him what he was doing, and do you know what he said?"

"No—what?"

"He said he was looking for the angels." Joseph chuckled. "He was extremely disappointed when none appeared to herald Joses' birth."

"Well, I suppose after having four brothers and two sisters, he's caught on that his birth story was unique."

Joseph nodded. "Whether or not he understands why is an entirely different matter."

The next morning, as Joseph and Jesus left for the temple, Mary took the younger children to help Elisabeth prepare for the Passover meal. This year would be a different Passover for Mary, as her mother Rebekah had died the previous spring. Heli had elected to stay home, as he felt the journey would be too long for "his old bones," as he called them. Mary worried at first that he would spend the feast alone, until he assured her that he and Jacob would be spending the Passover meal together. She had never seen either man cook and wondered how they would fare, until Mary's older sister Salome, who was expecting another child and was too far along to make the journey, informed her that she had invited both men to her home for the day. Greatly relieved, Mary was able to go without feeling guilty, but she still missed both his presence, and especially her mother's.

Elisabeth greeted her with hugs and kisses when she arrived and they quickly caught up on all the news in their respective families. While the women prepared the Passover meal, John left to meet Joseph and Jesus at the temple. John knew Jesus loved to learn and especially loved to study the scriptures whenever he could, so while they waited for Zechariah to finish in the temple, Joseph, Jesus, and John sat and listened to the Teachers of the Law.

"The teachers were quite impressed with you, Jesus. Especially that newest teacher, Nicodemus. He seemed quite flustered with the questions you were asking him," John observed. They were walking toward the Garden of Gethsemane, having left Zechariah and Joseph back at the temple. The garden was a favourite spot of John's for praying and was fast becoming Jesus' favourite place to pray as well.

Jesus smiled as he remembered the look of shock on the priest's face. "It is hard for one who is a slave to the Law to conceive of any other way to God—but I just had to ask him if he thought a relationship with Yahweh was possible. I believe it is, don't you, John?"

John nodded. "Oh, yes—why would Yahweh tell us so much about Himself if we were not to know Him?"

"It is peculiar." They arrived at Gethsemane and made their way to a huge gnarled olive tree which stood in the center of the garden. Taking a seat beneath the tree, each boy silently meditated on the glory of God. After a while, John pulled bread, cheese, and water out of a sheepskin sack and offered some to Jesus.

"I wish I could stay here in Jerusalem," Jesus moaned. "I've so much to learn."

"I think it would be wonderful if you could stay. However, I think you know more than the rabbis do, so I don't think studying more Scripture is what you need." John broke another piece of bread off the loaf his mother had packed for them and handed it to Jesus.

"Do you think you will get married, Jesus?" John asked, changing the subject.

"I don't know. I do not think so. I have too much within me that is restless and agitated by the sin around me. I just want to yell at the Pharisees and their hypocritical ways. I want to see people repent and return to God." He shook his head. "No, John, I do not see myself getting married." He smiled and shrugged. "However, who knows what Yahweh's plans are?"

Jesus closed his eyes and leaned his head against the trunk of the tree. "I do know that my birth was prophesied, and so was yours. We are destined for service to God, but it will not be easy. I see hard days ahead for us, John."

John nodded his agreement. "I know what I have to do, Jesus, but are you prepared for the cup you will have to take?"

"Isaiah says, 'He was oppressed and afflicted, yet he did not open his mouth; he was led like a lamb to the slaughter and as a sheep before her shearers is silent, so he did not open his mouth.'"[8] Jesus sighed and looked at John. "I am not prepared right now, John, to accept this prophecy. I am only twelve years old. I don't want to die. But I know that in the future, Yahweh will carry me through and I will partake of whatever cup He has set before me."

"Do your parents know you are aware of who you are?"

Jesus shrugged. "I'm not sure. They need to know soon, though, for I have to be about my Father's business. They need to be prepared."

The days passed quickly and before they knew it, it was time for them to leave. John and Jesus spent their remaining time in the temple studying with the teachers of the law. As the cousin of Zechariah, Jesus was a welcome guest. Most of the teachers knew John, of course, and were quite impressed with him, but they had been especially impressed at the knowledge Jesus possessed. They congratulated Joseph on a job well done, but Joseph felt he had little to do with it. Jesus' wisdom frightened Joseph sometimes, as it made him realize with amazement just who he had the honour of bringing up.

---

[8] Isaiah 53:7.

As the Passover celebration ended, Mary and Joseph said their goodbyes to Elisabeth and Zechariah and began the long trek home. As usual, the children were running back and forth to visit their friends, so neither Mary nor Joseph thought it odd that Jesus was not with them. Thinking he was in their company, they traveled on for a day. Then they began looking for him among their relatives and friends.

"I saw Rachel and talked to her, but she has not seen him since we left Jerusalem," Joseph said as he came back to camp that night.

"Joseph, I'm worried. Where could he be?" Mary's eyes were round with concern.

"My guess is that he is still in Jerusalem somewhere. No one has seen him at all."

"This is not like Jesus, Joseph. He is a very responsible boy. Something must have happened to him. What if he is hurt?"

"Do not fret, Little Mary. In the morning, we will turn back for Jerusalem. We will see if Elisabeth or Zechariah have seen him. We will find him. Don't worry."

It took them three days, but they finally found him in the temple courts, sitting amongst the teachers, listening to them and asking them questions.

"He has been here all along?" Mary cried when Joseph gave her the news. "Joseph, how could he have been so thoughtless?"

"Calm down, Mary. I'll go get him. Then you can yell at him—not me."

"Forgive me. I didn't mean to lash out at you."

He squeezed her hand. "I know. I'll be right back."

Mary had to wait in the Women's Court while Joseph fetched him. She paced in front of the entrance to the Men's Court and craned her neck to see past the bodies and pillars that blocked her view. Then she saw him. Joseph had his hand on the boy's shoulder and was guiding him out of the Men's Court toward her.

Mary watched Jesus' face light up when he saw her. He hurried to her side and hugged her. "Hello, Ima."

She returned his hug, then cupped his chin in her hands. "Son, why have you treated us like this? Your father and I have been searching for you for three days."

"Three days? But why were you searching for me?" he asked. "Didn't you know I had to be in my Father's house?"

Mary looked at Joseph, who shrugged and said, "Jesus, enough of your riddles. We have lost a day's journey already because of you."

"I am sorry, Abba." Jesus turned to his mother and hugged her again. "Ima, forgive me. I did not mean to cause you grief."

As they made their way back to Nazareth, Joseph and Mary kept a watchful eye on him, and Jesus, who was aware of their fears, stayed close to them, refusing to join the other children who were running back and forth to visit their friends. He was sorry he had caused his parents, relatives, and friends so much trouble. It had not even crossed his mind that they had been worried. He had been about his Father's business, so he naturally assumed they would know where to find him.

Even now as he watched her, he noticed that his mother was still upset. He determined then and there that he would not cause her anxiety again. He would always be respectful and obedient to his parents.

So Jesus grew in wisdom and stature and in favour with God and men.[9]

---

[9] Luke 2:52.

Part Two

"Come unto me, all ye that labour and are heavy laden, and I will give you rest. Take my yoke upon you, and learn of me; for I am meek and lowly in heart: and ye shall find rest unto your souls. For my yoke is easy, and my burden is light."
(Matthew 11:28–30, KJV)

CHAPTER
— 20 —

H e could tell as he came up the path toward her that she was in poor health. The doctor in him wondered how long she had been suffering. Luke knew that at eighty-three, Mary was nearing the end of her days, which was why the Apostle John had asked him to visit her again.

Two months ago, John had sent Mary a letter requesting that she move to his home in Ephesus. When she did not respond to his invitation, he became concerned and prepared to go to Jerusalem to bring her back, but since Luke was traveling there, he offered to bring her back to Ephesus with him. Over the years, Mary had traveled from Ephesus to Jerusalem to Nazareth—wherever her family or John happened to be. As she aged, her journeys became less frequent, until she finally settled in John's home in Jerusalem to stay. It was a concern to everyone, of course, for the situation in Jerusalem was getting worse and there was talk of a revolt against the Roman government. Yet again, John believed Mary was in danger and was anxious that she return to live with him.

As he came closer, Luke noted that she was sitting on her beloved bench once again, her head bowed over the bowl in her lap. He watched her quietly for a time, taking in her white hair and gnarled hands. How he would miss this dear woman when she was gone.

He cleared his throat, letting her know of his presence.

"The first time I met you, you were pitting olives," Luke said as he leaned over to look in the bowl. "What is it today… dates?"

She nodded, winked, and said, "Start pitting these and maybe I'll let you stay for supper."

He laughed, sat beside her, and did as she requested, touched by the way Mary had always treated him like a son.

"It's good to see you, Luke. Did you come all the way from Ephesus to help me pit dates, or is there something on your mind?"

He grinned. "I see your sense of humour is still intact—and how did you know I was in Ephesus?" he asked as he leaned over to plant a kiss on her cheek.

She shrugged and replied, "John's in Ephesus. I received a letter from him about two months ago—to which I have not responded. I was actually expecting him to show up on my doorstep. So why are you here?"

"Why haven't you answered him?" he countered.

"I'm still thinking about it."

"You don't want to move to Ephesus?"

"I'm old—it's a long journey and, to be honest, I'm not sure I would survive the trip."

Luke nodded and continued pitting dates. "You realize it's not safe to be here now, Mary. You think things were bad when Nero started burning Christians and throwing us to the lions." He closed his eyes to banish the memories. "If the Jews rise up as we've been hearing, the Romans will destroy Jerusalem. In truth, that is why I wanted to come. I could never forgive myself should anything happen to you. Since I am returning to Ephesus, it would be best for you to come with me. If we travel together, you will have a doctor with you, someone who would know how to help you should you need it. Would it make you feel better about traveling if I was with you?"

She smiled and patted his cheek. "I always enjoy your company, Luke. Having a doctor with me would definitely be an advantage—especially since it is you. But I will still have to think about it."

Remembering that she could be stubborn, and not wanting to force the issue, Luke decided to change the subject. He looked at the now finished bowl of pitted dates and said lightly, "Well, I guess my work here is done, unless you have any bread for me to bake?" he teased.

She laughed. "No need to bake bread today and no need to work for your supper. I was just teasing you."

She stood up slowly and groaned, "Oh dear! My body does not like it when I move." She rubbed her hip. "I'm certainly not the young woman you met so many years ago. Before you know it, I will be as stiff as my kissing bench."

Luke stood to help her, his brows drawing together in concern. "Please come back with me, Mary. You should not be alone."

She waved her hand in dismissal and, grasping the bowl of dates, she shuffled into the house. "I watched Jesus die a gruesome death on the cross. I've seen His followers—some my own flesh and blood—martyred for their beliefs. I have outlived my husband. My sister and my children no longer live close by. I rarely get to see my grandchildren." She placed the dates on the table and turned toward Luke. His face held the same concern John's had so many years ago. But there was something else she could see in his eyes. It was the fear of losing her. She was seeing that look on all who came to visit her of late. It was only natural. She was an old woman and her days were coming to an end. *Perhaps my son wants me to make this journey,* she thought. She glanced around the room. The believers took such good care of her that she had become too set in her ways—too complacent. She frowned. *This will never do.*

She nodded and smiled. "You are right. There is nothing to keep me here—not really. But…" Doubt set in again. She was weary of traveling. She just wanted to stay put in one place, yet her spirit sensed it might be the last time she would see John. "Are you sure John will not be coming here anytime soon, Luke?"

He shook his head. "The church in Ephesus needs him right now. With Paul's death,[10] they lack direction and are easily led astray. He cannot leave. I'm sorry."

She heaved a long, drawn-out sigh. "I suppose you can tell him that I will come visit him—for a while."

She sat at the head of the table that now graced the room. Gone were the throw pillows and low table from years ago. When

---

[10] The Apostle Paul.

her son Jude had seen her difficulty in bending down to sit, he had made a table with long legs and four matching chairs. She indicated with a nod that Luke should sit.

"Not just a while, Mary," Luke clarified as he sat opposite her. "He wants you to live with him in Ephesus. He worries about you being here in Jerusalem at your age. As I already told you, the situation here is dangerous. You could be hurt even if you are not directly involved. Please, Mary," Luke pleaded, "We have lost so many of our brothers and sisters. John is fearful for you. I'm to bring you to him to stay."

"Ephesus or Jerusalem—either place is dangerous, Luke."

"Granted. But John…" He hesitated, groping for words. "He needs to have you near him right now, Mary. These are stressful times. Do you understand what I mean?"

She nodded. "I do. He has many concerns for the church. Worrying about my welfare shouldn't be one of them." She was quiet as she pondered the change this would bring in her life. "Ephesus is so far, Luke. Will we be traveling by sea?"

"Yes, of course. It's the quickest way."

"I remember the horrible ordeal you and Paul went through when you were shipwrecked. I don't think I could endure something like that, Luke."

"I cannot guarantee you a safe voyage. I can only promise that I will not leave your side throughout the journey."

She smiled and reached over the table to squeeze his hand. "Well then, I suppose that's good enough for me. When will we leave?"

"There is a ship that will leave the port of Joppa in two weeks' time. If we leave next week, that should give us enough time to pack your belongings, travel to Joppa, and book passage."

She nodded. "It will be good to see John again. He has not been here to his own home for quite some time."

The servants came with bowls of stew and he offered up a prayer before they began to eat. As Luke watched Mary, he noticed her hands tremble as she drank from her cup and he wondered what other symptoms she might be experiencing at her advanced age. He prayed she would make it to Ephesus.

As Mary ate, she could feel Luke's eyes watching her. She knew the good doctor was dying to question her about her health and she appreciated his concern. She would not tell him of her fears. Let him think it was just old age for now, so he would not fuss over her. A journey at sea would surely lift her spirits. It would be nice to spend the following weeks in his company. She prayed she would survive the journey.

They arrived in Joppa with little time to spare. Their belongings were loaded and they put out to sea within the hour. Mary was thrilled at the feel of the ship beneath her feet. She loved the smell of the sea air and the spray of mist off the water that occasionally sprinkled her face. It made her feel like a young girl again.

They were travelling on a Roman ship that held over two hundred people. There was a place to sleep below, but the cramped quarters made the air stale and humid, so Luke and Mary spent most of their time above deck. During their weeks at sea, they had several opportunities to share the Gospel with their fellow passengers, and with the crew. Although there was some danger in sharing the Gospel, both Mary and Luke trusted God to keep them safe. As it turned out, there were very few women on board, so the passengers and crew tended to treat Mary as a surrogate mother of sorts, due to her advanced age.

She often found herself telling stories to the men to relieve the boredom of the long journey. It was during one of those times that Mary cleverly shared her story and that of her son's death and resurrection. She had brought her kissing bench with her, which Luke placed above deck and secured to the bottom of the mast. Each day she would sit there and greet the crew and passengers inviting them to join her. As she chatted with them, Luke felt transported back in time to when she had first shared her stories with him and Matthew. Mary began by talking about her cousin John and of how he had gone before Jesus to announce his coming.

"He went into all the country around the Jordan, preaching a baptism of repentance for the forgiveness of sins," Mary explained to the men before her. "It is written in the book of Isaiah the prophet: 'A voice of one calling in the desert. Prepare the way for the Lord; make straight in the wilderness a highway for our God.'[11] That scripture came to pass through my cousin John, called the Baptist."

"I heard about him," a sailor said. "My father told me Herod had him beheaded. He was your cousin?"

"Yes, he was," Mary said with a nod. "You remember that Herod married his brother's wife, while his brother was still alive?"

---

[11] Isaiah 40:3.

Some men nodded, remembering the treachery of Herod toward his brother Philip.

"For those of you who don't know John's story," Mary continued, "Herod had John arrested and bound, and put him in prison, because, well, he married his brother Philip's wife Herodias while Philip was still alive, and John was quite vocal in denouncing him for this deed. For that reason, Herod wanted to kill John, but he was too afraid of the people, because they considered John a prophet. From what I understand, he wanted to keep John locked up, but Herodias wanted him killed. So on Herod's birthday, the daughter of Herodias danced for him and all of his assembled guests. And she pleased Herod so much that he promised with an oath to give her whatever she asked."

Mary swallowed as she tried to tell the story of her cousin's death. To her it still felt like yesterday. A few moments passed as Mary struggled to gain control of her emotions.

Luke reached out and grasped her hand while whispering into her ear, "Would you like me to finish?" Mary nodded and Luke picked up where she left off.

"Herodias hated John for pointing out her sin so publicly," Luke began, "so she told her daughter to ask Herod for the head of John the Baptist on a platter. So, because of his oaths and his dinner guests, Herod granted her request and had John beheaded. His head was brought in on a platter and given to the girl, who carried it to her mother."

In unison, the sailors looked with compassion at Mary, knowing she was reliving that moment in time. "John's disciples came and took his body and buried it," she added. "And then they went and told Jesus."

"Jesus?" someone asked.

"Yes, he is the one I would like to tell you about."

"Who was he?" another sailor asked.

"He was my son."

"Woman," interjected a Roman centurion who had been listening to the conversation, "is this Jesus the same one the Christians preach everywhere?"

"He is."

"You could be arrested for talking to us about him, you know," the soldier said as he moved closer to her.

"I know… but, sir… is it against the law to talk about my own children?"

The centurion smiled at the clever old woman sitting in front of him and said, "I've heard of no such law that could prevent you."

"Thank you, sir." She smiled, then turned back to those sitting at her feet. "Listen, gentlemen, to what the scriptures say: 'Every valley shall be filled in, every mountain and hill made low. The crooked roads shall become straight, the rough ways smooth. And all mankind will see God's salvation.'[12] Do you know what that means?"

Mesmerized, they shook their heads and said as one, "No, what?"

Mary rejoiced inwardly at their eagerness to learn. "What once was hard to understand will now be made known unto you, and

---

[12] Isaiah 40:3–5.

you will know what the one true God did for you. You will see His salvation."

The perplexed looks on the faces before her caused her to pause and think of an illustration to help them. "For example," she said after a moment, "the Romans have built many fine roads that take us to all kinds of places. Traveling is easier because of these roads. Without knowing it, the Romans themselves have helped make it easier for the Word of God to go forth, because they have made it easier for Christians to travel from town to town."

"Woman!" the centurion growled. "I have great respect for the elderly, but I repeat, be careful. Mind what you say. Your life may depend on it."

"Sir, I meant no disrespect," she said, her tired eyes pleading for understanding. "I know the Roman Empire honours many gods. It is the belief of many of its citizens that they are on a safe path for life, by the many sacrifices they make to these gods. Unfortunately, the good people of Rome have been deceived. They paved the path so that the good news of the one true God, the Creator of the entire universe, could be known throughout the world—but they know Him not. It is my desire to tell everyone here about the one true God and the way to the path of salvation."

"The true God?" He scoffed. "Are you trying to make us believe there is only one God? That is very presumptuous of you, woman. It is also very hard to prove. What can your one true God offer me that my many gods cannot? Hmm? True God!" he sneered. "I'd like to see that."

He laughed and turned away with several others joining him, but as he started to leave he was overcome with fear that he might have offended this woman's god. Not sure of what her god could do, he stopped, turned, and said, "Go ahead then, woman. State your case. Show us the one true God."

Luke looked at Mary in surprise, shrugged, and silently lifted her up in prayer. Mary swallowed and began to tell her story once again.

CHAPTER
— 21 —

I don't understand why he is doing this," Mary said to Jesus. They had just returned from the annual Passover Celebration in Jerusalem. Exhausted, they sat down on Mary's kissing bench to catch their breath before unloading the wagon.

"It makes no sense for John to live in the desert when he has that huge home to himself." Both Zechariah and Elisabeth had died the previous year, one month apart, leaving John alone. He had refused to come to Nazareth to be with his family and had spent the year secluded in prayer and reflection. Now, he was apparently living out in the desert and Mary was anxious and confused over his behaviour. "He should be looking for a wife and settling down."

"Ima," Jesus said, taking her hand in his, "you are thinking in worldly terms. You are not thinking of what is best for John."

"How can you say that? Of course I am!" Mary huffed and folded her arms across her chest, offended that Jesus thought she didn't care.

"This is not a time for John to be thinking of his own needs, Ima. God has called him for greater things. You have told me that countless times. I have known this and John has known this since we were small children. Now it is time for him to reflect on what God has called him to do. He needs guidance and direction, and to be alone with Yahweh."

"Does he have to go into the desert to do that?" Mary asked, throwing up her hands in frustration.

Jesus chuckled. "You are too close to this situation," he said as he kissed the knuckles of her hand. "Soon John will be called to fulfill that for which he was chosen. Would you deny him the destiny God has called him to?"

Mary felt her emotions rising to the surface. She wiped her tears away with the sleeve of her robe and sighed. "Of course not—I've just lost so many of those I love. Your father, my parents, Elisabeth, Zechariah … I feel so alone and I feel like I have just seen John for the last time."

"Woman," Jesus began, placing his arm around her shoulder, "you have a very big heart, but it is getting crowded with the cares and woes of this world. Lay your head on my shoulder and I will give you rest."

Mary relaxed against her son and felt his peace imparted to her almost immediately. They sat there quietly, enjoying the sunshine, each lost in their own thoughts. Mary reflected on how Jesus had grown and changed into the man who would be the Messiah. He was now twenty-nine years old. Like John, he should have married by now and had children.

When Joseph was alive, both he and Mary had often discussed if they should arrange a marriage for Jesus. Muscular in build after years of hauling and cutting lumber with Joseph, talented in the art of carpentry and respected by all who did business with him, Mary knew that her son was a desirable match for any young woman. He was extremely talented and produced the most beautiful chests with ornate carvings on them, similar to the ones Joseph had created while they had been in Egypt. Several young women had expressed an interest in him already and he had close friendships with some of them, but he chose none of them for his bride. Joseph had become concerned about this and asked Jesus what it was that was holding him back from choosing a wife and starting a family. Jesus had replied that his purpose in life was to be in service to the Lord.

"In what way?" Joseph had asked. "As a temple priest? Like your uncle? They can get married, you know."

"I know that, Abba. I just feel that I am to keep myself wholly unto the Lord. Do you understand that?"

Joseph remembered once again Jesus' conception, his birth, and their flight into Egypt. He sighed, placed a hand on Jesus' shoulder, and said, "I do understand, son—sometimes I just forget."

Jesus nodded his understanding, absently patting Joseph's hand. "You have been a great teacher and father to me. I am the man I am today because of your love and instruction. I must serve the Lord and be ready for when He calls, Abba. To be married with children would hinder my service. For the cup I have to bear will not be an easy one."

"Do you know yet? About what you have been called to do?"

146

"I know the Father and He knows me. I do nothing on my own but wait for His guidance, and I know that my time is coming soon to begin my calling."

Mary sighed as she reflected on that conversation Joseph had repeated to her so many years ago. They came to realize then that their relationship with Jesus would soon change. She would always be his mother, but at some point he must become her teacher, her master—her Messiah. The transition was not always easy for her to make, for no mother finds it easy to let her son grow to become a man—to move away—to leave her. But how many mothers had to let their sons grow to become the Saviour of the world? Sometimes she simply could not come to terms with the little boy becoming the man, let alone the man becoming the Messiah.

As Mary relaxed against his shoulder, Jesus was lost in thought as well. From a young age, he had spent much time with his teachers at the synagogue. He had studied the scriptures until he knew them by heart. He listened to his parents' advice. He meditated, prayed, and fasted as he awaited his calling. He knew who he was, because his parents had told him countless times of his miraculous birth and the circumstances surrounding it. Nevertheless, he did not know when he was to start his ministry. He realized, like the prophets before him, that he would have to wait upon the Lord.

He recalled how, throughout his youth, the feeling of expectation had grown—a feeling that told him he was destined for something bigger than carpentry. When he was twelve, he began to realize that he was to be in service to the Lord. As he aged, it became apparent to him, and to his cousin John, that his life was to be one of discipline and sacrifice. It was hard at first, especially when his parents wanted to see him married. However, Jesus' love for Yahweh was so intense that at times he felt as if the two were one entity. He could not explain it in a way that anyone could understand, but even now he felt that he was not of this world.

"Ima?" Jesus nudged her head with his arm. "It grows late and I should finish unpacking the wagon. Are you rested now?"

She did not move.

"Ima?"

Realizing she had fallen asleep, Jesus carefully picked Mary up and carried her into the house where he placed her on her bed. Protectiveness for her overwhelmed him as he watched her sleep. He realized with an aching heart how important she was to him. It would be hard to leave her when his time came; he knew it would cause her grief, for they were very close.

―

"The months passed and word came to us again of John." Mary was becoming tired but was determined to tell her son's story to the men who had gathered near to listen. "The hardest part for me was knowing that John had completely abandoned his parents' home to live in the wilderness of Judea. Not only that, he had stopped wearing the beautiful clothes his parents had provided for him and instead began wearing clothes made of camel's hair and he was eating nothing but locusts and wild honey."

"Why would anyone in their right mind do something like that?" one of the guards asked.

Mary folded her hands in her lap. "It does sound strange, doesn't it? But, despite his appearance, many people went out to him from Jerusalem, all Judea, and the whole region of the Jordan."

"Why? What was the attraction for them?" someone asked.

"To become right with God, of course," Mary stated. "They would confess their sins and be baptized by John in the Jordan River."

———

Jesus knew right away that John was the one who was spoken of through the prophet Isaiah. Even now, he could feel his time growing short at home. Soon he would fulfill his destiny, as John was now fulfilling his.

He tried to prepare his mother for this in subtle ways, for he did not want her to suffer when he left home. He was, after all, the eldest male in the family, and since Joseph's death five years before he had handled all the responsibilities associated with the task of being head of the household. As the days passed, he slowly started handing those responsibilities over to his brothers James, Joses, Simon, and Jude. He made sure they continued in the trade of carpentry, taught to them by their father. He assured himself that even though two of his brothers were married with children of their own, they would continue to provide for Mary's needs. He reminded them often of their duty to care for their mother.

He spoke to his younger sisters and their husbands, ensuring that they would visit Mary often, as she was the type of woman who needed to have those she loved close by.

Most of all, he started speaking differently to Mary for her own sake. He would speak to her in a formal tone—calling her "woman" instead of the more endearing "Ima." He did this for her sake, as well as his own. He needed to separate himself from her, for her love for him was great and he would often find himself becoming a child again just being in her presence. She provided a peace that he did not want to leave behind. He carried fond memories of being held in her arms when he was a child and of being sung to sleep when he was afraid of the dark. He smiled as he remembered how she could make the pain of scrapes and cuts disappear just by kissing them.

She also needed to separate herself from him, to remember he was a grown man with a mission. For she constantly fussed over him and coddled him as if he were still a small child and not a grown man. He was her firstborn. She found it very hard to let him go.

One year later, he was ready. They had heard by this time that John had a huge following. Many people wondered if he John himself was the Messiah, but he assured them he was not. However, when he started rebuking Herod the Tetrarch, Jesus knew it was time to go. Mary was upset that he was leaving, of course, but relieved when he told her that he was going to see John. She feared for John's life once he had started speaking out against Herod and secretly hoped Jesus would be able to talk some sense into him.

"How long will you be gone? What will you do when you find John? How long do you think it will take?" She rattled off question after question as she helped him pack food and water for his journey. He would be walking on foot to find John, taking only what he needed and no more. He had heard that John was preaching in Bethany, which was on the other side of the Jordan River, so it would take him some time to get there.

"I don't know how long I'll be gone," Jesus replied, as Mary handed him some bread wrapped in cloth, "and I'm not sure what to expect once I get there. I only know I have to find John and that all will be revealed to me when I do. How long it will take, I have no idea, dear woman. Only our Heavenly Father knows that."

Mary swallowed as she tried not to cry, her eyes misting up. "Well then—you take care of yourself and try to hurry home in time for Matai's wedding."

"I will be here for Matai's wedding, Ima, don't worry. I would not want to disappoint Aunt Rachel." Matai was the son of Mary's best friend Rachel, whose firstborn had been killed by King Herod the Great, father of the current King Herod.

"You called me Ima," she said with a smile, her eyes filling with tears. "I didn't think I was ever going to hear that from you again."

Jesus shook his head in mock disbelief, his dark eyes widening. "Woman, you must be hearing things. I would not let my guard down at this late date when I am about to leave you for a while. To use a term of endearment with you now would be foolishness."

"But you did… I heard you, I…" She sputtered, not sure if she had really heard him, or if she had only wished for him to say it.

Jesus' eyes twinkled with merriment as he saw her confusion and wrapped his arms around her in a big bear hug. Laughing, he kissed her cheek and said, "Ima… I love you… I will see you again in time for Matai's wedding."

Tears spilling out of her eyes, Mary hugged Jesus back and said to him, "The Lord go with you, son."

"With you also, woman," he said, returning her hug. "With you also."

CHAPTER
— 22 —

Jesus found John baptizing people in the Jordan River. He looked like a prophet of old. His hair was a mess, his clothes dirty and worn thin from use. His beard was full, nearly reaching his eyes and Jesus wondered how it was that people trusted his cousin, for he looked like a madman. Then he heard him speak. When Jesus saw the fervour in John's eyes and the zeal in his voice, he knew why people were drawn to his cousin.

He did not approach John the day he arrived. Instead, Jesus mingled with the crowds on the banks of the Jordan, attentively listening to what John had to say. His heart was encouraged by his cousin's preaching. It seemed to Jesus that John was not afraid of anyone—not of Herod, the chief priests, or the teachers of the law. He told people what they needed to hear, not what they wanted to hear. It was a lesson that Jesus took to heart.

A sudden stir in the crowd made Jesus sit up. The crowd was being pushed back from the edge of the Jordan where John stood. He craned his neck to see what was causing the grumbling in the crowd and was surprised to see some of the same religious leaders who had taught John as a boy. They were pushing people out of the way so that they could get to the front. Jesus frowned and shook his head, wondering what his cousin would do.

"You brood of vipers!" John yelled at them, causing Jesus to laugh aloud at his cousin's courage. "Who warned you to flee from the coming wrath? Produce fruit in keeping with repentance and do not begin to say to yourselves, 'We have Abraham as our father.' For I tell you that out of these stones God can raise up children for Abraham! The axe is already at the root of the trees, and every tree that does not produce good fruit will be cut down and thrown into the fire."

The crowd began to murmur amongst themselves at John's audacity. To think that someone would dare insult the religious leaders both scared and delighted them. As one, they waited to see what their priests and teachers would do. Moments passed as the inscrutable faces of the leaders stared John down. Then, unexpectedly, the men turned and walked away. A collective sigh and a few chuckles could be heard throughout the crowd. Then someone asked, "What should we do then?"

"The man with two tunics should share with him who has none, and the one who has food should do the same," John answered as he returned to baptizing the people.

The day passed slowly but with much rejoicing as Jesus watched his cousin fulfill his ministry. It wasn't too long before he once again felt a shift in the attitude of the people. A murmuring went up from the crowd as before and Jesus turned to see what was causing the commotion. This time, tax collectors had appeared seeking John's baptism. Jesus knew many people regarded these men as pagans and traitors to the Jewish faith, who had defiled themselves because of their frequent contacts with the Gentiles. They were notorious for imposing more taxes than were required so that they could get rich quickly.

He searched for his childhood friend Matthew amongst the collectors. Matthew's mother Miriam was a good friend of his mother, Mary. Jesus recalled how disappointed Matthew's family had been when Matthew chose to become a tax collector. It was as if Matthew had ceased to exist in the eyes of his family. So it was with great joy that Jesus saw these men kneeling in repentance at John's feet. Regrettably, he did not see his friend among them.

"Teacher," one of the tax collectors asked John, "what should we do?"

"Don't collect any more taxes than you are required," he told them.

"And what should we do?" asked some Roman soldiers who had come to control the crowds.

Unafraid, John looked at them and said, "Don't extort money or accuse people falsely—be content with your pay."

The people gasped at John's fearless answer, but the soldiers did not take offence.

As Jesus watched, a number of priests and Levites from Jerusalem arrived and pushed their way through the crowds to confront John. Jesus shook his head at their behaviour. John walked back into the water, ignoring them. The priests waited at the river's edge and yelled out to him, "Are you the Christ?"

"I am not the Christ," he answered as he helped an old woman into the water.

"Then who are you? Are you Elijah?"

John shook his head. "I am not." He tenderly placed his hand behind the woman's neck and whispered in her ear. She nodded and pinched her nose between her fingers.

"Well then, are you the Prophet?" they yelled from the shore.

John dunked the woman's head beneath the water and she came up sputtering. Chuckling, John hugged her and helped her back to the river's edge to where the priests were standing. When they did not move to help her out of the water, John stared hard at them and said, "No."

One of the priests threw up his arms and yelled, "Who are you then? Give us an answer to take back to those who sent us. What do you say about yourself?"

John handed the old woman off to a friend and turned back toward the river. He walked to the middle, raised his arms, and shouted, "I am the voice of one calling in the desert, 'Make straight the way for the Lord.'"

"Why then do you baptize if you are not the Christ, nor Elijah, nor the Prophet?" the same priest asked.

"I baptize you with water," John explained. "But one more powerful than I will come, the thongs of whose sandals I am not worthy to untie. He will baptize you with the Holy Spirit and with fire. His winnowing fork is in his hand to clear his threshing floor and to gather the wheat into his barn, but he will burn up the chaff with unquenchable fire."

And just like that, Jesus knew his time had come. John's words made everything clear to him. Slowly, he stood and made his way to the front of the crowd. When John saw his cousin coming forward for baptism he was startled to see him and smiled a greeting. But when he saw the look on Jesus' face, his greeting died on his lips.

Jesus walked right into the water and stood face to face with his cousin.

John shook his head. "I need to be baptized by you, and yet you come to me?"

Jesus placed his hand on John's shoulder. "Let it be so now," he replied. "It is proper for us to do this to fulfill all righteousness." John nodded his understanding and baptized him.

When Jesus came up out of the water, heaven opened and Jesus saw the Spirit of God descending like a dove and lighting on him. A voice from heaven said, "This is my Son, whom I love. With him I am well pleased."

Jesus looked at John to see if he had heard the voice or seen what had happened to him. John grinned and laughed, patting his cousin on the back. He was thrilled with the knowledge that Jesus had at last begun his ministry, but he did not indicate to Jesus if he had heard Yahweh's voice.

The two men had barely spoken a word, a brief moment in time that was powerful for them both. Each had a calling from God and knew what they had to do. For it was at that moment, as the Holy Spirit descended on him, that Jesus knew what was going to happen to John and what was going to happen to him.

"Look, the Lamb of God, who takes away the sins of the world!" John suddenly proclaimed to the crowd, as he pointed at Jesus. "This is the one I meant when I said, 'A man who comes after me has surpassed me because he was before me.' I myself did not know him, but the reason I came baptizing with water was that he might be revealed to Israel." John looked at Jesus and smiled. "I saw the Spirit come down from heaven as a dove and remain on him." Jesus waded back toward the riverbank, pleased with the knowledge that John had seen the Spirit of God. "I would not have known him, except that the One who sent me to baptize with water told me, 'The man on whom you see the Spirit come down and remain, is he who will baptize with the Holy Spirit.' I have seen and I testify that this is the Son of God!"

The crowds of people surrounding John looked at the man he was pointing to and wondered why John was so excited, for he looked as ordinary as they did. However, two sisters, Mary and Martha of Bethany, and their brother Lazarus approached Jesus and invited him to stay in their home.

"Why is it that you invited me into your home?" Jesus asked later that evening, as they reclined over their meal.

"We have been followers of John for some time now," Lazarus said as he stroked his beard. "When he said you were the Son of God, we knew right away we should make sure your needs were provided for."

"And you believed him?" Jesus asked, amazed at their faith.

"We have offered our home to John several times, and our food," explained Mary, "but he is very strict in his commitment to

Yahweh. The only thing he accepts from us is the water we bring from our well. He would not come to us, so we went to him. We have listened to him daily. No one teaches as John does. He speaks the truth and sees people as they really are. Repentance is so important... and that is what John preaches. The Pharisees and Sadducees hate it, and that is why John rebukes them when they come and try to be baptized without first repenting of their sins."

"It's hard to repent of your sins when you believe you have none," Jesus stated.

They nodded and Martha said, "It is because of John's forthrightness that we believed him when he said you were the Son of God."

"No one else approached me after John said that. Even if I were not who John claims, custom alone would dictate that as a stranger in your midst, I should be invited for a meal or a place to stay. Only you three offered me shelter and food. Your faith and obedience to God will be rewarded."

The next day, Jesus went to hear John preach again, but as soon as John saw him he pointed at him and shouted, "Look, the Lamb of God!"

Jesus, not ready yet to begin his ministry, disappeared into the crowds but two of John's disciples, Andrew and Philip, ran after him. Turning around, Jesus saw them and asked, "What do you want?"

They answered, "Rabbi, where are you staying?"

"Come," he replied, "and you will see."

He took them to Mary and Martha's house. Martha invited everyone inside and she went to prepare a meal. While they waited, Andrew and Philip talked with Jesus and peppered him with questions. They listened to him expound on several subjects and soon the two men became convinced that Jesus was the Messiah, as John had claimed.

When they had finished their meal, Andrew excused himself to find his brother Simon. He found him selling fish outside the city gates of Bethany.

"We have found the Messiah!" Andrew exclaimed breathlessly as he raced up to his brother.

"You've what?" Simon asked as he finished selling the last of his wares. He looked at the people who had stood patiently in line for the fish he had brought from Galilee, threw up his hands, and said, "I'm sorry, my friends, but that is all I have until next month." Groans of disappointment rose up in chorus and the people started to disperse.

"We have found the Messiah!" Andrew repeated, his chest heaving as he tried to catch his breath.

"Oh, really?" Simon said sarcastically, disgruntled that Andrew had left him alone once again. "Do you have any idea, Andrew, how long it took me to sell these fish on my own? You said you were going with Philip for one hour. You promised me before we began our journey that this time you would be available to me. Yet you have spent our entire time here with Philip, listening to the Baptist. The day is almost gone and we have yet to find a place to spend the night. How could you be so irresponsible?"

"I'm sorry, Simon. Really, I am. If you would just listen to me—!"

Simon waved him off. "I am returning to Galilee tomorrow, with or without you. Now, if you'll excuse me, I need to find us a place to stay." He grabbed his meagre belongings and started walking towards the city gates.

"Philip and I have found the Messiah," Andrew repeated, his raised voice causing Simon to stop, turn, and give him a withering look. "Just come with me, Simon." he begged, holding out his hands. "Please?"

Simon sighed. "John the Baptist is not the Messiah, Andrew." He ran his hands through his hair in exasperation. "We've been through this before."

"You're right. He's not." Andrew nodded. Simon stepped closer to him and put a hand on his shoulder.

"I'm glad you realize—at long last—the truth. Now let's go before it gets dark."

"Simon… John is not the Messiah, but he has shown Philip and I who is. We spent the day with this man and we are convinced that Jesus—that is his name—is the one John has talked about for so long. Would you come with me? Please? We have been invited to stay at the same place he is staying. Then you can see for yourself."

Simon shook his head and smiled at his younger brother. "I must be mad." Andrew laughed, grabbed one of his brother's satchels, and said, "You won't be sorry. I promise."

Andrew took Simon back to Mary and Martha's, house where they found everyone seated inside, in deep discussion. When they entered, Jesus looked at Simon and, because the Holy Spirit had empowered him on the day of his baptism, Jesus knew things he had not known before, and he said, "You are Simon son of Jonah. You will be called Peter."

Simon stood in shocked silence, his face a mask of confusion.

"Rabbi, that's amazing. How did you know my brother's name—and my father's?" Andrew exclaimed as he made his way over to Jesus. "I know I never mentioned them to you."

"Of course you said something, Andrew," Simon replied, a hint of scepticism in his voice. "Either that or Philip told the Rabbi about me."

"Not I," Philip said shaking his head. "We have been talking about God's kingdom and John the Baptist and… well… everything but you." He started to laugh. "Sorry, Simon, but you're just not that interesting."

Simon scowled and sat beside his brother, who was sitting beside Philip. "It amazes me, Philip, how much you are like my brother. Neither of you has any concern for me at all, it would seem."

"Ah… yes, well… we try to think about you, Simon, but you are so easy to forget." Philip playfully punched Simon in the arm and everyone started laughing. It would be next to impossible to forget Simon son of Jonah, for he was over six feet tall, with broad shoulders, red hair, and no eyebrows whatsoever. Fortunately, he was able to laugh at himself and he joined in the fun.

Jesus grinned at the camaraderie between the two men and thought of his brothers back home. They were always having fun with each other. *How will they treat me now*, he wondered, *once I make it known I am the Messiah?*

"Andrew tells me that John the Baptist said you were the Lamb of God." Simon directed a challenging gaze at Jesus. "Neither he nor Philip told you my name or our father's name, yet you knew about me. How is that possible?"

Jesus smiled at Simon, pleased that he was unafraid to question him. "Do you care more about how I knew these things than about why I renamed you Peter?"

Simon shrugged. "Peter—it means Rock. I thought you were referring to my height."

Jesus chuckled. "It means so much more, my friend, but right now you are not ready to hear it. In the future, you will know why I called you Peter. For now, eat and we will talk and get to know each other."

They spent the rest of the evening doing just that, and in time their discussion turned to Galilee.

"When you come to Capernaum, Teacher, you must stay with us," Simon offered.

"I will be sure to." Jesus grinned and patted Simon on the back.

"I can't wait to tell my partner and his brother about you," Simon said. He had understood why Andrew had taken a liking to the charismatic young Rabbi. His ideas about sin, repentance, and God's coming Kingdom intrigued him more than he could say.

"Your partner?" Jesus asked.

"Yes... we're fishermen... we supply fish to the local markets and make our living that way."

"Then you must know my cousins, John and James. They are fishermen as well. In fact, the last I heard they were also living in Capernaum."

"John and James? Not the sons of Zebedee?" Simon asked, shock registering on his face.

"Why, yes! The very same!" Jesus laughed. "Do you know them?"

Simon started laughing. "Know them? They're our partners! Andrew, remind me to chastise those two for not telling us about the Teacher sooner."

Jesus joined in the laughter. "It's not their fault, my friend. They do not yet know about me."

"But you are their cousin. How could they not know who you are?" Andrew questioned.

"They know *of* me ... but they do not know *who* I am," Jesus replied.

Andrew sent Simon a questioning glance and remained silent. Many of the things the Teacher had said this day were strange, as if he were keeping a secret. John had called him the Lamb of God, a fact Jesus had neither confirmed nor denied. Both men wondered how long it would be before they knew the truth.

They would not have long to wait.

CHAPTER
— 23 —

"Following John's example, Jesus went out into the desert, led there by the Holy Spirit," Mary said as she began another day at sea, this time with the captain of the ship listening to her story. She was both delighted and surprised to find he had been led to Christ by the Apostle Paul during one of Paul's many crossings at sea.

"What happened to him there?" the captain asked as he sat beside her on her bench.

"He told me that he was tempted by the devil to use the power and knowledge God had imparted to him. After fasting for forty days and nights, Jesus was hungry, weak, and tired. It was when he was most vulnerable that he was tempted, for just as Adam and Eve were tempted in the garden to disobey our Heavenly Father, so now Jesus was tempted as well. This was the first of many tests for him and the devil was determined that Jesus would fail."

He tried to lick his dry, cracked lips, but his swollen tongue and parched mouth made it impossible after so many days without liquids. He could feel his body weakening and he wondered how much longer he would last.

Jesus knew that his journey into the Judean wilderness would be a difficult one. The farther he walked the more isolated he became, until he was surrounded by miles of sand, rocks, and a few sparse trees. The terrain was hilly in some places, smooth in others, but always there was sand and rocks—so many rocks. But the time spent alone communicating with God, finding out where he was to go and what he was to do, was a blessing and he felt strong in spirit.

He hadn't told anyone where he was going. He had simply left Martha's after the morning repast. With one final sip of cool spring water from the well in her courtyard, he had turned to her and said, "I am going away to spend some time in prayer. I will return here when I am done. Please tell the others not to search for me. I will find them."

Now, forty days had passed and he wondered how he would make it back to civilization. He was too weak. Lack of food and water had taken its toll. He now stood at the highest point he could find in the desert, searching for the road back to Bethany. Jesus shielded his eyes from the sun with his hand. He was amazed at how far he had wandered.

Although he felt spiritually strong, his journey had not been without its difficulties. The tormentor had followed him into the wilderness. He had first heard him ten days into his journey.

"If you are the Son of God, tell these stones to become bread."

Jesus looked at the rocks and stones on the ground and heard his stomach growl once again. He had dismissed Satan with Scripture and said, "It is written: 'Man does not live on bread alone, but on every word that comes from the mouth of God.'"[13]

He remembered that verse once more as the hunger pangs consumed him. He spotted something moving in the distance. A camel? A tree swaying in the breeze? He was too far away to see.

The devil tried to tempt him again on his twentieth day in the desert. Jesus had succumbed to the sun and in his delirium found himself in Jerusalem standing on the highest point of the temple.

"It could all be over in an instant," Satan had whispered in Jesus' ear. "No more hunger, no more thirst. If you are the Son of God throw yourself down from here. For it is written: 'He will command his angels concerning you, and they will lift you up in their hands, so that you will not strike your foot against a stone.'"[14]

Jesus had answered him, "It is also written: 'Do not put the Lord your God to the test.'"[15]

Jesus smiled, wincing when his bottom lip cracked and started bleeding. Satan had been furious that even in Jesus' most confused moments he was spiritually strong.

"Do you see it?"

Jesus started at the now familiar voice of his enemy. He bowed his head in prayer, seeking spiritual strength once more.

"Open your eyes!" Satan hissed. "I have something to show you."

[13] Matthew 4:4.
[14] Psalm 91:10–12; Luke 4:9–11; Matthew 4:5–7.
[15] Luke 4:12.

He knew he shouldn't, that it was another attempt to seduce him to give up his mission. But he also knew that he was stronger now. One didn't spend forty days in the desert and not call out to one's Maker. He smiled inwardly and opened his eyes. The desert was gone and in its place all the kingdoms of the world and their splendour were before him. Jesus pursed his lips. He was crafty, this Forsaken One.

"All this I will give you, if you will bow down and worship me."

"Away from me, Satan!" Jesus waved his hand as if swatting a fly. "For it is written: 'Worship the Lord your God, and serve him only.'"[16]

"I am not finished with you yet, Son of God!" The scream started low and built till it pierced the sky with thunder, and then there was silence. Jesus shook his head. He knew Satan would try to trap him again, but for now he was prevented.

Jesus lifted his head up and felt a cooling breeze caress his face. Gentle whispers accompanied the breeze and then he heard their heavenly voices. He smiled as he tasted the cool water sent from heaven above. God's holy angels had come to attend him and he rested in their ministering hands.

"Rabbi! You have returned!" Mary clapped her hands in surprise and called for Martha and Lazarus.

"Shalom, Mary." Jesus stopped at the well and lowered the bucket in. Mary ran forward and grabbed it from his hands.

---

[16] Luke 4:8; Deuteronomy 6:14

"Please, Master. Let me get you a drink. Sit. I can see you have had a long journey and have much to tell us."

He nodded his thanks and crossed the courtyard toward the house and sat on a mat covered with cushions. A lush vine of grapes hung over his head like a canopy, providing shade from the hot sun. He breathed a sigh of thanksgiving that he was back with friends. Mary filled a pitcher with water and placed it on the mat before him. She stepped inside to retrieve a cup and bumped into Martha who, having heard the Master's voice, came out with a tray laden with fruits, vegetables, and bread. She laid it before him and backed away while Mary went into the house.

"Master, we are so happy to see you again," Martha said.

"It is good to be back."

"Consider this your home as long as you are here, Rabbi," Lazarus said, stepping out of the house and sitting beside Jesus.

Jesus patted Lazarus on the back and glanced at Martha. "Will you sit and eat?"

"Sit with you, Master? Oh, no! That would not be right. I will eat after you have eaten, or in the house with Mary."

"Did someone speak my name?" Mary came back with four cups and filled them all with water. She handed Jesus a cup and then sat opposite him.

"Mary! What do you think you are doing?" Mary turned towards Martha's scowling face.

"Oh! I am so sorry, Master. I forgot myself."

Martha relaxed and stepped into the house. She turned at the door and waited for her sister. It wasn't proper for the women to sit and eat with the men. She shook her head and realized that for all she had taught her, Mary still forgot simple etiquette.

Mary offered bread to Jesus and Lazarus and sat back on her heels, her hands folded in her lap. Jesus broke the bread and passed some to her and Lazarus. Then he crooked his eyebrow and glanced at Martha, who was still standing in the doorway.

"Are you going to eat in the doorway, friend Martha? Or are you going to sup with us?" he asked, his eyes holding a certain merriment that gave Martha the feeling she was being tested. She moved forward and stopped. "Master, this goes against everything I know and believe. Women do not eat with the men."

"We eat with Lazarus everyday," Mary said, smiling at Martha who glared at her in dismay.

"You, my sister, have long been without the guidance of our mother." She stepped towards her. "Lazarus is our brother and he is not a guest."

"Martha, Martha!" Jesus chuckled and held his hand out. "Your brother has offered me his home and I am going to take him up on his offer. Come, sit and eat with your family."

Martha frowned and bit her lip, hesitant to move from her post at the door. Mary patted the cushion beside her and giggled. Lazarus started to chuckle and Jesus held out his hand and smiled. "Martha, I have news that I wish to share with the three of you and I don't want to repeat it twice. Now come, enjoy the bounty you have prepared."

"Humph. I can't believe I'm doing this." She leaned on Mary's shoulder and plopped herself down on the pillows. "There is another reason I eat in the kitchen, you know," she said as she settled her corpulent body in the pillows.

Jesus arched his eyebrow. "Oh, what is that?"

She grinned and lowered her eyes. "I have a tall table with chairs and they are much easier for this body to get in and out of." She nudged Mary with her shoulder. "Good luck helping me out of these cushions, Sister. I think I'm stuck here now!"

Jesus chuckled to himself as he remembered his last night with Mary, Martha, and Lazarus. While Martha continued to fuss over dinner preparations, refusing to sit still, Mary had convinced the men to come and eat at Martha's tall table for Jesus' last meal before he left for Matai's wedding. He shook his head and smiled. The look on Martha's face when they had all followed her into the kitchen was priceless, but one he would carry with him in the days ahead.

"Rabbi?" He turned at the sound of a familiar voice.

"Philip! How are you my friend?"

Philip, a tall, lean young man, bounded toward him. "I've been looking all over for you."

"Have you?" Jesus asked. "Well, I am on my way to Cana for a friend's wedding. Why don't you come along?"

Philip hesitated. "I will go with you, Rabbi, but first I must find my friend Nathanael. I have been telling him about you for quite some time and he wants to meet you."

"Well then, by all means go and find him. I will wait over yonder under the sycamore tree."

"I will hurry." Philip dashed down the road, leaving a trail of dust behind him. Jesus smiled, crossed the road to sit beneath the shade of the sycamore, and waited for Philip to return.

Half an hour later, he saw them coming up the road.

"Here is a true Israelite," Jesus said as he greeted Nathanael, "in whom there is nothing false."

"How do you know me?" Nathanael asked, his young face a picture of bewilderment.

Jesus answered with a laugh, "I saw you while you were still under the fig tree before Philip called you."

Nathanael fell to his knees in awe. "Rabbi, you *are* the Son of God; you *are* the King of Israel!"

"You believe because I told you I saw you under the fig tree? You shall see greater things than that, my friend," Jesus laughed. He helped Nathanael up, playfully slapping him on the back. "I tell you the truth, you shall see heaven open, and the angels of God ascending and descending on the Son of Man."

They arrived on the third day of the wedding celebration. It was a tradition that the wedding feast last for at least seven days, so Jesus had not rushed to get there. Upon their arrival, the three men were surprised to see Simon and Andrew. Also present were James and John, Simon's partners and cousins to Jesus. Rachel, the mother of the groom, greeted them as they arrived.

"It's so good to see you again, Jesus. We have missed you," she said as the servants brought them food and drink. "We are blessed to have you here at Matai's wedding."

"Thank you. I'm honoured to be here. Since I have known Matai since we were children, I would never have missed this very important time in his life," Jesus responded as he settled himself on a cushion.

"Unca' Jesus!"

All eyes turned toward a chubby little girl with curly black hair running toward Jesus. He held his arms out for her and she ran into his embrace, flinging her arms around his neck, peppering him with kisses.

Jesus laughed so hard tears came to his eyes. The disciples chuckled at the little mop who had obviously won the heart of their Master.

"Who is this then, Rabbi?" Simon asked as he playfully grabbed one of the curls on the child's head.

"This, my friends, is Sarah, the two-year-old daughter of my sister Ruth." He cuddled her on his lap and said, "Sarah, these are my friends—can you say hello to them?"

She promptly stuck her thumb in her mouth and shyly muffled hello to the disciples. They laughed and tried to get her to talk, but she would only content herself with sitting on Jesus' lap, talking to him and playing with his beard. Ruth caught Jesus' eye and he motioned for her to go and enjoy herself. Sarah was a handful at times and Jesus knew Ruth needed a break, especially since she was expecting again. After a time, Sarah fell asleep and Jesus was just beginning to feel his arms go numb when he heard his mother's voice.

"Aha, so you're the one with my granddaughter!" Mary said as she kissed him on his head. "How are you, son? Are you keeping well?"

"Very well, woman, and you?" he replied as she sat beside him.

"Wonderful!" Mary said as she looked at the men sitting beside her son. She immediately recognized her nephews James and John, the sons of her sister Salome and her husband Zebedee. She informed them that their parents had just arrived, so the two men excused themselves and went to greet them. Jesus then introduced Mary to Simon, Andrew, Nathanael, and Philip. After the introductions, the conversation flowed from how Mary's cousin John was faring to Jesus' temptation in the wilderness, and finally to the bride and groom. At this point, Sarah began to stir and Mary took her to Ruth so she could tend to her.

"Your mother is a delightful woman, Master!" Philip said. "She has a wonderful sense of humour and she seems very knowledge-able in regards to the scriptures."

Jesus smiled and nodded his head. "When I was a child, while learning and memorizing the scriptures, she insisted on learning them as well. That is why she is so well-informed." Jesus stood up. "Well, gentlemen, I believe it is time I congratulated the bride and groom." His disciples agreed and they made their way with him through the crowds to offer best wishes to the happy couple. Afterwards, the men began to circulate and mingle with family and friends.

Jesus noticed that Miriam was present with her husband Cleopas and their son James. Matthew, their other son, a tax collector, was not present, which disappointed but did not surprise Jesus.

Mary returned, minus Sarah, and pulled Jesus aside to talk to him.

"Walk with me?" she asked him. Offering her his arm, they began to walk toward the house.

"Did you know that Matai has run out of wine?" Mary asked.

"Really? That is a shame," he replied as they approached the house.

"Yes… but it doesn't have to be," she said with a hopeful voice. When Jesus did not respond, she changed the subject. "Simon told me you knew all about him before you even met."

"Did he?"

"Yes… Nathanael also mentioned something to that effect." She paused. "That's quite remarkable, don't you think?"

"What is?"

"Knowing about people before you meet them… and apparently you knew Simon's father's name as well."

"Yes, indeed—quite remarkable." He arched one of his eyebrows, looked down at her, and grinned.

Exasperated, she removed her arm from his, put her hands on her hips and glared up at him. "They have no more wine."

"Dear woman, why do you involve me?" Jesus groaned. "My time has not yet come."

Undeterred in her efforts to keep the guests happy, Mary approached a servant who was pouring wine. She pointed at Jesus and said, "Do whatever he tells you."

Nearby stood six stone water jars which were used for ceremonial washing, each capable of holding from twenty to thirty gallons of water. Jesus sighed as he realized his mother would have her way no matter what. So he said to the servants, "Fill the jars with water." So they filled them to the brim.

"Now draw some out and take it to the master of the banquet," he said, and as they drew the water out it turned a deep burgundy color. The servants gasped in amazement and immediately took the wine to the master of the banquet.

After tasting it, the banquet master called Matai aside. "Everyone brings out the choice wine first," he said, "and then the cheaper wines, after the guests have had too much to drink; but you have saved the best till now." He turned to his guests and lifted his cup high. "Drink up, everyone! Drink up! For this is the best wine I have ever tasted!"

Matai, confused over this new batch of wine, asked the servants where it had come from. "I know we didn't have any more left. Where did you get this?" he asked. They pointed to Jesus and explained to Matai what they had seen. Confused, Matai turned toward Jesus, who nodded and smiled. He had just performed his first miracle and news of it was spreading to all the wedding guests.

"Look around you, son. Do you see?" Mary touched his arm. "You have just revealed your glory and your disciples are already putting their faith in you."

Jesus smiled down at the diminutive figure of his mother and kissed her cheek. "Woman, it appears I still need to listen to you." He crooked his eyebrow. "Once in a while."

Her laughter filled the night air and brought a lightness to Jesus' steps he had not felt in some time. Tomorrow would be a day full of new beginnings.

"After the wedding we—Jesus, his disciples, my sons and I—visited Capernaum. My sister Salome lived there with her husband Zebedee, John and James' parents. Peter and Andrew lived in Capernaum and Jesus stayed with them while my sons and I stayed with Salome," Mary explained to those who had gathered around her on the deck of the ship. "My nephews, along with Peter and Andrew, made arrangements with Zebedee and Jonah, Peter and Andrew's father, to manage the fishing business on their own for a time. All four men wanted to get to know Jesus and his teachings better, so they followed him out into the Judean countryside where they spent some time baptizing. My cousin John, they called him the Baptist by then, was also baptizing people in the same area. It was some time after this that John stepped up his attacks on Herod Antipas and his sinful lifestyle. John was constantly reminding them both of their sin. So, fed up with John's constant attacks, Herod sent his soldiers out one day while John was speaking, had him arrested and thrown in prison. When Jesus learned John had been arrested, he returned to Nazareth at once to inform me."

CHAPTER
— 24 —

He found her beside the outdoor oven kneading bread. So immersed was she in her task that she didn't notice he was there until he spoke.

"Woman, are you going to ignore me all day?"

Mary turned her head and gasped, her eyes and mouth open wide with surprise. Jesus laughed and held out his arms as she ran into them.

"Jesus!" She stood on tiptoes to hug him. "Oh, my boy, I have missed you so!"

"I missed you as well." He bent lower to return her embrace.

"Let me look at you… why, you've lost so much weight!" she said as she reached up to cup his face in her hands. "Have you been eating?"

"Merely fasting and praying Ima… Woman," he stammered.

Her eyes sparkled as he stumbled over what to call her. "Old habits are hard to break, are they not?" She winked.

He smiled and said, "I've been preparing myself for the cup the Father has set before me and what do I do when I see you?" He shook his head and leaned in to kiss her cheek. "It is only for your benefit that I call you woman and not Ima. You must try to remember, for your own sake, who I am."

"I know, son... Yahweh has been dealing with me since you have been gone. I am ready for whatever must be." She patted his arm soothingly.

He nodded, took hold of her hand, and sighed. "I have news of John."

Her brows furrowed in concern and she led him to sit with her on her bench. "Tell me everything."

As he related the circumstances of John's arrest, Jesus found His Heavenly Father had indeed given Mary a stronger spirit and a peace he had not seen before. After telling her all he knew, they prayed together and then began to talk of other things. Mary resumed her breadmaking and listened to Jesus as he told her of his experiences thus far. He talked of Simon and Andrew, of James, John, Philip, and Nathanael.

"They have left me for a time to attend to their businesses. When the time is right, I will go and call them to follow me," he stated.

"How will you know when the time is right?" Mary asked, turning her head to look at him.

"When I am no longer welcome here," Jesus replied.

"But you are always welcome here, son." Mary frowned. "Why ever would you think such a thing?"

"I don't mean at home, dear woman. I mean in Nazareth itself."

"The people of Nazareth, not welcome you? Why, they have known you since you were a small child. Forgive me, son, but that's absurd," she said as she put the bread dough in the oven.

Jesus raised his eyebrows and stood. "You will see what I mean on the Sabbath. For now, I shall go and greet my brothers and sisters to let them know I am back."

"Tell them to come for supper and we will celebrate your homecoming," Mary said to him as he walked down the path toward his sister Ruth's home. He acknowledged her request with a wave of his hand and continued on his way.

On the Sabbath day, they went to the synagogue. The day shone brightly, the sky a deep azure blue. A soft breeze carried the smell of wildflowers lining the road. As they entered the synagogue, Mary went to sit with her friends in the women's section while the men went to their own seating area.

When it was discovered that Jesus was home again, he was asked to read from the Holy Scriptures. An attendant handed the scroll of the prophet Isaiah to him. Unrolling it, he found what he wanted and began to read, "The Spirit of the Lord is upon me, because He has anointed me to preach good news to the poor."

Mary's heart quickened, as she knew immediately what Jesus was going to declare.

"He has sent me to proclaim freedom for the prisoners," Jesus continued, "and recovery of sight for the blind, to release the oppressed, to proclaim the year of the Lord's favour."

Then he rolled up the scroll, gave it back to the attendant, and sat down. All eyes in the synagogue fastened on him as he said, "Today this scripture is fulfilled in your hearing."

"Mary, you must be so proud of your son," Rachel, Mary's friend, whispered to her.

"Thank you, Rachel."

"He is very well spoken and seems to be telling the entire synagogue that he is going to serve the Lord. Is it possible that he will be a Rabbi? I never would have imagined it; I always thought he would follow in Joseph's footsteps."

Mary pulled her shawl closer and absently nodded her agreement, half-listening to the voices around her.

"Isn't this Joseph's son?"

"The carpenter, right?"

"Isn't that his mother?" Someone pointed at Mary. Three young women strained their heads forward in their seats to catch a glimpse of her.

"I heard he turned water into wine in Cana!" one of the girls said.

Someone gasped and added, "Did you hear what he did in Capernaum? He healed the son of a royal official!"

Rachel leaned forward and glared the three women into silence just as Jesus started speaking again.

"Surely you will quote this proverb to me: 'Physician, heal yourself! Do here in your hometown what we have heard that you did in Capernaum.' I tell you the truth," he continued. "No prophet is accepted in his hometown."

"Prophet?" Rachel stiffened and frowned. "He thinks he's a prophet now?" She turned her head toward Mary. "What is he saying Mary?"

Mary closed her eyes and began to pray.

"I assure you that there were many widows in Israel in Elijah's time," Jesus said, "when the sky was shut for three and a half years and there was a severe famine throughout the land. Yet Elijah was not sent to any of them, but to a widow in Zarephath in the region of Sidon. And there were many in Israel with leprosy in the time of Elisha the prophet, yet not one of them was cleansed—only Naaman the Syrian."

Mary bowed her head as voices around her exploded into shouts of anger. Rachel gasped in surprise and clasped Mary's arm. "Is he saying what I think he's saying Mary?"

"Rachel, I—"

"What are you saying, Jesus?" A burly man jumped from his seat and pointed his finger at Jesus. "That we are not good enough to receive God's help? You compare us with lepers? How dare you!"

Jesus stood from his seat and turned to face his accusers.

"Who do you think you are anyway?" another yelled. "If Yahweh's prophet stood before us, we would certainly know it! And we know you are not him!"

As one, the men in the synagogue rushed toward Jesus, but his brothers jumped from their seats and surrounded him. Curses flew from mouths that had begun the day with prayer. The mob forced its way through the four brothers, carrying them off their feet. Jesus held up his hands to signal peace, fearful that his brothers would be trampled, but no one listened. His eyes searched for a way of escape for himself and his brothers.

Rachel stood and stared with Mary at the rioting crowd on the other side of the room. She was stunned by what she had heard but her love for Mary kept her from joining the mob. *What was Jesus thinking?* She glanced at Mary and saw her fear.

She held her fast. "No! You mustn't try to get near him, Mary. You could get hurt." But Mary shoved her arm away and fought with the rioting crowds to get to Jesus. She could hear Rachel yelling her name, but she was swept away in the crowd.

She was caught in a maelstrom of hate so violent that she found her feet leaving the floor of the synagogue as bodies pressed in all around her. As she struggled to escape the crowds, she suddenly found herself in James' arms. He carried her through the crowd and out of the synagogue.

Panting, James deposited her beside a huge acacia tree that grew outside the synagogue. Together they turned and waited for Jesus and the others, but the voices grew louder as people began to spill out of the building yelling and screaming in fury at the words of her son.

"James?" She looked toward the doors of the synagogue but couldn't see Jesus. "We have to go back." She darted forward, but James grabbed her hand and held her fast.

"No! Ima, it isn't safe."

"James, please! Let me go. Oh, my sons, my sons!" He heard the fear and heartache in her voice but refused to give in to her demands. He could see the rioting crowd surrounding Jesus and feared the worst. They were going to shove him off the cliff the town was built on. Mary was screaming Jesus' name, struggling to break free of James' hold on her. James took one last look at the crowds and steered his frantic mother back toward the center of town.

They stood panting and waiting at the well in the middle of town. Mary sat on the stone ledge that surrounded the well, rocking back and forth, her arms folded across her stomach. Her eyes were red from crying. She shook with fear over Jesus' whereabouts, and relief that the rest of her family was safe.

"What was he thinking? Has our brother gone mad?" Joses fumed as he paced back and forth. "You could have been seriously harmed, Ima!"

The brothers stood around their mother in a protective circle, far away from the crowds that had chased Jesus out of town. As far as they could tell, Jesus had escaped, but they weren't certain because the crowds had kept them pushed back.

Mary had never seen such a horrible display of disrespect for a place of worship in her life. Nevertheless, she was not ashamed of Jesus or embarrassed; she understood why he said what he did. She had suspected what Jesus had to say might cause a stir, but never in her life had she imagined it would cause a riot. Her emotions were a tangled, gnarled mess. On the one hand, she was proud of Jesus. On the other, she had to live with the people of Nazareth—how would they treat her now?

Her worst fears were confirmed when her friends and neighbours returned from trying to harm her son. When they saw her with her sons in the middle of town, they began yelling and cursing. James suggested they get Mary home as quickly as possible. It was incomprehensible to her that the people she had known since childhood would now treat her so badly.

She spotted Rachel in the crowd and her heart leapt.

"Rachel!" she stood and reached out a hand to her longtime friend. "Is my son safe?"

"Until your son repents of his words this day, woman, my wife will no longer be talking to you!" Levi pushed Rachel forward, causing her to stumble. Mary stepped forward, anxious for her friend and for an answer to her question. As Rachel recovered her footsteps, she turned toward Mary and her answer came in an imperceptible nod. Mary mouthed her thanks and bowed her head. Jesus had escaped Nazareth, yet one question remained—where had he gone?

CHAPTER
— 25 —

I don't understand why he is here." Perpetua leaned against a smooth rock that jutted out from the shoreline. "Not that I'm complaining, mind you. But James and John are his kin. Why isn't he staying with them?

Simon frowned. "Pet, it is an honour to have the Rabbi stay with us." He motioned for her to move and threw his net over the rock to dry.

"Simon, don't misunderstand me. I am pleased to have him honour us in this way. I just don't understand why he is choosing us over his own family."

Simon shrugged. "The Teacher is… different in his approach. You have much to learn, which is why I think he has favoured us this way."

Perpetua stared out to sea and sighed. "I hope I do not disappoint him." Her hazel eyes grew pensive and Simon could tell by her stance that she was worried. He spied his surroundings to see if anyone was about. Satisfied that they were alone, he came up behind his wife and wrapped his arms around her. "You could never disappoint anyone."

Perpetua smiled and leaned into him. "Andrew says Jesus is going to travel throughout Galilee to preach to the people. Will you be going with him?"

Simon straightened and turned her to face him. "Is that what is bothering you? You think I'm going to follow him all over the countryside?"

"I don't know what to think. Isn't that why he chose you? Don't you have to go with him to learn? All rabbis have disciples, Simon. He has chosen you for a reason." She lowered her gaze and stepped back from him. "What does he want from you?"

Simon struggled to maintain his emotions. He suspected Jesus had chosen him for something the moment he changed his name to Peter. The revelations at Martha's house consumed him. Why would Jesus change his name if he wasn't preparing him for something? Yet, at the same time, Jesus had not demanded anything of him. He feared that one day Jesus would ask him to join him, but he wasn't ready to give up his fishing business to follow someone he had known less than three months. He stroked his beard as he thought about Perpetua's questions. "Philip and Nathanael, even Andrew—they all believe Jesus is the Messiah."

"I have heard them say the same." She swallowed a fear that was slowly rising within her. This Jesus could bring them much pain and heartache if the Sanhedrin ever found out what his disciples were saying. "I fear things will be changing soon. What will you do?"

"Continue to fish. If Jesus is the Messiah, it will be revealed to me in time." He handed her a basket of fish. "Nothing is going to change. Now, I think it is best you go back to the house. I heard Jesus leave earlier, but I'm sure he'll be back soon to break his fast."

She nodded, turned to leave, and stopped. "He calls you Peter. Yet he knows that is not your name. He has already begun to change things, my husband."

He began preaching throughout Galilee in synagogues, on hillsides, and wherever people congregated. His message was always the same: "Repent and believe, for the Kingdom of Heaven is near!" He echoed the words of his cousin John, which was not lost on John's followers. John had proclaimed to everyone that he was the forerunner of one to come and the people began to wonder if Jesus was that One.

Philip and Nathanael went everywhere with him, having chosen to follow him at Cana when he had turned water into wine. Simon, Andrew, James, and John would occasionally go out and listen to him speak, but they were reluctant to follow him everywhere, as that meant giving up their fishing income and their families depended on them.

One hot summer day, Jesus walked down to the cove where the four men were washing their nets. The breeze off the water provided a welcome respite from the heat of the day and some of the people who had followed Jesus began to settle themselves on the rocky hillside that surrounded the shoreline. Others took the opportunity to get closer to Jesus, making it impossible for him to move about.

"Peter, I need to borrow your boat." Jesus waded into the water and heaved himself into the boat. "Would you put out a little from shore?"

Simon grinned at the use of his new name, set aside his net, and said. "Of course, Rabbi." He pushed the boat out into the water and scrambled aboard. When they were a fair distance out, Jesus threw the anchor overboard.

"I think this is far enough for them to hear me," he said, clapping his hands.

"But Teacher, how will the people hear you? We are too far out."

"Not at all, Peter. This particular shoreline has excellent acoustics. Listen and you will see."

The people on the shore spread out in a semi-circle to listen to him. When Jesus started speaking, Simon was amazed at the power in his voice. It seemed to echo throughout the hillside. No one yelled at Jesus to speak up; no one suggested he come closer. All were attentive and respectful.

Sometime later, when Jesus finished speaking and the people started to disperse, he rubbed his hands together and said, "Put out into deep water now, and let down the nets for a catch."

Simon shook his head wearily. "Master, we've worked hard all night and haven't caught anything." Jesus arched an eyebrow. Simon shrugged. "But, since you say so, I will let down the nets."

Jesus grinned and settled into the bow of the boat. When they got out further, he joined Simon and helped him lower the nets into the water. Simon sighed, wondering if Jesus realized how fruitless an activity this was. He watched as the nets sank into the dark water. Jesus sat back in the bow, turned his face toward the sun, and smiled. Simon sighed again and was wondering how long he should wait before he told the Rabbi he was wasting his time— when suddenly the boat heaved to one side. Startled, Simon sprang forward to pull up the nets. Jesus laughed and helped him pull, but they had caught such a large number of fish that the nets began to break.

"James! John! Andrew!" Simon yelled to shore. "Help us quickly before these nets capsize our boat!"

The men sprang into action and soon had their boat pulled alongside Simon's. As they pulled the nets into the boats, it soon became apparent that both boats were sinking due to the large catch.

When Simon saw this, he fell to his knees at Jesus' feet and cried, "Go away from me, Lord. I am a sinful man!"

Jesus placed a comforting hand on Simon's shoulder and looked at the fear in the faces before him. "Don't be afraid," he said. "Follow me and from now on I will make you fishers of men."

The four men looked at each other and did not hesitate. They had seen the miracle at Cana when Jesus had turned the water into wine and now they were witnessing yet another miracle. Without another thought, they immediately pulled their boats ashore, left everything with Zebedee and their hired men, and followed Jesus.

CHAPTER
— 26 —

The Sabbath day brought a chill to the air in Capernaum. A breeze carried a fine mist that picked up from the Sea of Galilee. Morning doves cooed greetings as Jesus and his disciples made their way to the synagogue Peter and Andrew attended regularly. As they entered, Simon introduced Jesus to the people around him. When the ruler of the synagogue realized that Jesus was the same man he had heard speak the day before, he invited him to teach. Simon sat up straighter, feeling honoured that his Teacher was going to preach in his synagogue. Andrew nudged him with his elbow and beamed. Jesus looked at them with arched eyebrows. Without Jesus saying a word, both men felt thoroughly chastised for their pride. They lowered their eyes and squirmed in their seats, uncomfortable that they had somehow failed the Teacher. But when Jesus started to speak, they raised their heads and saw a look of forgiveness that almost had them crying like babies.

As he spoke, Simon could hear the whispers of the men around him.

"He's amazing."

"He speaks as if he has authority, as if he wrote the words himself."

"He is not like the teachers of the law at all."

Simon jumped at the next voice that echoed off the walls. "Ha! What do you want with us, Jesus of Nazareth? Have you come to destroy us?"

Everyone gasped at the man who had entered the synagogue. His hair was wild, his body filthy, and his clothes rags. But his face was recognized by everyone. Hanan ben Judah had been cast out of the community the previous year. Declared mad by the leaders of the synagogue, he now lived in a cave far removed from civilization. Andrew stood from his seat in the front along with Simon, James and John. *How did he come to be here?* Andrew wondered.

"It is the demon man," Simon muttered.

"I know who you are—the Holy One of God!" Hanan shouted.

"Be quiet!" Jesus commanded. "Come out of him!"

A loud scream came from deep within Hanan's throat. He arched his back and collapsed on the ground, still and silent.

"What is this teaching?" the ruler of the synagogue asked. He pointed a trembling finger at Jesus. "With authority and power he gives orders to evil spirits and they come out!"

Jesus ignored the stunned looks of his disciples and the murmurs of awe and fear from the people. Kneeling, he whispered in Hanan's ear and lifted him to his feet. The voices in the synagogue grew quiet as they waited to see what Hanan would do. To their amazement, he hugged Jesus and wept with joy and relief. "I am healed! Praise God, I am healed!"

And word spread about Jesus throughout Galilee.

Simon was stunned by the scene he had just witnessed. Everyday Jesus was proving to him that he was the Messiah. He wasn't just a great teacher, as some thought, and he knew he had made the right decision in following him. As they turned up the road toward his house, Simon knew immediately that something was wrong. Perpetua came running from the house, wailing and screaming that her mother was dying.

"Simon! Simon! Oh, that you had been here sooner. I don't know what to do!"

"Calm down, woman!" Simon took his wife firmly in his arms, forcing her to look up at him. "What is it that has you so distressed?"

"Ima!" she whimpered.

"Your mother? Is something wrong with her?" Simon brushed the tears from his wife's face. "Please, tell me what the problem is."

"I'm sorry." She took a deep breath, grabbed Simon's hand, and pulled him toward their home. "She took ill. Right after you left for the synagogue. She is in bed now with a raging fever. Simon—she is as hot as the noonday sun and I cannot rouse her!"

Simon saw the fear in his wife's eyes and he along with Jesus and the others followed her into the house.

When he saw how red her face was, Simon was devastated. He placed his hand on her fevered brow and recoiled at the heat radiating from her body. He shook his head in despair. This kind of illness usually ended in death. He knew his mother-in-law was beyond his help.

Perpetua saw the hopelessness in her husband's eyes and began to cry, but Jesus placed his hand on her shoulder and whispered in her ear. She looked at him as if seeing him for the first time. Blinking back tears, she nodded and said, "Her name is Esther."

Jesus moved closer to the bed and, bending down, he took Esther's hand and helped her to sit up. When she opened her eyes and saw everyone standing around her bed, she was startled.

"Is something the matter? Did I oversleep?" she asked, blinking her eyes.

"Ima!" Perpetua threw herself down upon her mother, hugging her with such intensity that Simon had to pull her away.

The shouts of joy and delight that emanated from their home were heard by many who passed by. "A miracle! A miracle!" Perpetua cried repeatedly as she thanked Jesus and kissed his hands for the return of her mother.

"A miracle? What are you talking about, Perpetua?" Esther asked as she got out of the bed. "Why are all these people here?"

Jesus laughed as Perpetua and Simon hugged Esther and proceeded to tell her how sick she had been. She found it hard to believe they were telling her the truth, because she felt just fine. And to prove it, she got up and began to serve them the evening meal.

———

"Word spread quite quickly after that," Mary continued as she spoke with the men who had gathered round on the ship. "People showed up at Simon Peter's house and stayed until early morning. Jesus healed everyone. Then he went throughout Galilee, teaching in the synagogues, preaching the good news of the kingdom, and healing every disease and sickness among the people. News about him even spread all over Syria, and the people there brought to him all who were ill with various diseases. Those suffering severe pain, the demon-possessed, those having seizures and the paralyzed, lepers, the blind… and he healed them all. Large crowds from Galilee, the Decapolis, Jerusalem, Judea, and the region across the Jordan followed him. He was never alone for very long. After a time, I rarely got to see him."

"So he was doing good things?" The centurion tilted his head in confusion. "I recall that your son was crucified… am I correct?"

Mary nodded.

"And we are to believe that he was crucified for doing all these wonderful miracles?"

"There's a bit more to it than that," Luke interrupted.

The centurion glared at him. "Was I addressing you?" He turned to Mary and said, "Why?"

"Why?" She blinked several times, her brow furrowed in concentration.

"Yes… why did they crucify him, if he was so great? I don't understand."

"It's not easy to explain."

"Well, woman, we're about three days from Ephesus. You have plenty of time to enlighten us."

"Very well." She breathed in deeply, squelching the pain that was beginning to form like a knot in her back. "After a time," she began again, "Jesus had many followers, whom he called disciples. Out of these disciples he chose Twelve that he designated as apostles, so that they might be with him and that he might send them out to preach and to have authority to drive out demons … "

———

He had spent the night in prayer on a mountainside. It was that night when God told him who his apostles should be. He had pictured them in his mind as each was revealed to him. Simon— whom he now called Peter—was a tall man with a ruddy complexion. He had a short, thick beard and eyebrows that were so thin they looked like they were not even there. Jesus smiled warmly as he thought of this disciple. Peter could be impulsive and headstrong, but he loved God and desired to serve Him.

Next was Andrew, Peter's younger brother. Although alike in appearance, their personalities were quite different. Andrew was quiet and thoughtful, where Peter was loud and impetuous. The two would need to rely on each other's traits for strength in the days to come.

His cousins James and John came to mind next. James was rugged and self-assured; he would be an excellent fisher of men. John was the younger brother of James. He was like his brother in temperament. Jesus called these two the "Sons of Thunder," for you always knew when they were around. He had called them this since childhood. He loved their boisterousness, their sense of humour, and knew they would be great choices as apostles. There was

Philip, Nathanael, and Thomas, another fisherman and someone who was always asking questions.

He was greatly surprised and pleased as the Father showed him the next candidate. For it was his childhood friend Matthew, the tax collector. Only yesterday, he had seen him down by the lake at his collection booth. Matthew had tried to hide his face in shame when he saw Jesus coming, but Jesus walked right up to him and asked him to follow him. The look of surprise, followed by uncertainty, on Matthew's face made Jesus want to weep. After years of rejection, someone actually wanted him. Matthew looked stunned.

"Follow me, Matthew," Jesus repeated, as he gazed into his eyes. For a moment, Jesus wondered if Matthew would turn down his offer. An offer, Matthew knew, meant repenting of his sins of extortion and giving up everything he had worked for over the years. However, Jesus was not disappointed. Matthew was so excited that he brought Jesus to his home. He held a great banquet in Jesus honour, with many of Matthew's friends, who were tax collectors and prostitutes. Jesus quietly laughed to himself as he remembered how the Pharisees had reacted when they heard about that event. They actually had the audacity to go into Matthew's house and confront Jesus about why he was associating with "sinners."

Jesus had glared at them and said, "It is not the healthy who need a doctor, but the sick. I have not come to call the righteous, but sinners to repentance." After that, the Pharisees had left in a huff and the banquet continued.

Jesus smiled as he continued thinking of his choices for apostles. He thought James the Younger, Matthew's brother, would be an ideal apostle, for he was bold and courageous, unafraid to speak his mind. Finally, there was Thaddeus, Simon the Zealot—and Judas Iscariot.

Jesus bowed his head once more in prayer. He knew that Judas would betray him, but he hoped Judas would learn something in the years ahead and repent of his sins when the time of betrayal arrived, lest it consume him.

When he came down from the mountain the next day, a large crowd of his disciples were waiting for him. Out of the crowd, he called his chosen Twelve and blessed them. Once again, the number of people who had come to see him surprised him. They had come from all over Judea, from Jerusalem, and from the coast of Tyre and Sidon, because they had heard he could heal them of their diseases. Jesus, strongly affected by the scene before him, waded into the crowd to do what he could. His love for the lost was evident by his actions and his heart broke to see them so in need.

One man who had stood far away from the crowd tried to approach him. Many people started screaming when they saw him and yelled at him to go away, but he would not relent. Instead, he focused his eyes on Jesus and as the crowd parted to get away from him, the man, ravaged by leprosy, fell at Jesus' feet.

"Lord, if you are willing, you can make me clean," he begged.

"I am willing." Jesus, filled with compassion, reached down and touched him. The people surrounding Jesus gasped in surprise. "Be clean!" Jesus commanded and immediately the leprosy left the man. Jesus helped him to his feet and said, "Don't tell anyone, but go, show yourself to the priest and offer the sacrifices that Moses commanded for your cleansing, as a testimony to them."

News of this miracle caused the crowds to swell even more, so Jesus stood on a rock so that all present could see him. Chattering voices in the crowds soon became still as the people waited for Jesus to begin teaching. Although he spoke to every one of his disciples there, he kept glancing at the chosen Twelve, as if he wanted them to realize the importance they played in the establishment of His kingdom.

"Blessed are the poor in spirit, for theirs is the kingdom of heaven." As he spoke, Jesus hoped that the people understood what he was saying. He wasn't speaking of not having enough money or food. He was speaking about how poor they were in spirit. He wanted them to know that when they truly hungered after God, they would be satisfied. "Blessed are those who mourn, for they shall be comforted. Blessed are the gentle, for they shall inherit the earth. Blessed are those who hunger and thirst for righteousness, for they shall be satisfied.

"Blessed are you when men hate you," he continued, "when they exclude you, insult you, and reject your name as evil, because of the Son of Man. Rejoice in that day and leap for joy, because great is your reward in Heaven! For that is how their fathers treated the prophets."

The Apostles listened intently to Jesus as he spoke. They understood what he was saying. They knew the risks involved in following him and they were willing to take them.

The rich, the poor, the young, and the old spread over the hillside like a colourful blanket of flowers. Mothers with little ones listened attentively to Jesus while trying to amuse their children. One mother of two tried to quiet the cries of a hungry baby and calm a fidgety three-year-old to no avail. Seeing her dilemma, Jesus swept the child up in his arms and, putting the youngster on his shoulders, carried him around while he continued speaking.

Peter and John laughed at the squeals of delight coming from the little one perched on Jesus' shoulders.

"There is one thing about Jesus that has always been constant with him, ever since he was a child," John remarked.

"And what is that?" Peter asked.

"He has always loved to laugh. He particularly loves to surprise and delight those around him. And joy—he is so joyous, it's infectious!"

Peter nodded in reply. "I think that's what draws people to him. He is showing them what God is really like. The love of God draws us to him. Look at his face, John—it is the face of God!"

John knew what Peter meant, of course. No one would ever be able to look on the face of God and live to tell about it, but God's love could be seen here on earth through one man and they both agreed they were blessed to be part of Jesus' chosen Twelve.

CHAPTER
— 27 —

While John the Baptist suffered in prison, he began to hear through his disciples of the miracles and wonders Jesus was performing. His disciples faithfully visited him each day of his imprisonment, bringing news of the one John himself had declared to be the Messiah.

"You are positive that the man performing these wonders is the same man I baptized?" John asked through the bars of his prison cell. He was frightfully thin and the look of despair in his eyes told his disciples that he needed encouragement.

Herod had not killed him right away, for he feared the repercussions from the Jews who thought John was a great prophet. Instead, he kept him chained like a dog in a cold, dank prison cell, made to sleep in his own filth and eat off the floor. He was covered with sores and crawling with lice. There was nothing his followers could do for him except bring him news of the outside world.

"We are, John. We went to Jesus and said this, 'John the Baptist sent us to you to ask, "Are you the one who was to come, or should we expect someone else?"'"

"What did he say?"

"He said, 'Go back and report to John what you have seen and heard: The blind receive sight, the lame walk, those who have leprosy are cured, the deaf hear, the dead are raised, and the good news is preached to the poor.'"

John sighed and nodded, contemplating this information.

"He also said something else, John," his disciple added.

"What?"

"He said, 'Blessed is the man who does not fall away on account of me.'"

To their surprise, John started to weep. The two men glanced at each other, not knowing how to comfort this great man who had suffered so much for God's Kingdom.

"Master? Why do you weep?"

It took a moment for John to compose himself. Once he had recovered himself, he explained haltingly, "The Lamb of God is my cousin… his name is Jesus… he is the man I sent you to. I weep because of what you just told me. He is concerned that I will fall away from God because of what I am enduring. He has become greater and I have become less. He does not want me to be discouraged or to lose faith in God."

After John's messengers had questioned Jesus and left, Jesus began to speak to the crowd about John.

"What did you go out into the desert to see? A reed swayed by the wind? If not, what did you go out to see? A man dressed in fine clothes? No, those who wear expensive clothes and indulge in luxury are in palaces. But what did you go out to see? A prophet? Yes, I tell you, and more than a prophet! This is the one about whom it is written: 'I will send my messenger ahead of you, who will prepare your way before you.' I tell you, among those born of women there is no one greater than John; yet the one who is least in the kingdom of God is greater than he."

———

"One of the Pharisees, by the name of Simon, invited Jesus to have dinner with him." Mary was talking privately to the centurion who had taken an interest in her story. She learned that his name was Julius, that he was twenty-three years old, and his wife had just given birth to a baby boy. He had gradually opened up to her over the course of the voyage and Mary had discovered that he was discouraged with the many gods he and his family worshipped. He had told her that they did not seem to have any power at all. At least, he said, not like her son. Eager to learn everything he could about Jesus, he would often seek her out privately so she could tell him more.

"A Pharisee? Weren't they always trying to trap him?" Julius interrupted her.

"Yes, they were," Mary responded.

"So did Jesus go? Did they catch him then?"

Mary grinned and shook her head. "No, they didn't catch him then, and yes, Jesus did go to his house."

"So what happened?"

"If you will stop interrupting me, I'll tell you," she admonished with a smile.

Julius blushed. "I'm sorry, Mary. I won't interrupt you again. Please tell me what happened."

"There was a woman present," she said. "Her name was Mary Magdalene." Mary rose from her bench and walked over to the ship's railing. Julius followed her. "Jesus had cast several demons out of her and she had followed him ever since. She brought an alabaster jar of perfume into the room where Jesus and Simon were, and she fell at Jesus' feet weeping—in fact, she wept so much that she began to wet his feet with her tears. So she wiped them with her hair, kissed them, and poured perfume on them."

"She uncovered her head?" Julius shook his head in disbelief. Even he knew that was not proper for a Jewish maiden. "What did the Pharisee do?"

"Jesus could tell what Simon was thinking. He knew that Simon regarded Mary as a sinner. In his eyes, she had no right to touch Jesus, much less be in his house."

"What did Jesus do then?"

"He said to Simon, 'Two men owed money to a certain moneylender. One owed him five hundred denarii, and the other fifty. Neither of them had the money to pay him back, so he cancelled both of the debts. Now which of them will love him more?' Simon shrugged and replied, 'I suppose the one who had the bigger debt.' Jesus replied, 'You have judged correctly.' Then he turned toward Mary Magdalene and said to Simon, 'Do you see this woman? I came into your house. You did not give me any water for my feet, but she wet my feet with her tears and wiped them with her hair. You did not give me a kiss, but this woman, from the time I entered, has not stopped kissing my feet. You did not put oil on my head, but she has poured perfume on my feet. Therefore, I tell you, her many sins have been forgiven—for she loved much. But he who has been forgiven little, loves little.'"

"Your son was very wise," Julius said, gazing out to sea. His brow furrowed in concentration.

Mary nodded. "He was that and so much more. That story is my favourite. But it doesn't end there."

"What else happened?"

"Jesus placed his hand on Mary's head and told her that her sins were forgiven, that her faith had saved her and to go in peace."

"But how could your son forgive sins?"

"It's strange you should ask that question, Julius. For it was the very question the other guests at the party began asking."

"What do you think we should do then? He has healed many people, James—he is fulfilling that for which he was called," Mary said to her son who was concerned about the people associating with his eldest brother. Jesus had been gone for over a year, visiting as often as he could, but as far as Mary was concerned it was not often enough.

James and his brothers—Joses, Jude, and Simon—were annoyed with their mother. They had heard since birth the story of Jesus' unique calling by God. They had come to believe that their brother was at best a prophet of God, but certainly not the Messiah as their parents had always claimed. But lately, James wasn't putting much stock in Jesus being a prophet either, not after recent reports of him forgiving people of their sins and associating with prostitutes, tax collectors, and the like. James did not believe this was what God had intended for Jesus.

"Ima, I will not stand by and let him ruin his reputation, as well as ours," James said. "He's gone too far! Clearly, he is rejecting all that he was called for. Why else would he be associating with such people?"

Mary perused the faces of her sons, who all seemed to agree with James. She wondered what to do, but trusted Jesus and knew that his ways, although a bit unconventional, always had a greater purpose towards God's glory. She had tried to explain this to her sons, but they were of the opinion that Jesus needed to come home for a while and get things in perspective.

"He's not just healing people, Ima. He is casting out demons. Demons, Ima! Where does he get such authority to do something like that?" Joses reasoned.

"There is talk against Jesus, Ima. Neither the Pharisees nor the Sadducees like him, for the people are claiming him to be a great prophet. Some are even calling him the Messiah," Jude added. "In public, Ima! It is one thing for you to think that, but if the Sanhedrin hears these people, Jesus' life will be in danger. For it would be considered a great blasphemy."

Mary eyes grew round with fear, for she knew the danger that would come to Jesus if people started declaring him the Messiah. Simon noticed his mother's look of dread and, taking advantage of it, said, "Ima, we cannot let happen to Jesus what happened to our cousin John. John would not listen to anyone—and now he is in prison. Would you have us let our brother go about the country-side spouting blasphemies against God and against the teachers of the law? We have heard that they are already plotting Jesus' de-struction. We must go and bring him home."

Trembling with fear for her firstborn and forgetting all she knew to be true, Mary let herself be convinced that they had to go and find him. So they left immediately to find Jesus and bring him home.

CHAPTER
— 28 —

They found him in Capernaum in the home of Peter and Andrew. They tried to get in to see him, but the vast assembly gathered outside prevented them from getting closer. Yet Jesus knew his family had arrived and why they had come. He was saddened that his brothers thought so poorly of him and was equally disappointed that his mother had listened to them. However, he knew her heart and trusted that she was just concerned for his well-being.

As the crowds continued to swell, Mary and her sons found it harder and harder to get in to see Jesus. James decided to tell his cousin John that they were there. As he pushed his way to the front of the crowd, he noticed a man standing before Jesus. He was blind and appeared to be mute.

"He is demon-possessed!" someone muttered. Jesus shook his head and smiled. James watched as his brother walked up to the blind man and whispered in his ear.

A look of utter astonishment spread over the man's face. He raised his hands to his eyes, as if to block the sun, then fell on his knees before Jesus. "Thank you, Lord!" he cried. "Thank you!"

James gasped, along with everyone else present.

"Could this be the Son of David?" someone asked.

"It is only by Beelzebub, the prince of demons, that this fellow drives out demons." A few Pharisees had pushed their way through the crowd and stood before Jesus, daring him to deny the charge.

Jesus turned to the people around him and said, "Every kingdom divided against itself will be ruined, and every city or household divided against itself will not stand. If Satan drives out Satan, he is divided against himself. How then can his kingdom stand?"

James' heart stirred with pride at Jesus' words, but he was confused. Jesus didn't sound crazy. Perhaps they had made a mistake?

Jesus glared at the religious leaders and continued, "And if I drive out demons by Beelzebub, by whom do your people drive them out?"

James' eyes widened in shock at Jesus' audacity.

"So then," Jesus said when the religious leaders did not respond, "they will be your judges. But if I drive out demons by the Spirit of God, then the kingdom of God has come upon you."

By this time Joses, Jude, and Simon pushed their way through the crowd with Mary and were close enough to see Jesus. He turned to them and said, "Or again, how can anyone enter a strong man's house and carry off his possessions unless he first ties up the strong man? Then he can rob his house."

Gazing into Mary's eyes, he said, "He who is not with me is against me, and he who does not gather with me scatters.

"And so I tell you, every sin and blasphemy will be forgiven men, but blasphemy against the Spirit will not be forgiven," he continued. "Anyone who speaks a word against the Son of Man will be forgiven, but anyone who speaks against the Holy Spirit will not be forgiven, either in this age or in the age to come."

He directed his words to those who opposed him: "Make a tree good and its fruit will be good, or make a tree bad and its fruit will be bad, for a tree is recognized by its fruit. You brood of vipers, how can you who are evil say anything good?"

"Our brother is asking to be arrested," Jude muttered to James. "His words incite only anger within the religious leaders." James placed his finger to his lips and shushed his brother. He needed to hear what Jesus would say to these Teachers of the Law.

"For out of the overflow of the heart, the mouth speaks. The good man brings good things out of the good stored up in him, and the evil man brings evil things out of the evil stored up in him. But I tell you," Jesus continued, "that men will have to give account on the Day of Judgment for every careless word they have spoken. For by your words you will be acquitted, and by your words you will be condemned." Then he turned and walked back into the house.

"Master!" his disciples called. "Your mother and brothers are here outside waiting for you."

"Who are my mother and my brothers?" he asked. Then he pointed at the crowd surrounding him, "Here are my mother and my brothers. Whoever does God's will is my brother and sister and mother."

When Mary heard what he said, she bowed her head in shame. She had doubted him and knew instantly it was not God's will for her to take him home.

"Oh, my sons!" Mary lamented as they led her away from the house. "We have done a dreadful thing. I have done a dreadful thing."

"No, Ima! You have done nothing wrong." Joses pushed the people out of the way so they could pass. "I can't believe our brother is treating you so badly. How dare he imply that we do not do the will of God!"

"Joses, you do not understand what Jesus meant…" Mary wept.

"He has disrespected you, Ima," Simon interrupted. "He has denied us all!"

"Oh no, Simon! He did not mean it that way." Mary tried to explain to her sons what Jesus meant, but they would not listen to her. They were furious with the way Jesus had treated her. They had taken Jesus' comments as a personal insult—a rejection of them.

"Jesus was just trying to make a point with his disciples."

"Ima, I do not like to be ridiculed by my own brother. We are leaving—*Now!*" Joses declared as he and Simon steered her away from the crowd.

James and Jude were less judgmental, for they had not dismissed the healing of the demon-possessed man that had taken place before their eyes. Although they still were not convinced Jesus was the Messiah, they were more willing to listen to him now that they had seen him perform a miracle.

211

"Joses, wait!" James cried. "Do not do this, my brother. Do not leave! Think about what you are doing. Jesus would never insult our mother. His love and respect for her is too great."

Jude agreed and added, "Let our mother see the son she has not seen in many months. She has come all this way, Joses; do not let her leave without seeing him again."

"At least take the time to listen to him, my sons," Mary pleaded. "He is your brother. He deserves that much."

After much coaxing, the two men relented and by the time the crowds dispersed their anger had abated. It was hard for them to look upon the sea of desperate faces and not wonder how Jesus was able to perform so many miracles—if he was just a normal man.

Jesus sought Mary out later that evening. He knew she was waiting, that she was remorseful, and his heart went out to her. He brought them all to Peter's house, where they spent the night. They met his chosen Twelve and the others who were also traveling with him. James felt guilty right away over his thoughts of the "sinners" Jesus had been associating with. After he met Mary Magdalene, he promised himself he would never think that way again. He found her and the others to be people filled with joy and hope, no longer slaves to their sin but free. This amazed and confused him, because his brother had helped them find that freedom. But he couldn't understand where Jesus' power came from.

"I'm staying with your brother," Mary decided as her sons prepared for their journey home the next morning.

"You can't be serious!" Jude's mouth fell open in surprise. "Why?"

"I want to get to know the women traveling with Jesus. I want to get to know his disciples. I want to hear him speak, to help in whatever way I can."

"But Ima, he has no place to lay his head. You will be spending many nights outdoors, sleeping on the ground. Are you sure about this?" James took Mary's hands in his, reluctant to leave her.

Mary nodded and caressed his face. "I'll be fine. You know that, James. Your brother is the Messiah. I must follow him, and if you would just look within yourself, you too would realize this truth."

James grimaced at Mary's words. "Ima! Please don't say that too loudly."

"Why not? It's true. Search yourself, James. You know I'm right."

He pursed his lips. "I will think on it." He turned to Jesus. "Be careful, brother. The Jewish leaders want you dead. They are very jealous of the power you have over the people. See that you don't give them a reason to harm you or our mother."

———

"As the months passed, Jesus attracted many followers," Mary said. When morning had finally broken, she was weary. She had found that Julius seemed to have a never-ending supply of questions. While eager to see him come to faith in Christ, she was so tired she feared she would fall over in a heap at his feet at any moment. Luke came to her rescue and ordered her to bed, promising to let her finish her story after she rested. Julius apologized for monopolizing her time and agreed with Luke. Six hours later, she was back on her bench and sharing her story with both the passengers and crew once again.

"Those who followed him were ordinary people. They were beggars, sick, poor, lame, or blind. Some were people who, until they met Jesus, had lived immoral lives—prostitutes, drunkards, thieves, adulterers, and the like. These people needed hope, for they had none. They needed love, for they were considered unlovable by many. They needed a reason to live and they found it in Jesus, who accepted them, healed them, and loved them all unconditionally. They came to him broken, and in their own eyes, beyond repair or saving, and by his precious touch they were healed. How he loved them! How his heart ached for them. They could see his compassion and gave themselves to him willingly, for they believed he was the Son of God." Mary arched her back and stood, pacing back and forth as she spoke.

"He also attracted many enemies. Those who rejected him felt threatened by him. They were the rich, the self-righteous, the arrogant, and the proud. These people placed their hopes in their good works, religious duties, money, and in themselves. They found their happiness and success in their wealth and power. They hated Jesus and all he stood for. Most of them made up the Jewish high council. They wanted Jesus dead, because he threatened their power over the people and their way of life.

"But oh, how Jesus loved them as well! How his heart ached for them. For they did not know, nor could they see, that they were lost and would perish—separated for all eternity from the God they claimed to serve, because they would not turn from their sins."

"Was there no one in the Sanhedrin who believed in Jesus?" someone asked.

Mary stopped pacing and returned to her bench. She stared out to sea, listening to the flap of the sails in the breeze and the first mate relaying orders to the crew. "There were a few believers on the council. Secret believers. I remember one man—his name was Nicodemus. He was a Pharisee and a member of the Jewish ruling council. He came secretly at night one year, while we were in Jerusalem for the annual Passover celebrations."

———

He found Jesus, with his chosen Twelve, gathered around a campfire in the Garden of Gethsemane, outside the walls of Jerusalem. Jesus sat hunched over the fire, stirring its embers with a stick while his disciples slept nearby.

"Nicodemus! Come join me." Nicodemus jumped at the sound of Jesus' voice. How was it possible that this man knew his name? Nicodemus shook his head in wonder as he approached.

He had been observing the young Rabbi from Nazareth for some time. At first, Nicodemus had ignored Jesus and the outrageous claims of his miraculous powers. However, as he listened to him speak and saw the wondrous miracles with his own eyes, he decided to investigate the mysterious Rabbi further. He secretly sought out information on his past—where he had been born, who his parents were, and if he came from the line of David. To his amazement, he discovered Jesus was the same child who had im-

pressed him and the other priests at the temple so many years ago.
He remembered Jesus coming into the temple and questioning the
teachers of the law for more than three days. They had found him
to be an extraordinary child, full of wisdom and knowledge. After
his parents had taken him home, Nicodemus questioned Zechariah, Jesus' relative, about the child. He remembered how Zechariah had told him of Jesus' birth and of Simeon's testimony about
him at his dedication ceremony.

Nevertheless, he had kept those things to himself, waiting
many years to see if the boy would one day proclaim his throne.
Yet Jesus had not made any such claims. Even so, many of his followers believed he was the long awaited Messiah and Nicodemus
believed the people were right. Still, he would not jeopardize his
position on the Sanhedrin, or his relationship with High Priest
Caiaphas, on false hopes. He needed to talk to the man himself.

"Come, sit beside me," Jesus said as he patted the ground. Jesus watched the teacher with amusement, knowing that sitting on
the ground was not something a prominent teacher of the law often did. Finally, with a grimace and a sigh, Nicodemus lowered his
corpulent body beside him.

"Rabbi, we know you are a teacher who has come from God.
For no one could perform the miraculous signs you are doing if
God were not with him."

Jesus knew that Nicodemus was a teacher of the law and therefore his whole life was guided by it, so he said to him, "I tell you the
truth, no one can see the kingdom of God unless he is born again."

Nicodemus stroked his beard as he contemplated Jesus' words.
It was several minutes before he spoke. "How can a man be born

when he is old? Surely he cannot enter a second time into his mother's womb to be born!"

Jesus smiled, knowing how difficult it would be for the learned teacher to understand. "I tell you the truth; no one can enter the kingdom of God unless he is born of water *and* the Spirit. Flesh gives birth to flesh, but the Spirit gives birth to spirit." He saw the look of confusion on Nicodemus' face and tried to explain. "You should not be surprised at my saying, 'You must be born again.' The wind blows wherever it pleases. You hear its sound, but you cannot tell where it comes from or where it is going. So it is with everyone born of the Spirit."

"How can this be?"

"You are Israel's teacher and you do not understand these things?" Jesus shook his head and stared at the fire. He knew it would be hard for Nicodemus to understand that while God had given His laws as a means of showing man right from wrong, He also wanted man to come into a relationship with Him—to have a transformed heart, filled with His Holy Spirit, where He would dwell forever. How could he explain to one of Israel's finest teachers that he needed a heart for God?

"I tell you the truth," Jesus continued. "We speak of what we know, and we testify to what we have seen, but still you people do not accept our testimony. I have spoken to you of earthly things and you do not believe; how then will you believe if I speak of heavenly things?"

Nicodemus ran a hand through his beard as he tried to understand Jesus' words. His brows drew together in concentration. He opened his mouth to speak, and then closed it. As a Pharisee, he followed the law to the smallest detail. He was a stickler for ceremonial purity. If anyone was to get into heaven—it would be him. Why then was Jesus saying he must be born again?

"No one has ever gone into heaven," Jesus continued after seeing the perplexed look on Nicodemus' face, "except the One who came from heaven—the Son of Man. Just as Moses lifted up the snake in the desert, so the Son of Man must be lifted up, so that everyone who believes in him may have eternal life. For God so loved the world that he gave His one and only Son, that whoever believes in Him shall not perish but have eternal life. For God did not send His Son into the world to condemn the world, but to save the world through Him. Whoever believes in Him is not condemned, but whoever does not believe stands condemned already, because he has not believed in the name of God's one and only Son."

Nicodemus shook his head, his eyes widening. "Rabbi, what you are saying is that one must believe in the Messiah to be saved, the one who will come to free us from Roman oppression. What about the law? The rules and regulations we have followed for centuries? Do they count for nothing?"

"This is the verdict," Jesus answered in a soothing tone. "Light has come into the world, but men loved darkness instead of light because their deeds were evil. Everyone who does evil hates the light and will not come into the light for fear that his deeds will be exposed. But whoever lives by the truth comes into the light, so that it may be seen plainly, that what he has done has been done through God."

Nicodemus stared at Jesus in disbelief. He believed himself to be a righteous man. He did not believe his deeds were evil. Yet Jesus said he needed a change of heart.

He stood up to leave and said, "Rabbi, I have waited anxiously for the Messiah all my life. If I knew he was here today, I would follow him." He waited, hoping Jesus would confirm that he was the Messiah, but Jesus turned toward the fire and stoked the dying embers with a stick once more.

Nicodemus sighed, disappointed that Jesus had not confirmed his identity to him. With one last look at the young Rabbi, he turned quietly and left.

"Who do the crowds say I am?" Jesus asked his chosen Twelve some time later.

John swiped at a fly buzzing near his head. "Some say John the Baptist."

"Others say Elijah," James added.

Matthew sat forward, his face earnest and hopeful. "Some say you are one of the prophets from long ago come back to life."

"But what about you?" Jesus asked. "Who do you say I am?"

"You are the Christ," Simon Peter answered. "The Son of the Living God."

Jesus reached out and clasped Simon Peter's arm. "Blessed are you, Simon son of Jonah, for this was not revealed to you by man, but by my Father in Heaven. And I tell you that you are Peter, and on this rock I will build my church, and the gates of Hades will not overcome it." He clapped Peter's back. "I will give you the keys to the kingdom of heaven. Whatever you bind on earth will be bound in heaven, and whatever you loose on earth will be loosed in heaven."

Peter gasped in surprise at the honour Jesus bestowed on him. Jesus held his finger to his lips and searched the faces of the people standing in a circle around the campfire.

"Repeat this to no one," he warned. "The Son of Man must suffer many things and be rejected by the elders, chief priests, and teachers of the law—and he must be killed and on the third day be raised to life."

"Never, Lord!" Peter looked to the others for confirmation. "This shall never happen to you!"

Jesus' body tensed, his nostrils flaring. "Get behind me, Satan! You are a stumbling block to me. You do not have in mind the things of God, but the things of men."

Peter dropped his gaze, avoiding the looks of the others. He blinked back tears that threatened to spill. Moments before Jesus had called him blessed, and now he compared him to Satan? He felt as if he had been slapped in the face.

Jesus saw the confusion and sorrow on Peter's face and patted his shoulder. "Listen to me, all of you, if anyone would come after me, he must deny himself and take up his cross daily and follow me. For whoever wants to save his life will lose it, but whoever loses his life for me will save it. What good is it for a man to gain the whole world and yet lose or forfeit his very soul? If anyone is ashamed of me and my words," Jesus continued, "the Son of Man will be ashamed of him when he comes in his glory and in the glory of the Father and of the holy angels."

Peter thought long and hard about all he had left behind to follow Jesus. He thought, too, about all Jesus went through each day and how he denied himself continually in order to show God's love to the people. People pushing, crying, begging for healing, for a touch, for deliverance from something—Jesus, hot, hungry, tired and sore, exhausted to the very marrow of his bones... yet he continually denied himself in order to reach the masses. Jesus did not seek his own will first, but that of the Father's. He did not satisfy his own needs first, but instead took the form of a servant and saw to the needs of others before seeing to his own.

Peter could see now why Jesus had rebuked him. Jesus needed to stay focused on his calling and not listen to the temptation of Satan to give it all up, to use his power to make things easier for himself. He regretted his words immediately, and when Jesus smiled at him Peter knew he was forgiven.

"I tell you the truth," Jesus said. "Some who are standing here will not taste death before they see the kingdom of God."

Finally! Judas Iscariot said to himself. *Now he is making sense. Perhaps when we go up to Jerusalem, Jesus will go into the temple and declare himself the Messiah.*

As the days and weeks passed, he waited anxiously for that moment to be revealed.

CHAPTER
— 29 —

S ometime after that we traveled back to Nazareth," Mary explained as the ship continued on its course to Ephesus. The men around her had started out as a small group, but now more were coming to listen to her as word spread throughout the ship. The sun beat down on the little group, causing many of the men to squint. Mary was thankful the wind had picked up, as it was providing a nice respite from the heat.

"Nazareth!" Julius exclaimed. "How could he journey back to Nazareth after almost being killed there?"

"I myself was greatly concerned," Mary replied, "but Jesus was preaching throughout Galilee and some of our friends from Nazareth had heard of his miracles and the claims about him. They urged us to stay. I suppose they wanted to determine if they had acted prematurely in their judgment of him, so once again we found ourselves in Nazareth."

"What happened when you got there?" someone asked. "Did they try to kill Jesus again?"

Mary shook her head. "No, it wasn't bad at all. Some people had heard of his miracles and he was able to help them. Others wondered where he got his power and wisdom. They could not forget that he was the son of a carpenter, though. They saw his brothers and sisters in the synagogue with me and refused to believe. He did heal a few sick people by laying hands on them. Unfortunately, most people lacked faith and he couldn't help them. So after visiting with his sisters and brothers, he left."

"Did you go with him again?" Luke asked. "Or did you stay home with your daughters?"

"I went with him. By that time, several women were traveling with him. Mary Magdalene, who was healed of several demons, Joanna the wife of Chuza … "

"Herod's steward?" Julius interrupted, surprised that some people in the palace had been followers of Jesus. "Men of influence followed Jesus?"

"Oh yes!" Mary's eyes lit with excitement. "He came to heal the poor in spirit, Julius—and many powerful people are very poor in spirit indeed. By that time, Peter's wife Perpetua and some of the other wives had joined us. Once we were all together, Jesus sent the Twelve out, two by two, and gave them authority over evil spirits."

"He could do that? Give his power to others?" Julius raised his eyebrows in doubt.

"Oh yes. The Apostles went out and preached that people should repent. They drove out demons and anointed many sick people with oil and healed them." She paused and was quiet for a moment. "It was around this time that John the Baptist was beheaded."

———

They were in Capernaum at Peter's house, when Chuza, Herod's chief steward, came running up the path toward Jesus. Behind him were several of John the Baptist's followers. They were clearly agitated and Chuza could barely get his words out when they reached Jesus.

"Lord... we have... news..." he panted. He hunched over, taking huge gulps of air. Jesus, sensing his struggle to breathe, placed his hands on him. Immediately Chuza's breathing came easier. He fell to his knees, grasping Jesus' hand. "Master... we have news of John the Baptist."

Mary had been talking with Perpetua when Chuza and the others ran up. She drew closer to Jesus, knowing instinctively the news was not good.

"Tell me, Chuza," Jesus said quietly. "What news have you?"

Chuza's shoulders started to shake as he and the others related the news of John's beheading. Mary moaned and started to sway. Jesus reached for her and held her steady in his arms.

"Sit here, Ima," Jesus said as he helped her onto a nearby tree stump.

"We have buried his body, Master. We are sorry for your loss."

Mary wept silently. Jesus sat beside her and rubbed her back. He whispered in her ear and she nodded. "Go—I am fine." Jesus squeezed her hand lightly, swallowing the sorrow that was building within him as he rose to comfort his flock.

He patted Chuza on the shoulders reassuringly, muttering words of encouragement, repeating the gesture with the rest of John's followers and his own disciples. All eyes were on Jesus, waiting to see what he would do. He could see the people gathering once again on the hills around him, waiting for him to perform more healings. However, everyone needed time to grieve their loss, so Jesus whispered to Peter and John to get the boat ready.

"We will go to the other side—over to Bethsaida. We all need time to grieve—to rest." Peter and John nodded and, after finding James, they went to get the boat ready.

"Woman, you will stay here with Perpetua and the others until we return," Jesus said to his mother, indicating to all present that he wanted to be alone with his Apostles.

Mary blinked back tears and hugged him goodbye. "We will see you when you return. Take as much time as you need." Her heart was breaking for Jesus' loss. He and John had been very close through the years and she knew he was suffering.

Within the hour, they put out to sea. All the people who had waited on shore to see Jesus saw him leave and ran by foot to the next village, and the next one after that, to see where he would land. However, Jesus was more concerned about his friends and their reaction to the news of John's death. As they rowed the boat out to sea, he told them stories of his childhood and shared his personal thoughts about his cousin. It was a time of friendship—a time for sharing and ministering to each other. It was one of those rare moments when they were able to spend time alone together—without crowds of people bombarding them with pleas of healing and cries for help. By the time they landed in Bethsaida, the men felt refreshed and rested despite their grief.

They were not surprised to see a large crowd of people gathered on the shore when they arrived. Jesus had compassion on them all and immediately began healing people. As evening approached, Peter along with the others came to him and said, "This is a remote place, and it's already getting late. Send the crowds away, so they can go to the villages and buy themselves some food."

Jesus replied, "They do not need to go away. You give them something to eat."

"That would take eight months of a man's wages!" Philip exclaimed. "Are we to go and spend that much on bread and give it to them to eat?"

"How many loaves do you have?" Jesus asked. "Go and see."

The men went throughout the crowds and half an hour later returned to Jesus.

"There's a small boy here who has five barley loaves and two small fish, but what is that between so many, unless we go ourselves and buy food for these people?" Andrew said as he showed Jesus the contents of the food basket.

Jesus nodded, reached out his hands, and said, "Give them to me." Andrew handed him the basket and Jesus told them to have the people sit down on the grass in groups of fifty. So the Twelve went out again amongst the crowd and had them sit as Jesus instructed. There were over five thousand men gathered, as well as women and children.

When everyone was seated, Jesus took the five loaves and two fish and, raising his face toward heaven, he gave thanks and broke the loaves. He then divided the loaves and fish between his disciples to give to the people.

It was an astonishing day for them all. As each Apostle broke off a piece of bread to give to someone, the bread miraculously continued to multiply. It never ran out. The same thing happened with the fish. The men rejoiced with each other and giggled like children each time they reached into their baskets to find more fish or bread.

"I feel like the widow whose oil did not run out!" Peter exclaimed as he handed a young woman a serving of fish and bread.

John nodded in agreement. "It is amazing, isn't it?"

When they all had enough to eat, Jesus said to his disciples, "Gather the pieces that are left over. Let nothing be wasted."

Once again, the Apostles walked through the crowd and they collected twelve baskets of leftover food. After the people realized Jesus had performed yet another miracle, they began to say, "Surely this is the Prophet who is to come into the world."

Judas heard their whispers and agreed. *Now is the perfect time for Jesus to reveal himself, but how and when will the Master do it?*

Jesus, knowing that the crowd intended to come and make him king by force, dismissed them, urged the apostles to return to Capernaum without him, and then withdrew to a mountain where he could be alone to pray.

Later that evening, when darkness descended like a velvet blanket across the land, Jesus looked out toward the middle of the lake and could see his disciples straining at the oars. A strong wind was blowing and the waters were rough. He could see that the men were having a difficult time making the crossing, so he went out to them, walking on the lake. When they saw him approaching, they thought he was a ghost and were terrified.

Jesus immediately said to them, "Take courage! It is I. Don't be afraid."

"Lord, if it's you," Peter replied, "tell me to come to you on the water."

Jesus smiled, held out his hand, and said, "Come."

Surprise and fear mingled on Peter's face like a tortured mask. Now was a time for faith, but his heart was thumping through his chest. He could hear the others whispering, wondering what he would do. Peter looked over the side of the boat at the churning waters below and immediately regretted his bad habit of speaking before thinking. He could shake his head and say he had changed his mind, but what would his friends think of his faith? Hesitantly, he put one leg over the side of the boat. His sandaled toes could feel the water lapping at them. He winced and pulled his leg back from the cold bite of the water. Jesus remained standing outside the boat, waiting for him, his hand extended.

The wind was picking up again and the waves tossed the boat up and down effortlessly. Keeping his eyes focused on Jesus, Peter slid his legs over the side of the boat once more. He felt the water envelop his feet again, but suddenly it became solid beneath him. Shock poured over him like the waves of the sea. Cautiously, he took a step and then another. The disciples sat in awe as they watched their friend walk on the rough water toward the Master, unsure of whom they should be more afraid—Jesus or Peter.

Peter was giddy with delight. He was walking on the water! Gradually he became more confident as he made his way toward Jesus. He could hear the others in the boat and their gasps of amazement. He started laughing. His wife would have died of fright if she could see him now!

Suddenly, a wave crested and slammed into Peter's chest. Jesus saw the alarm on his face and knew that if Peter did not keep his eyes focused on him, his faith would falter. But Jesus did not move. Instead he waited to see what Peter would do.

The force of the wave stunned Peter and as the wind continued to howl and the water rose higher he looked away from Jesus and became afraid.

At once, he began to sink and, reaching out his arms, he cried, "Lord, save me!"

Immediately Jesus reached out his hand and caught him.

"You of little faith," Jesus chided as he led Peter to the boat. "Why did you doubt?"

He helped Peter into the boat and as soon as they had climbed in the wind died down.

The apostles were dumbfounded. What they had just witnessed took away any lingering doubts they had harboured in their hearts. As one, they worshipped Jesus, saying, "Truly you are the Son of God."

CHAPTER
— 30 —

Jesus, I am afraid I have more bad news for you." Mary greeted her son with a quick hug, then waited while the rest of the Twelve gathered around. It had been two weeks since John's death. Jesus had left for Bethsaida with his disciples and was just now coming back to Capernaum.

"What is it, woman?" Jesus asked, taking Mary's hands in his.

"We received word from Mary and Martha while you were in Galilee. Their brother Lazarus is sick. I am very worried."

Jesus nodded and squeezed his mother's hand reassuringly. "This sickness will not end in death. No, it is for God's glory so that God's Son may be glorified through it."

Mary closed her eyes and sighed. "That is a relief. I was quite convinced he was so ill you would be too late to save him. But—if you say he will not die, I feel much better."

"Well, I for one am glad we are not going back to Judea," Perpetua said as she brought water and cloths to wash the men's feet.

"The Jews there are totally unreasonable! I still can't forget how they tried to stone you, Lord, the last time we were there."

Jesus smiled as he sat on a nearby stool. "It will be good to visit with you both for awhile."

Mary arched her eyebrows in surprise. "A visit, is it? For how long?"

Mary knelt at Jesus' feet, took his foot in her hands, and removed his sandals.

"Oh, I don't know. I suppose we will stay long enough for some good food, a little rest—maybe some fishing."

"Fishing?" Mary looked amused as she poured water over Jesus' dusty feet and proceeded to wash them. "You are going to fish—for fish?"

Jesus laughed aloud at the expression on his mother's face. "What—you think I can only fish for men?"

"You are teasing me! Do not think you can leave me behind so easily this time. It is one thing to receive bad news when you are nearby, but to receive it and not be able to tell you anything because I don't know where you are—well…"

"Woman," Jesus said quietly, "I will never leave you nor forsake you. Rest assured, when we do leave, you will be going with me."

Two days later, Jesus surprised the Apostles when he said, "Let us go back to Judea."

"But Rabbi," Peter protested, "a short while ago the Jews tried to stone you, and yet you are going back there?"

Jesus nodded. "Are there not twelve hours of daylight? A man who walks by day will not stumble, for he sees by this world's light. It is when he walks by night that he stumbles, for he has no light."

Peter shook his head in bewilderment.

"Our friend Lazarus has fallen asleep and I am going to wake him up."

John replied, "Lord, if he sleeps, he will get better."

Jesus shook his head. "You don't understand. Lazarus is dead and for your sake I am glad I was not there, so that you may believe. But let us go to him."

It took them a week to get there and upon arrival Jesus found that Lazarus had already been in the tomb for four days.

"Oh, my son, we are too late!" Mary pressed her hands against her chest as they passed a group of mourners who had come to comfort Martha and Mary over the loss of their brother. "Look—is that Martha?" She pointed at a woman running toward them.

"Lord! Lord!" Martha cried when she saw Jesus. Her tear-stained faced was evidence of her misery. "If you had been here, my brother would not have died. But I know that even now God will give you whatever you ask."

Jesus put a comforting arm around her and said, "Your brother will rise again."

As they walked together in the direction of her house, Martha nodded in response. "Yes, I know he will rise again in the resurrection at the last day."

"I am the resurrection and the life, Martha. He who believes in me will live, even though he dies. And whoever lives and believes in me will never die. Do you believe this?"

"Yes, Lord," she told him. "I believe you are the Christ, the Son of God who was to come into the world."

Jesus felt joy and grief at the same time. Joy that Martha had listened to him and grief that both she and Mary had to suffer for the loss of their brother.

"Go and tell Mary I am here, Martha. For I wish to comfort her as well," he said. She nodded and ran to the house and called Mary.

"The Teacher is here," she said, "and is asking for you."

When Mary heard this, she got up quickly and went to him. Jesus had not yet entered the village, but waited at the place where Martha had met him. When the people who had been with Mary in the house, comforting her, noticed how quickly she got up and went out, they followed her, supposing she was going to the tomb to mourn there.

When Mary reached Jesus, she fell at his feet and sobbed. "Lord, if you had been here, my brother would not have died."

When Jesus saw her weeping, and her friends who had come along with her also weeping, he was deeply moved in spirit and troubled. "Where have you laid him?" he asked, anxious to relieve their suffering.

"Come and see, Lord," she replied as she led him toward the tomb.

Jesus looked at the grief-stricken people around him and wept. He was moved by their sorrow and loss, filled with grief over what he now had to do. *How can I bring Lazarus back to this world when he is currently enjoying heavenly riches?* This saddened him most of all. He could not contain his tears.

Then the people said, "See how Jesus loved him!"

But some of them said, "Could not he, who opened the eyes of the blind man, have kept this man from dying?"

Jesus sighed when he heard what they said. He stood in front of the tomb. He could have healed Lazarus. He knew that. But what he was about to do would be far more miraculous than any one of them had yet experienced.

"Take away the stone," he said calmly as he wiped away his tears. His disciples looked on in shock. Surely the Master had not just asked to move the stone? John looked at Peter and shrugged.

"He's overcome with grief," John whispered to him. "He does not know what he is saying."

"But, Lord," said Martha, voicing everyone's concerns, "by this time there is a bad odour, for he has been there four days."

Mary nodded her agreement, hoping her son's sorrow had not overcome his judgment.

"Did I not tell you that if you believed, you would see the glory of God?" Jesus asked. So, reluctantly they took away the stone.

Jesus looked to the heavens and raised his arms in prayer. "Father, I thank you that you have heard me. I know that you always hear me, but I said this for the benefit of the people standing here, that they may believe you sent me."

He lowered his arms, then stretched them out toward the tomb and yelled, "Lazarus, come out!"

Martha and Mary came closer to the tomb and waited in silence. Nothing happened. Peter and John exchanged worried glances. The silence seemed interminable, when suddenly a groan was heard and then a slight rustling. A few moments passed, and then Lazarus was there—at the entrance of the tomb—alive!

Several people started screaming and ran away. Some fainted, overcome with fear. Others stood rooted to the spot, unable to comprehend what they were seeing.

"Take off the grave clothes and let him go," Jesus ordered.

Mary and Martha ran forward, along with Jesus' mother, to release Lazarus from his wrappings.

"There is no odour. I don't understand how this could happen," Mary said as she fumbled with the cloth on her brother's face.

"His flesh is also perfectly normal. There is no sign of decay at all," Martha said, amazed.

"My sisters," Lazarus moaned as he was released from his wrappings. "I have just been in a glorious place, surrounded by wonderful things. It was a beautiful city and there were many others there. Then I heard the Master's voice and my heart filled with joy. I had to follow his voice—and now—I am here again."

Jesus came with a robe and put it around Lazarus' shoulders. Hugging his beloved friend, Jesus said to him, "I am glad you are here."

Lazarus looked at him and said, "Lord, I could not live in another world without your presence there."

Jesus' eyes filled with tears once again and said to his friend, "Someday we both shall rejoice in my Father's presence together."

"Many people believed in Jesus that day and put their faith in him because of that miracle," Mary said as she continued her story on the last day of their journey to Ephesus. "I myself was never quite the same again. I saw Jesus differently—not just as my son, but finally as my Lord—my Saviour."

"No doubt that was a difficult transition to make," Julius remarked.

"It could have been, but I had been waiting for Him since the moment He was conceived. I was well prepared spiritually—it was the emotional cord of being a mother that was a little hard to cut." Mary smiled. "The Sanhedrin was angry when they heard Jesus had brought Lazarus back from the dead. More and more people began following him. Little by little, the Sanhedrin was losing the respect of the people. They feared for their futures. If the people made Jesus king, what would happen to them? For that matter, what would Herod do if the Jews proclaimed another as their king?" Mary shook her head. "They convinced themselves that the Romans would come and take away both our temple and our nation. So they plotted from that day on to take Jesus' life."

"What did Jesus do then?" someone yelled from the back of the crowd that had gathered on deck.

"He no longer moved about publicly among the Jews. Instead, he withdrew to a region near the desert, to a village called Ephraim, where he stayed with his disciples."

"I still don't understand how an innocent man could be offered up to be killed because of one group's fears and insecurities," Julius commented.

"They feared they would lose not only their power over the people," Luke explained, "but their station in life."

"Yes," Mary said, nodding. "These men were very wealthy and influential. They were our governing body, so to speak. They made the laws and had the authority to arrest whomever they wanted."

"But they had no power to execute anyone. That was up to the powers of Rome," Julius clarified.

"That's right," Luke agreed. "This is why they had to get permission from Pilate and Herod before they could do anything."

"Let me guess," Julius smirked. "They brought forward a lot of trumped up charges against him?"

"There was false testimony given," Mary replied. "But in the end … Jesus convicted himself by his own words."

CHAPTER
— 31 —

While they were in Ephraim, Jesus took the Twelve aside as they were walking in the fields and said to them, "We are going up to Jerusalem, and everything that is written by the prophets about the Son of Man will be fulfilled. He will be handed over to the Gentiles. They will mock him, insult him, spit on him, flog him, and kill him. On the third day he will rise again."

"What do you mean, Lord?" Thomas asked. "You think the Romans are going to kill you?"

"It is as I have said." Jesus nodded and continued walking.

"But Lord," Philip said, brow furrowed. "It is the Jews, especially the members of the Sanhedrin, who are threatened by you and want you dead. How can you be handed over to the Gentiles?"

"No! No! No! He is to start his earthly kingdom." Judas Iscariot rolled his eyes and shook his head. "That's what the Master means, Philip. Herod wouldn't like that at all!"

"But Judas," Matthew said, pointing his finger at him. "He can't start his kingdom if he is dead."

Jesus sighed and shook his head, amazed that his apostles were still trying to find a hidden meaning in everything he said. He removed himself from their discussion and went off to be alone. They could not comprehend why he was going to die, but soon they would understand everything.

Sometime later, they made their way to Bethany where they stayed once again with Mary, Martha, and Lazarus. Their house had a wonderful courtyard surrounded by a brick wall built for privacy. A grapevine, lush with fruit, wound its way overhead as a protective canopy from the noonday sun. The small group was very tired and Martha was soon tending to their needs, making sure everyone had water to wash with and a place to lay their heads if they needed to rest.

Later, Jesus began teaching his disciples once again. Taking that as her cue, Martha nudged her sister and with a nod indicated that she was to follow. After several minutes, she went in search of Mary and found her sitting at the feet of the Master, totally absorbed in his words. Martha sighed, her lips drawing to a thin line. *If she is not going to help, I shall do it myself!* As she fumed over Mary's thoughtlessness, Martha began dinner preparations. Whenever she had something to put on the table, she would nudge Mary. Unfortunately, she soon discovered that Mary was oblivious to her needs. As the evening progressed, she would often slip into the room where everyone had gathered. She would fold her arms and stand behind Mary, sighing and whispering about how hot it was in the kitchen, drawing the attention of everyone but her sister. Her anger building, Martha was incensed at her sister's insensitivity. *This meal is in Jesus' honour for all that he has done for our brother. Why isn't Mary helping me?* Finally, after several more attempts to solicit Mary's help, she decided to go to Jesus.

"Lord, don't you care that my sister has left me to do the work by myself? Tell her to help me!" she pleaded.

"Martha, Martha." Jesus grasped her hand and pulled her down to sit beside him. "You are worried and upset about many things, but only one thing is needed." He pointed at Mary and said, "Mary has chosen what is better, and it will not be taken away from her."

Martha's face crumpled in dismay. Mary, suddenly aware of all that Martha had been doing, grew red with embarrassment at her lack of concern for her sister's needs.

"Martha," Jesus spoke softly to her, "I do not mean that what you do for me is not appreciated. You have served me wonderfully and you will be rewarded. But even your servants have taken time to listen to me. Sit now, rest and listen to me as Mary does. It is a better choice."

Mary smiled at the look of surprise on Martha's face, then moved over and patted a place on the pillow beside her. Martha glanced back at the kitchen, and then reluctantly sat beside her sister.

The next night, they gathered at the home of a man named Simon. Jesus had healed him of leprosy some months previous and upon hearing that he had returned to Bethany Simon invited Jesus and his disciples to dinner.

It was after the meal that Mary showed Martha just how much the Master meant to her. She took a pint of expensive perfume and lovingly poured it on Jesus' feet, wiping them with her hair. Soon the house was filled with the fragrance of the perfume.

Judas Iscariot objected, "Why wasn't this perfume sold and the money given to the poor? It was worth a year's wages."

Jesus waved his hand in dismissal and shook his head. "Leave her alone. It was intended that she should save this perfume for the day of my burial. You will always have the poor among you, but you will not always have me."

Judas felt the sting of Jesus' rebuke. Embarrassed and angry, he withdrew to a corner of the room where he contemplated once again his reasons for following the Teacher. He was positive Jesus was the Messiah. The miracles alone proved that! However, Jesus' insistence on his impending death and his refusal to acknowledge that he was the Chosen One annoyed Judas to no end. *Why does the Master say such strange things? When will he claim his Kingdom? How much longer will we have to wait to be free from Rome's cruel hand?* He could feel the frustration building within him and decided that if Jesus did not declare himself as Messiah soon, he would go to Caiaphas himself and do it for him.

When it was time for the Passover, they went up to Jerusalem once again. When Jesus came near the place where the road sloped down the Mount of Olives, the whole crowd of disciples began joyfully praising God in loud voices for all the miracles they had seen.

"Blessed is the King who comes in the name of the Lord!"

"Peace in heaven and glory in the highest!"

"Hosanna! Hosanna to the Son of David!"

"Blessed is he who comes in the name of the Lord! Hosanna in the highest!"

"Blessed is the coming Kingdom of Our Father David! Blessed is the King of Israel!"

Some of the Pharisees in the crowd said to Jesus, "Teacher, rebuke your disciples!"

"I tell you," he laughed, "if they keep quiet, the stones will cry out."

"This is incredible! Can you believe this, John? Everybody is honouring the Master!" Judas was so excited with the prospect of what was to come he thought he would burst. He jumped around like a little boy, making John laugh at his antics. John had never seen this side of Judas before.

"Judas, I can't believe I'm saying this, but maybe you were right all along," John said as he watched the procession. Jesus had ridden into Jerusalem on a donkey, fulfilling what was spoken through the prophet Zechariah: "Say to the Daughter of Zion, 'See, your king comes to you, gentle and riding on a donkey, on a colt, the foal of a donkey.'"[17]

Everywhere, people were laying their cloaks on the ground and waving palm branches as he passed by. Their shouts of praise were deafening. They were proclaiming him King, something Judas had been wishing Jesus would do for some time now. John was amazed that it was now happening.

---

[17] Isaiah 62:11.

Judas stopped and smiled smugly, his curly brown hair sticking to his forehead, damp with sweat from the already sweltering heat of the day. He looked ahead to the crowds pressing around Jesus and once again was filled with awe that he was one of the chosen Twelve, handpicked by the Lord himself. Thousands had been healed, seen miracles performed, and listened to Jesus speak. They were, like Judas himself, convinced that Jesus would bring in a New Kingdom—free from oppression. He was the King of the Jews and his time had come to take his throne on earth. Just looking around at how the people adored and worshipped Jesus was proof enough for Judas. The time had finally come—after all these anxious months—for Jesus to announce His Kingship. *Just in time, too,* Judas thought. *I've had enough! I'm tired of crowds and tired of having so little money. Perhaps once Jesus has established His Kingdom, I can concentrate on how to make this whole adventure more profitable.*

However, as Jesus approached Jerusalem and saw the city, he did not rejoice but wept, crying, "O Jerusalem! Jerusalem! If you, even you, had only known on this day what would bring you peace—but now it is hidden from your eyes. The days will come upon you when your enemies will build an embankment against you and encircle you and hem you in on every side. They will dash you to the ground, you and the children within your walls. They will not leave one stone on another, because you did not recognize the time of God's coming to you."

CHAPTER
— 32 —

The procession of worshippers followed Jesus right to the temple steps, where he dismounted and entered the temple courts. In the court of the Gentiles, the moneychangers were present as always, charging exorbitant amounts for animals used in the daily sacrifices. Jesus watched as rich and poor alike purchased clean, unblemished animals to take to the priest as an offering for the cleansing of their sins. The very poor would buy doves, the more wealthy—cattle or sheep. Some came prepared with their own offerings but were turned away and told to buy them only from the temple, where they could be sure the offering was acceptable.

Jesus was appalled by what he was witnessing. He had seen this every year of his life, each year becoming more and more incensed by the complete lack of regard for God's Holy temple.

"Look at them." Jesus pointed toward the moneychangers. "They care nothing for my Father's house. This is where the people are to make atonement for their sins, but they are making it a den of thieves." Without warning, he grabbed the cords off a curtain which hung from a pillar and hastily fashioned a whip out of them.

Mary, alarmed that he was going to do something rash, grasped his arm and said, "Son, remember who you are!"

"Woman, it is because of who I am that I must do this!" He turned toward the moneychanger tables. Cracking the whip high above his head, he shouted, "Get out!" The whip slammed down onto the table nearest him, causing the coins to scatter over the ground. With a mighty shove, Jesus overturned table after table, their contents spilling to the temple floor. Shouts of outrage drew temple worshippers to the scene where some pocketed the coins that were lying on the ground. The courtyard was in chaos. The poor were gathering coins discretely while the moneychangers, temple guards, and priests were scrambling to save it all before it was lost. Amidst the confusion, Jesus began opening the cages of the sacrificial animals. Sheep and cattle were running amok throughout the temple. As he opened the cage which housed the doves, he said to those who sold them, "Get these out of here!" His wrath was frightening. The Twelve stood dumbfounded as they watched their mild-mannered teacher turn into a roaring lion. As Jesus herded the sheep down the temple steps and into the streets, he turned and pointed at the priests who had gathered. Fixing an accusing glare on them, he shouted, "How dare you turn my Father's house into a market!"

The poor were thrilled with him and looked on in awe. Never in their lives had they seen anyone stand up to the temple Priests. "Isn't he the man from Galilee?" they whispered. "The one whom everyone is talking about? Is he the one who has come to save us?"

Caiaphas, the High Priest, was furious. He bounded down the steps from the Men's Court, followed by his guards. "What miraculous sign can you show us to prove your authority to do all this?"

"Destroy this temple, and I will raise it again in three days."

Mary gasped, as did the others with her. Had she heard her son correctly? Had he just threatened to destroy the temple? She looked at the disbelieving faces around her. *They must think he is mad!*

Judas gritted his teeth. He was furious. Jesus had just ruined what could have been a perfect day. Now it would be impossible for him to proclaim his Kingdom.

Caiaphas narrowed his eyes and stepped closer to Jesus. "It has taken forty-six years to build this temple, and you are going to raise it in three days?" He smirked and arched his eyebrows. Looking around at the guards and other priests who had gathered, he started to laugh. "He's mad!"

However, no one understood what Jesus meant and before they were all arrested, his mother and the apostles quickly ushered him out of the temple.

———

"That was your son!" Julius' mouth hung open in surprise. "My father was there that day, watching from the streets. He used to tell me that was the best day of his life—watching Caiaphas turning three shades of red, I mean." He chuckled. "Father used to say that was the day the people fell in love with Jesus and the chief priests stepped up their attempts to trap him."

Mary nodded. "Indeed, they were constantly trying to find ways to arrest him. But they couldn't, not without causing a riot, because the people loved him."

"So, what did he do, this son of yours?" Julius stood at the bow of the ship with Mary watching the ship cut through the waters. They were alone again except for a few of the crew who, while working, were listening intently.

"He went back to the temple the very next day, and every day that week."

The men chuckled along with Julius. Mary smiled and laughed with them. "He was bold and they tried to trick him so many times into saying something blasphemous that it almost became comical whenever the priests and teachers approached him."

"Tell us, by what authority are you doing these things?" the priests demanded one day as they tried to get him to say something in front of the people. "Who gave you this authority?"

He replied, "I will also ask you a question. Tell me, John's baptism—was it from heaven, or from men?"

They discussed it amongst themselves and said, "If we say, 'From heaven,' he will ask, 'Why didn't you believe him?' If we say, 'From men,' all the people will stone us, because they are persuaded that John was a prophet."

So they answered, "We don't know where it was from."

Jesus scrunched up his nose and shrugged. "Neither will I tell you by what authority I am doing these things."

Keeping a close watch on him, they sent spies who pretended to be honest. "Teacher, we know that you speak and teach what is right, and that you do not show partiality but teach the way of God in accordance with the truth. So, is it right for us to pay taxes to Caesar or not?"

He saw through their duplicity and said to them, "Show me a denarius."

They brought one to him and he asked them, "Whose portrait and inscription is on it?"

"Caesar's," they replied.

He threw the coin back to them and said, "Then give to Caesar what is Caesar's, and to God what is God's."

They were unable to trap him in what he had said. Astonished by his answers, they became silent.

After the fiasco in the temple, Judas was sure that any opportunity for Jesus to claim his Kingdom had come and gone. His dreams of political power, money, and prestige had all but vanished before his eyes. Fortunately, the people still hung on Jesus' every word. However, the increased presence of the Sanhedrin and the temple guards had Judas worried. He knew they were looking for ways to arrest the Master and Judas knew it was only a matter of time before they carried out their plans. When the time came, he did not want to be among the ones arrested. If Jesus was not going to use his power to release them all from the tyranny of Rome and proclaim himself king, then he would have to find a way to make it happen himself.

As Passover drew nearer, Judas fumed that Jesus had done nothing to establish his kingdom. Since Jesus' tirade in the temple, the people were falling on his every word while the temple priests, teachers, and guards did nothing, as if they were afraid to intervene. Judas waited almost the entire week to see what Jesus would do, but the only thing the Master would do was talk about his death and preach to the people. *The people adore Jesus—why can't he see they would follow him anywhere? Now is the time to act—when the odds are in our favour!*

"Judas?" Startled at the Master's voice, Judas jumped. They were once again in Bethany at the home of Mary and Martha. Everyone had retired for the evening, but Judas still sat outside warming himself by the fire.

"Master! I thought you were asleep."

Jesus squatted beside Judas. He rubbed his hands and held them closer to the fire for warmth. "I have been praying. What of you? What have you been doing?" Jesus asked.

Judas shifted uncomfortably and shrugged. "I've been thinking."

Jesus turned toward him. "Guard your thoughts, lest they lead you into temptation."

Judas looked into Jesus' eyes and quickly turned away. "Y–yes, Master." Jesus stood and patted his shoulder. "Good night, Judas."

"Good night, Rabbi." Judas remained seated as he watched Jesus walk into the house. As soon as he was gone, he stood up and began to pace.

Guard my thoughts? Judas struggled to find the meaning behind Jesus' words. *Is it possible he knows what I am thinking? If so, what does he mean?* He stopped pacing and stared back at the house, imagining Jesus laying his head down to rest with the others in the small home. *The Messiah shouldn't have to share a corner of ground to sleep. He should be sleeping at the temple! He needs to realize that. Is that what he meant by guarding my thoughts? Am I to be the one who gets him closer to his goal?* Judas grinned as a plan began to form in his mind. *Caiaphas! He must be made to realize that Jesus is the Messiah. If I meet with him and tell him that I can bring Jesus to him, perhaps they could talk. Surely, the Master would welcome the opportunity to present his case before the High Priest and Caiaphas will finally see that Jesus poses no threat, that he really is the Messiah. I might even be able to get some money out of the old coot for all my troubles.*

Judas clapped his hands together and almost laughed aloud. Tomorrow he would go see Caiaphas and together they would usher in a new kingdom.

When the temple guards announced to Caiaphas that one of the Teacher's disciples had come, he was both surprised and curious, so he ordered that Judas be brought in immediately to see him.

Judas could not believe his eyes when he saw the luxury Caiaphas enjoyed. *Obviously, the old priest enjoys his power and alliance with Rome,* Judas surmised as he watched a corpulent Caiaphas lower himself onto a cushioned cedar chair inlaid with ivory and gold.

Caiaphas narrowed his eyes and leaned forward. "What is it you want?"

Judas cleared his throat and said, "Sir, I know you have heard of the great things my Master Jesus has done."

"That I cannot deny. I have heard many things," Caiaphas replied as he sat back in his chair. "What of it?"

"He has come to free the oppressed. He has healed the sick and even raised the dead; he is a king worthy of a throne." Judas cleared his throat again and said, "I have come to ensure that he receives his rightful place of authority in this temple."

Caiaphas raised his eyebrows at the audacity of the man standing before him. Was he that naïve? Did he not realize that he and the other temple priests had been trying to find a way to arrest Jesus all week long? That they had wanted him dead for months? Caiaphas tried to keep a stern look on his face, but inside he was laughing. For surely the Lord God Himself would deliver the impostor Jesus into their hands through one of his own errant disciples!

"How do you propose that he receive his 'rightful place,' hmm?" Caiaphas clasped his fingers and grinned.

"You will talk to him and he will let you know what needs to be done."

"Will he?" Caiaphas studied Judas for several minutes, then asked, "How much do you want for him?"

Judas was startled that the High Priest could so easily read his thoughts. He would indeed want something in return for bringing the King of the Jews to them. He should be handsomely rewarded for that. After all, once Jesus announced his kingdom, they would all be freed from Roman tyranny.

"Thirty pieces of silver!" Judas blurted, lest Caiaphas change his mind.

"Done!" Caiaphas said, slapping his hand on his knee. "But how will you bring him to us?"

"He won't come of his own accord. He has this crazy belief that he must first be handed over to the Gentiles."

"Handed over to the Gentiles? We have the authority in this matter! Not the Romans! If he desires to be 'handed over' to someone, let it be to us."

Judas did not like the sound of where this conversation was going, but he had heard the Master say he would be handed over to the Gentiles. According to Jesus, they would mock him, insult him, spit on him, flog him, and kill him. He could save Jesus from all that.

"You can see him in the temple everyday," Judas offered. "He is always preaching there. Talk to him then."

"We have talked to him enough!" Caiaphas' face turned red with rage. "His claims disturb us greatly. He needs to be arrested for what he has said about himself."

"No! You cannot arrest him. He's done nothing wrong!"

"I am not a fool! The people would riot if we even attempted such a thing. They believe he *is* the Messiah. He has deceived many with his blasphemy!"

"If you could just get him alone and talk to him, you would believe also." Judas stepped forward, raising his hands in supplication.

Caiaphas snorted, waving his hands at him. "It is impossible to be alone with him and well you know it! There are people constantly surrounding him. Unless you can think of a better way for us to see him, this conversation is over!"

Judas thought about the money he had yet to receive. He was not going to let Caiaphas spoil his plans. The realization that he would have to deliver Jesus to the High Priest dawned on him like a new morn. *I am the one who will usher in the Messiah's reign of peace! This is why I am one of the chosen Twelve.* "I will watch for a time when he is alone," Judas said. "Then I will come to you, so that you may come and talk to him."

Caiaphas nodded. "He will have to come to me, for the other chief priests and teachers of the law will want to question him as well."

"Very good. I will let you know the moment he is alone."

"Agreed!" Caiaphas stood, retrieved a leather purse from his belt, withdrew thirty pieces of silver, and handed them to Judas. "I will see you again." He waved his hand in dismissal. "You may leave."

A deal had been struck, yet as he was leaving Judas felt as if he had set something horrible in motion, and he could not shake the feeling that he had just betrayed his Lord.

CHAPTER
— 33 —

The day of Passover dawned bright and clear. Caravans had been arriving all week as families arrived for the celebrations. The hillsides were dotted with makeshift tents by those who could not find room at an inn, or couldn't afford one. The disciples had spent the night in Bethany at the home of Mary, Martha, and Lazarus. Early in the morning, Jesus sent John and Peter into Jerusalem to make special preparations for the Passover meal. Peter had frowned at his request, wondering why the women weren't preparing the meal, but he said nothing.

"Where do you want us to prepare for it?" he had asked.

"As you enter the city, a man carrying a jar of water will meet you. Follow him to the house he enters and say to the owner of the house, 'The Teacher asks, "Where is the guest room, where I may eat the Passover with my disciples?"' He will show you a large upper room, all furnished. Make preparations there."

The two men had nodded and left.

As they approached the city gates, they scanned the area for a man carrying a jar of water.

Peter shook his head. "So many people. How will we ever spot him?"

"We won't spot him," John said. "He'll spot us."

Peter turned a quizzical eye to him. "Explain."

"Jesus no doubt gave the man your description."

"Why me?"

John threw back his head and laughed. "Peter, you have red hair and are a giant of a man! No one amongst all these people even comes close to looking like you. Of course the Master told this man what you look like."

Peter threw up his arms in defeat. "It's always my hair and my height. Isn't there anything else about me that stands out?"

John pursed his lips, looked at his friend, and said, "No." He shook his head. "I just don't see anything else." He started to chuckle at the downcast look on Peter's face. "Oh, come on, Peter! You know I'm only teasing."

Peter chuckled, knowing his friend's taunts were all in good fun. "The sad thing is, I know what you say is true."

John frowned. "Now, Peter, don't get all melancholy on me."

"I'm not. Really, I'm not. It's just that fellow over there—the one with the water jug on his head. He is waving his hands at us. So, I'm guessing he might have been told who to look for."

John turned, saw the man waving frantically, and started to chuckle. Peter slapped him on the back and they walked toward the man.

"Follow me," the man said as soon as they reached him, allowing no room for introductions. Without looking back to see if Peter and John were behind him, he began making his way through the crowded streets. The two disciples followed without hesitation. It wasn't long before the servant brought them to a large two-story home not far from the temple. However, when they realized whose home it was, the two apostles stood in disbelief, hesitant to enter through its courtyard gates.

"This can't be right," Peter whispered to John. "It's a trap!"

John shook his head. "I am thinking the same thing, and yet how can it be a trap, Peter? We met a man with a water jar—just as Jesus said we would."

The servant carrying the water jar disappeared through the doorway and in his place stood a powerful member of the Sanhedrin.

John stepped forward. "Are you the owner of this house, sir?"

"I am."

John cast Peter a questioning look. Peter shrugged his shoulders and said with authority, "The Teacher asks, 'Where is the guest room, where I may eat the Passover with my disciples?'"

"Upstairs—follow me."

Fear turned into surprise as the disciples followed this obviously secret disciple of Christ into his home.

"Don't look so astonished," the man laughed. "Not everyone on the council feels the same way about the Master."

Peter and John laughed nervously as they climbed stairs that led into a large room, where everything was waiting for them just as Jesus had predicted.

The room was generous in size, yet cozy. The vaulted ceiling made it seem spacious and yet the tables, rugs, and scattered pillows provided a warm and inviting atmosphere. Oil lamps attached to huge chains hung from the ceiling, giving the two men just enough light to begin their preparations. Everything they needed was laid out before them —food, wine, bread, water, and of course, the Passover Lamb.

"I hope this is to your satisfaction," the homeowner said.

Peter nodded, awestruck by his surroundings. "It is more than adequate. Thank you, sire."

"My servants are at your disposal should you need anything." He bowed and left.

Sometime later, as Peter and John were finishing, Jesus arrived with his brothers and mother. His brothers had arrived from Nazareth at Mary's request, having put aside their doubts of their eldest brother in order to spend the Passover with their family. Mary's sister Salome and her husband Zebedee followed close behind them. Mary, Martha, and Lazarus were present, as well as Mary Magdalene, Miriam, and her husband Cleopas... and of course, the Apostles. When all had arrived, their host shut the door and locked it.

Jesus and the Twelve reclined at a table at the front of the room while his family and friends sat at separate tables.

"I have eagerly desired to eat this Passover with you before I suffer," Jesus said, "For I tell you, I will not eat it again until it finds fulfillment in the kingdom of God."

John poured wine into Jesus' cup and, taking it, Jesus gave thanks and said, "Take this and divide it among you. This cup is the new covenant in my blood, which is poured out for many for the forgiveness of sins. For I tell you I will not drink again of the fruit of the vine until the kingdom of God comes."

The cup passed from table to table as everyone poured a small portion into their own cup. The room was silent as everyone drank, quietly pondering Jesus' words and actions. These were not the usual words for the Passover Seder and usually everyone had their own cup of wine; they did not share from one. Mary could see the looks of consternation on her sons' faces and wondered if they would protest. But they drank their wine and remained silent. The meal continued and everyone took a bowl of water and washed their hands. Then they dipped a green vegetable into a bowl of salt water, remembering the bitter tears of the Jews who had fled Egypt so long ago. Mary relaxed, as Jesus seemed to be following the rest of their Passover traditions, but as he took the bread before him, he gave thanks to God, broke it, and gave it to everyone, saying, "This is my body given for you. Do this in remembrance of me."

They ate their bread in silence. Once again, pondering Jesus' words. A small tremor of sadness permeated the room, for half of this bread represented the bread of affliction and the other half the Pesach sacrifice.[18] What was Jesus saying to them?

The evening progressed and as the rest of the meal was eaten everyone began to relax. As they chatted amongst themselves, Jesus got up, took off his outer robe, and wrapped a towel around his waist. He then filled a basin with water, knelt down before John, and proceeded to wash his feet. The room grew silent once more as

---

[18] Passover.

258

everyone watched in amazement as their Master humbled himself before them. When he finished with John, he moved on to Peter and it was then that everyone realized that Jesus intended to wash all their feet.

"Lord, are you going to wash my feet?" Peter asked, pulling his foot away from Jesus' outstretched hand.

Jesus knew what he was thinking and smiled. "You do not realize now what I am doing, but later you will understand."

"No." Peter pushed Jesus hands away. "You shall never wash my feet."

Jesus sat back on his heels and looked at Peter. "Unless I wash you, you have no part with me."

"Then, Lord…" Peter thrust out his hands and bowed his head. "Not just my feet, but my hands and my head as well!"

Jesus chuckled, grabbed Peter's foot, took his sandals off, and began to wash his feet. "A person who has had a bath needs only to wash his feet; his whole body is clean. And you are clean." He dried Peter's feet and moved on to Judas, took his foot, removed his sandals, and after a moment added, "Though not every one of you."

When he had finished washing everyone's feet, he put on his robe and returned to his place. "Do you understand what I have done for you?" he asked them. "You call me 'Teacher' and 'Lord,' and rightly so, for that is what I am. Now that I, your Lord and Teacher, have washed your feet, you also should wash one another's feet. I have set you an example that you should do as I have done for you. I tell you the truth, no servant is greater than his master, nor is a messenger greater than the one who sent him. Now that you know these things, you will be blessed if you do them."

Mary was proud of her son as she watched him. He had even washed her feet and silently whispered to her the words she always longed to hear from his mouth. How tenderly he had stooped to place her tiny foot in his hand as he said, "Thank you, Ima, for your obedience to the Father. I love you dearly." Then he had moved on. She had felt her eyes tear at once and ducked her head so that no one would notice. Now he was teaching them a final truth... she could feel it, to love and serve one another. Never would they forget this night.

"I tell you the truth—one of you is going to betray me."

All chatter in the room ceased. They stared at one another, at a loss as to which of them he meant. Since John was reclining next to Jesus, Peter whispered to him, "Ask him which one he means."

Leaning back against Jesus, John asked him, "Lord, who is it?"

Jesus whispered into John's ear, "It is the one to whom I will give this piece of bread when I have dipped it in the dish."

Then, dipping the piece of bread, he gave it to Judas Iscariot. John watched in dread as Judas took the bread and ate it.

"What you are about to do, do quickly," Jesus said to Judas.

"Master?" Judas questioned, taking the bread from Jesus' hand.

"What does Jesus want Judas to do?" Thomas asked Peter. Peter shook his head and watched John, who was watching Judas with something akin to revulsion.

"He's probably going out to buy something else for this fine feast, or to give something to the poor," Andrew responded to Thomas. "After all, Judas is in charge of the money."

Judas ate the bread Jesus offered him. Then, with a subtle nod of his head, he left.

After Judas left, Jesus said, "Now is the Son of Man glorified and God is glorified in Him. If God is glorified in Him, God will glorify the Son in Himself, and will glorify Him at once." Jesus looked with earnest at all his followers. "My children," he said, "I will be with you only a little longer and where I am going, you cannot come. A new command I give you: Love one another. As I have loved you, so you must love one another. By this all men will know that you are my disciples, if you love one another."

Peter asked, "Lord, where are you going?"

"Where I am going, you cannot follow now, but you will follow later."

"Lord, why can't I follow you now?" Peter frowned. "Even if all fall away on account of you, I never will."

Jesus put his arm around Peter's shoulders. "Will you really lay down your life for me, Peter? I tell you the truth, before the rooster crows, you will disown me three times!"

Jesus perused the faces before him. "This very night you will all fall away on account of me, for it is written: 'I will strike the shepherd, and the sheep of the flock will be scattered.'[19] But after I have risen, I will go ahead of you into Galilee."

Peter shook his head. "Even if I have to die with you, I will never disown you." All in the room echoed their agreement.

---

[19] Zechariah 13:6–8.

When the temple guards announced to Caiaphas that Judas Iscariot had arrived, he saw him immediately.

"Is he alone then?" Caiaphas asked.

"Not yet. He's still finishing his Passover meal," Judas replied. "But after he is finished, they are all going to the Garden of Gethsemane."

"Why?"

"He likes to pray there."

Caiaphas grimaced. He did not want to arrest a man in the throes of prayer. Somehow that just didn't feel right to him. It also occurred to him that they might arrest the wrong man, since the garden was quite dark at this time of night.

"We must arrange a signal of some kind, so we will know who to approach."

"Certainly..." Judas thought a moment, then said, "I will kiss him on the cheek. The one I greet will be the one you want to talk to."

"Very good. You have done well."

The doors opened and a large crowd entered the room along with some temple guards. Some carried torches while others had clubs and swords.

"What is this?" Judas demanded.

"There is nothing to worry about." Caiaphas waved his hand. "They are here on behalf of the chief priests, teachers of the law, and the elders. They will go with you to find Jesus and bring him back here. He has many charges to answer to, you know."

"Charges? You said nothing about charges! What charges?"

"He thinks he is the Son of God, you fool! He must answer to the charge of blasphemy," Caiaphas said as he prepared to leave for the council chambers.

"You have deceived me!" Judas wailed. "You said you only wished to speak with him to find out who he really was."

"And so we do." Caiaphas feared that Judas would not cooperate, so putting an arm around him he said, "Calm down, Judas, my friend. We do wish to talk with Jesus, but you must understand that we must be convinced, beyond any doubt, that he is in fact the Messiah, as you claim. You are doing Jesus and us a great service. There will be no more animosity between us—just truth. If he does not come with us willingly, we must, as a mere formality, arrest him."

"No!"

"If we arrest him, my friend," Caiaphas said, his voice softening, "he will be protected from the Romans. Herod wouldn't like to know another King was after his throne now, would he? We are simply trying to do our best for him and for you. Do you understand?"

"I suppose so." Judas frowned. "But you must not hurt him."

"Of course not! We will treat him as we would any great teacher or prophet."

Judas felt a sudden coldness sweep over his skin. Caiaphas' words disturbed him. The Jewish people were notorious for killing the prophets God sent them. However, he held his tongue for fear he would lose his money. He saw Nicodemus then, talking to Joseph of Arimathea. He knew they were both secret followers of Jesus. Since they sat on the council, he knew they would not let any harm come to the Master. Judas relaxed as he thought things through and willingly followed the crowd into the night to look for Jesus of Nazareth.

CHAPTER
— 34 —

After they had finished their meal, they sang a hymn and prepared to leave. Jesus made plans to go to the Mount of Olives in the Garden of Gethsemane where he often went to pray. The Twelve were going with him and some others in the room decided to follow as well, but Mary was feeling tired and took Jesus aside to inform him she would not be coming.

"Your Aunt Salome has invited me to stay with her this evening, Jesus. She and Zebedee have a room not far from here," she said with a weary look on her face. "I'm sorry, son, that I cannot come and celebrate the rest of this Passover with you, but I am utterly exhausted."

"I understand." He took her hands and kissed them. "You will need to rest—the days ahead will be trying for you."

"What do you mean?" she asked, gripping his hands.

"Woman," he said with a smile, "the time has come for me to fulfill my calling."

"Fulfill your calling? But you have done that already. The people believe you are the Messiah. Are you to claim your throne now?"

"Woman," he said, looking into her eyes, "my kingdom is not of this world. I thought I made that clear to you. If you do not remember that, the days to come will be very hard for you indeed."

"Jesus, you are frightening me—what are you about to do?"

"Nothing that my Father in Heaven has not already planned."

"Will I see you again?"

"In the coming Kingdom, we will spend much time together. Go now—and do not worry." He kissed her cheek, handed her over to his brothers with instructions to see her safe, and left with the Twelve.

When they reached the Mount of Olives, it was already late in the evening. Jesus took Peter, James, and John with him into the Garden of Gethsemane while the other disciples waited at the bottom of the hill. He led them to the olive tree in the center of the garden where he and John the Baptist had sat so long ago as young boys.

"Sit here while I pray," he said. "My soul is overwhelmed with sorrow, to the point of death. Stay here and keep watch."

He withdrew about a stone's throw beyond them, knelt down, and prayed, "Father, if you are willing, take this cup from me, yet not my will, but yours be done." He felt a sob lodge in his throat and his body trembled. He was not sure if he would be able to go through with what he knew would be a horrendous ordeal.

After a while, he returned to his disciples and found them sleeping.

"Peter," Jesus said as he nudged him awake, "are you asleep? Could you not keep watch for one hour? Watch and pray so that you will not fall into temptation. The spirit is willing, but the body is weak."

Peter, feeling guilty that he had fallen asleep, opened his weary eyes, rubbed them, and began to pray. Jesus, in anguish, withdrew again and prayed so earnestly that his sweat was like drops of blood falling to the ground. He wanted to please the Father, he wanted to be obedient, but he knew everything he was going to endure. *Will my body be able to withstand the torture to come?* He rose from his knees and went back to the disciples, for he needed their comfort and friendship. Once again, he found them asleep on the ground.

"Peter? James? John? Can't one of you stay awake with me?"

Startled, the men sat up and mumbled their apologies. They could see Jesus was upset, but they didn't know what to say to him. The wine from dinner had made them sleepy. John yawned, squeezed his eyes shut, and then opened them wide in a bid to stay focused. Ashamed, the men once again lowered their heads, but their eyelids were heavy and when he left they drifted back to sleep.

I had hoped my closest friends would have been a comfort to me this night. Jesus fell to his knees and sobbed. *I need their strength! Not because of the torture I will have to endure from the hands of sinful men, but because of the sinful state I am about to enter. I am about to die for humanity! After living a sinless life, I will take upon my body the sins of the world. Abba! Help me! I have never known sin. Give me strength to endure!*

A gentle breeze touched his shoulder. He turned and smiled. An angel from heaven appeared to strengthen him. Restored in both mind and spirit, he returned to his disciples.

"Are you *still* sleeping and resting? Enough!" He clapped his hands, waking them. "The hour has come. Look, the Son of Man is betrayed into the hands of sinners. Rise. Let us go. Here comes my betrayer."

The three men turned toward the sloping hill and noticed a crowd of people coming up the path toward them.

"What's going on?" Peter slowly stood and turned around. "Is that Judas?"

Peter and John flanked Jesus' sides. "What has he done?" John asked.

James stayed low to the ground and slipped behind a tree. His body trembled with fear. He could see the soldiers coming, could hear the grumbling voices shouting, "Death to the blasphemer!" He had to leave. His eyes darted toward Jesus, John, and Peter. Someone had to tell the others! *If we're all caught here with the Rabbi, who will tell Mary?*

Judas waved a hand in greeting, walked up to Jesus, and kissed his cheek. "Rabbi!"

"Judas." Jesus arched his eyebrow as he shook his head. "You betray me with a kiss?"

"What?" Judas chuckled nervously, his eyes widening. "No, no, Master! You don't understand!"

But as he tried to explain himself, the guards seized Jesus. "You are under arrest!" Malchus, servant to the High Priest announced.

Jesus nodded and stepped between two guards. John, James, and Peter all started yelling.

"Judas!" Peter spun toward Judas and grabbed the front of his robe. "What have you done?" Judas shook his head, his eyes bulging in fear.

The guards began to lead Jesus away. James watched from his hiding place in horror.

"No!" Peter shouted. Running forward and drawing his sword, he cut off Malchus' ear.

Screaming in agony, Malchus dropped to the ground, desperately trying to stem the flow of blood pouring from his head.

"Enough of this!" Jesus shouted as he reached out and healed the servant's ear. Amazed at the miracle they had just seen, some of the soldiers fell back and were afraid to approach Jesus any further.

"Am I leading a rebellion that you had to come out with swords and clubs to arrest me? Every day I was with you, teaching in the temple courts, and you did not arrest me." Jesus glared at the men before him and held out his arms. "But this is your hour— when darkness reigns."

"Seize him!" someone shouted from the crowd. James turned and ran to escape as more men poured into the garden. Peter and John slipped into the darkness and watched as their Teacher was taken away in chains.

CHAPTER
— 35 —

When the crowds dissipated, the two men came out from the cover of darkness to find Judas standing beneath the olive tree in the centre of the garden. Together they watched the mob approach the disciples who had waited at the bottom of the hill. They could hear shouts of fear and the clash of swords. Soon there was silence as those who only hours before had shared the Passover with the man they believed to be the Messiah turned and ran away.

Peter glared at Judas. He clenched and unclenched his fists.

John gritted his teeth, barely able to contain his anger. "Why? Why did you betray him, Judas?"

Judas raised his hands in defence, anticipating a beating from the two angry men. "No! No! You do not understand. Please, I meant him no harm. They were supposed to come and talk to him. Just talk to him! I told Caiaphas that Jesus was the Messiah, and that it was time for him to take his rightful place on the throne—to start his kingdom!"

"Start his kingdom?" John exclaimed, his mouth open in astonishment. "Judas! Have you not been listening to our Lord at all? How many times have you heard him say his time had not yet come? What did you think that meant anyway?"

"His time has come! He's just too foolish to recognize it!" Judas spewed. "He has the power to overthrow Rome. He has the power to rain down money from heaven! Yet he wasted his power on beggars and lepers and prostitutes! I was only trying to get him to step up and use his authority and power for what it was meant for." His eyes darted between them, taking in the grief, shock, and disgust on their faces. "Don't you see? Are you so blind?"

Peter shook his head and started to weep. "Oh, Judas—what have you done?"

"They'll be taking him to Caiaphas, Peter—he *wants* to prove that Jesus is the Messiah! He told me so—you will see. No one will harm him. Come with me, see for yourself," Judas said as he turned to follow the soldiers. "By daybreak, it will all be over and Jesus will be proclaimed Messiah by the Sanhedrin."

"I know Caiaphas," John said to Peter as they watched Judas disappear into the dark night. "Let's hurry, Peter, we can find out for ourselves. He'll let me into his courtyard."

Peter agreed and they followed the contingent of soldiers at a distance.

As expected, John gained entry into Caiaphas' courtyard. At first, Peter had to wait outside the door, but John talked to the servant girl on duty who then let Peter in.

"You are not one of his disciples, are you?" Her eyes narrowed as Peter entered the courtyard.

He lowered his head and shook it. "I am not."

It was cold, and the servants and officials stood around a fire they had made to keep warm. Peter stood with them, warming himself while John went to find out what was happening to Jesus.

Another servant girl stood across the fire from Peter. She stared at him and said, "This fellow was with Jesus of Nazareth!"

"What?" Peter chuckled nervously and backed away from the fire. "I don't even know the man!"

Meanwhile, John had gotten close enough to hear what was going on and saw that they had bound Jesus' hands. It seemed to him that the whole Sanhedrin was trying to find evidence against Jesus so they could put him to death. Only one man on the council made it clear he disapproved of their actions—Joseph of Arimathea. This was the same man who only hours before had lent his home to their use for the Passover meal. John offered up a quick prayer for him and Jesus.

The proceedings carried on with witnesses coming forward bearing false testimony. No two stories were ever the same. John knew they would not be able to convict Jesus of anything with the "eyewitnesses" they had found. After a while however, it became clear to him that the chief priests would take false evidence if it would sentence Jesus to death. *Judas is wrong*, John thought. *They don't want to prove he is the Messiah—they want to prove he isn't.*

Finally, two witnesses came forward and declared, "This fellow said, 'I am able to destroy the temple of God and rebuild it in three days.'"

Then Caiaphas stood up and glared at Jesus. "Are you not going to answer? What is this testimony that these men are bringing against you?"

But Jesus remained silent.

About an hour later, after Peter had drawn closer to listen to the proceedings, another person approached him and said to those around him, "Certainly this fellow was with him, for he is a Galilean."

Fearful that he would be arrested as well, Peter shouted, "Sir, I don't know what you're talking about!"

Just as he was speaking, the rooster crowed and Jesus turned his head and looked straight at Peter. Then Peter remembered the words Jesus had spoken to him: "Before the rooster crows, you will disown me three times." Horrified and ashamed that he had denied his Lord, Peter went outside and wept bitterly.

Caiaphas glared at Jesus. "I charge you under oath by the living God—tell us if you are the Messiah, the Son of God."

Jesus stared Caiaphas in the eye and said, "Yes, it is as you say." He turned to those gathered in the room. "But I say to all of you: In the future you will see the Son of Man sitting at the right hand of the Mighty One and coming on the clouds of heaven."

"He has spoken blasphemy! Why do we need any more witnesses?" Caiaphas cried. He turned toward the members of council. "Look, now you have heard the blasphemy. What do you think?"

"He is worthy of death," the council answered.

"No!" John cried, but his voice was lost among the many who were now crying out for justice.

The men who were guarding Jesus began mocking and beating him. Someone blindfolded him. One hit him in the mouth and split his lip open, another sent a jarring pain through his head. Beneath his blindfold, Jesus could feel his left eye begin to swell.

"Prophesy, Messiah! Who hit you?" A blow to his head sent him spinning to the floor.

Their verbal and physical assaults continued and John was powerless to stop them.

Early in the morning, while the citizens of Jerusalem were still asleep, Caiaphas and several elders of the people had Jesus bound and handed over to Pilate. If he could, Caiaphas would have executed Jesus on the spot. However, Roman law dictated that he be handed over to the governor, as he was the only one who had the authority to put Jesus to death.

When Judas heard what they had done to Jesus, and that he had been condemned to death, his guilt overwhelmed him. He decided to return the thirty silver coins to the chief priests and the elders and rushed to the temple looking for Caiaphas. Levi, one of the elders present, recognized him immediately. He and Annas, who was the father-in-law of Caiaphas, approached him.

"Judas!" Levi greeted him. "What has happened? Don't tell me the blasphemer was freed?"

Judas' eyes were wild with terror. "I have sinned," he cried out as he looked for some sort of absolution, "for I have betrayed innocent blood!"

"What are you talking about?" Levi frowned. "Surely you don't think that man was innocent? He claimed to be God!"

Judas looked at the money in his hand. "I can't keep it. I have to give it back... he is innocent of all charges."

"You are talking foolishness!"

"I have sinned," Judas repeated.

"What is that to us?" Annas snorted. "That's your responsibility."

Judas thrust his hand out. "Please, take it back! It is anathema to me!"

"We are holy priests of the Most High God. If you want forgiveness, buy an offering like everyone else. Then we will make atonement for you," Annas said as he turned his back on him.

"But don't buy your offering with that blood money!" Levi warned. "It will not be accepted into Yahweh's Holy Temple."

Out of the corner of his eye, Judas saw Nicodemus hiding behind a pillar. "Will you not help me?" Judas knew the answer before Nicodemus did. The look of shock and shame on the old priest's face said it all. He wanted to defend his Lord, but he wanted to keep his position on the council as well. Nicodemus remained silent.

Disgusted, Judas threw the money onto the temple floor and left.

Annas looked at the coins and said, "It is against the law to put this into the treasury, since it is blood money."

"Yes, we would not want to break the law," Levi agreed as he bent down to retrieve the scattered coins. "What shall we do with them then?"

Annas' brow furrowed as he thought about what to do. "Ah! I know!" He snapped his fingers. "Caiaphas was talking the other day about the need for a burial place, especially in the city. You know, for criminals, paupers and the like. Perhaps we should put it toward that. After all, it is money attained putting a criminal to death. We might as well use it for that."

Then that which was spoken of by the prophet Jeremiah was fulfilled: *"They took the thirty silver coins, the price set on him by the people of Israel, and they used them to buy the potter's field, as the Lord commanded me."*[20]

---

[20] Zechariah 11:12; Matthew 27:9–10.

CHAPTER
— 36 —

I t was discovered later that Judas hung himself."

"The coward." Julius shook his head. "Did he ever seek forgiveness?"

"No," Mary said as the city of Ephesus came into view. "We do know he was filled with guilt as he tried to give the coins back. Who knows?" She shrugged. "Though he did realize he had betrayed Jesus. Nicodemus heard him say those very words, 'I have betrayed innocent blood.' It was devastating for all of us when we found out. We had such hopes for Judas. We knew the kind of man he was, a petty thief—Jesus knew the kind of man he was. I suppose that is why he chose him. Perhaps Jesus hoped that Judas had been with him long enough that he would repent and seek his forgiveness. But it was not to be."

She had been talking to the people on board about Jesus throughout the entire voyage. At least, it had felt that way to Mary. She was so tired. Her back pain had increased with each passing day. However, every day someone would find her and ask her to continue her story, and she simply could not turn them away. When she was unable to continue, Luke would step in. Between the two of them, it had been joyous to share the Gospel, and sad to relive some of the more difficult memories. Now they were nearing the end of their journey and it was time to tell the people what her son—the Son of God—had endured for them.

———

They took him before Pilate, spewing out lies as they went. A formal bill of indictment given to Pilate from Caiaphas read: "We have found this man subverting our nation. He opposes payment of taxes to Caesar and claims to be the Messiah, a king."

John had slipped in quietly to listen to the priests and elders present their case against Jesus. They were now at the Fortress Antonia, northwest of the temple area. Pilate sat in the judge's seat on a raised dais overlooking the plaza to the east.

"We know this man," Caiaphas said, pushing a bound Jesus out in front of him, "that he is the son of Joseph the carpenter, begotten of Mary. He says that he is the Son of God and a king. He is polluting the Sabbaths and he would destroy the law of our fathers."

Pilate could see that the man standing below him had already received a beating today. He shook his head and sighed. It appeared to him that these people had already found this man Jesus guilty.

"I would talk to him alone. Bring him inside," Pilate ordered his guard. He went back into the palace and waited for Jesus.

"Are you the king of the Jews?" he asked once Jesus had arrived.

"Is that your own idea, or did others talk to you about me?" Jesus asked.

"Am I a Jew?" Pilate grunted. "It was your people and your chief priests who handed you over to me. What is it you have done?"

Jesus sighed. "My kingdom is not of this world. If it were, my servants would fight to prevent my arrest by the Jews. But now my kingdom is from another place."

"You are a king, then!"

Jesus nodded. "You are right in saying I am a king. In fact, for this reason I was born, and for this I came into the world, to testify to the truth. Everyone on the side of truth listens to me."

"What is truth?" Pilate waved his hand. "Take him outside!" The guard grabbed Jesus' arm and pushed him outside onto the raised dais, while Pilate crossed over to his chair and sat down. He waited for the murmuring in the crowd to stop and said, "I find no basis for a charge against this man."

Caiaphas cringed. The entire council of the Sanhedrin had put Jesus on trial and found him guilty of blasphemy. He was determined that their verdict stand.

"Procurator! He stirs up the people all over Judea by his teaching. He started in Galilee and has come all the way here," Caiaphas retorted.

On hearing this, Pilate asked Jesus, "Are you a Galilean?"

Jesus nodded. "Yes, I am."

"How fortuitous!" Pilate arched his eyebrows, a smug look playing across his face. He tented his fingers below his chin and grinned. "Since Herod is in Jerusalem as well, and Galilee is his jurisdiction, I will send you to him."

"My lord, the miracle worker from Galilee is here." Chuza, Herod's chief steward, announced. As a secret follower of Jesus, he knew better then to tell Herod that the true King of Israel had arrived. When Chuza and his wife Joanna had heard the news about Jesus, he had immediately rushed to the palace, hoping to convince Herod to free him. But when Caiaphas had taken him to see Pilate first, Chuza was unable to gain an audience with the king—until now.

"You mean Jesus? The Nazarene? The one who can raise the dead?" Herod reclined on a couch where a table of fresh fruit sat before him. He took a handful of grapes from a bowl in the middle of the table and began popping them one by one into his mouth.

"The very same, sire."

"How delightful! Do you think he will perform for me?" Herod asked. He had been ecstatic when he heard Jesus was coming to see him. He had wanted to see the Nazarene for a very long time and had hoped he could get Jesus to perform some sort of miracle for him.

Chuza gritted his teeth in an attempt not to shout at Herod. "I have heard he is a generous man, sire. A man, I might add, not given to violence … "

"I did not ask you for a description of this man's temperament! I asked you whether or not he would perform for me!"

Chuza bowed low in fear. "Who would deny you, my lord?"

A smile of smug satisfaction spread over Herod's fat face. "Send him in at once."

"Did you see him, Chuza? Were you able to talk to him?" Joanna asked her husband when he returned to their quarters.

Chuza shook his head. "I had no chance to speak to him, but Joanna, I saw him." He buried his head in his hands and began to weep. "He has been badly beaten. I fear Herod will inflict even more punishment on him."

"What can we do?"

"There is nothing we can do but pray. Only Yahweh can help the Master now."

"So, you are the Miracle Worker from Galilee?" Herod grunted. "You can't be much of a miracle worker if you haven't yet escaped your chains." He laughed as he stood up from his couch and walked closer to Jesus, who stood between two guards.

"I see by your face that you have met the fists of the temple guards. I do hope it will not interfere with your performance here today."

Jesus remained silent.

Herod removed his scarlet robe and draped it around Jesus' shoulders. He shook his head and laughed. "Pilate says you claim to be the Messiah—the king of Israel. I thought this might help you look the part." He shook his head and sighed. "But no, you still don't look like much of a king to me."

"Pilate also tells me that the Sanhedrin has found you guilty of subverting our nation. Do you have anything to say in your defense? If you are innocent of all crimes, you will be free to go—after you have performed for me, of course. Who do you get your power from?"

A slap across his face from the guard standing beside him startled Jesus. "Answer your King!"

Jesus winced, but said nothing.

At Herod's nod, the guard slapped Jesus again.

"You refuse to talk to me?" Herod's eyes narrowed as he considered the man before him. "If you are truly the king of Israel, why don't you defend yourself? Why don't you use your powers to escape?"

When Jesus still refused to speak, Herod grew annoyed. "You are either a very brave man or a very foolish one. Send him back to Pilate!"

Pilate's irritation grew as Jesus stood before him once again. As soon as word reached the Sanhedrin that Jesus was back, the Fortress Antonia filled once again with his accusers. Pilate rolled his neck and sighed. He had not slept at all and was losing patience. Most of Jerusalem would soon be awake. *Will the people wonder why the Sanhedrin conducted a trial secretly at night? Will they riot when they find out it is the prophet from Galilee?* Pilate was in Jerusalem specifically to keep the peace during the Passover Celebrations. *What will happen if I have to pronounce a guilty verdict on this man?* Once again, Pilate asked himself why the priests were so anxious to do away with Jesus. *Why do they fear him?* Before this day was over, he was determined to find out.

"You brought me this man as one who was inciting the people to rebellion." Pilate looked at the sea of faces below him. He saw many angry faces and only a few who actually seemed to grieve over the fate of this prisoner. "I have examined him in your presence and have found no basis for your charges against him." The priests started grumbling and Pilate could see they were going to object. "Neither has Herod." He raised his voice and held up his hand for silence. "For Herod sent him back to me—as you can see. This man has done nothing to deserve death. However, it is your custom for me to release to you one prisoner at the time of the Passover. Do you want me to release the King of the Jews?"

To Pilate's surprise, the people cried out with one voice, "No! Away with this man! Release Barabbas to us!"

Pilate shook his head in disbelief. *Barabbas? They want me to release a murderer and insurrectionist? These people make no sense!* Wanting to release Jesus, Pilate appealed to them again. But they kept shouting, "Crucify him! Crucify him!"

"Why?" he yelled. "What crime has this man committed? I have found in him no grounds for the death penalty." He tried to reason with the crowd, but their lust for blood could not be sated.

"Very well!" Pilate shouted, his face turning red with rage. "Be quiet then! I will have him scourged and release him." Hoping that would satisfy them, Pilate turned away, but the protests grew louder and more demanding.

"CRUCIFY HIM! CRUCIFY HIM!"

Pilate's shoulders slumped. He turned back toward the crowd and faced Jesus. "Have him flogged," he said to the guard. "And release Barabbas."

Rough hands pawed at him. They tore off his robe, exposing his bare back to the chill of the morning. He groaned as someone lifted his arms above his head. A soldier chained him to a stone pillar that stood in the center of the courtyard. Cold, alone, and exposed, he waited for the first crack of the whip.

At some point, he could not remember when, he had lost his blindfold. *Not that I need it*, he reasoned, since his left eye was almost completely swollen shut. Unfortunately, he managed to catch a glimpse of the whip before it struck him. It was leather, several feet long, and embedded with lead balls and pieces of sheep bone. Jesus knew the damage it would inflict and tried to steady his breathing as he waited.

At the signal of his commanding officer, a Roman soldier struck his back. Jesus gasped with shock as the sting of the whip ripped into him. With each continuing blow, his body recoiled in agony and he prayed for strength to endure.

After several blows, he could no longer contain the groans coming out of his mouth. It was impossible to try. Like a hiccup, they were involuntary. The pain was indescribable. He could feel the sheep bone from the whip digging into his back, tearing pieces of flesh away. It was becoming harder to breath. He knew he was bleeding heavily.

As the scourging continued, his back became a bloody pulp of torn flesh. *Should I call my angels to put a stop to this? How much more can I endure? Father! Father!* he cried inwardly. Then mercifully, he passed out.

When the soldiers finished, they untied Jesus from the post where he collapsed in a heap on the ground. Seizing his arms, they hauled him to his feet once more. They did not know who this disfigured man was before them and they did not care. To them, he was just another prisoner.

"Apparently, this one thinks he's King of the Jews!" laughed a soldier who had gathered a crude vine of thorns. "I say we treat him like one!" He twisted the thorns together to form a crown and pressed it on Jesus' head. Jesus cried out as the sharp spikes cut into his scalp and caused more blood to pour down his face.

"Ha!" laughed another soldier, oblivious to Jesus' pain. "I've an idea! Let's clothe him in royal robes, shall we?"

Grabbing the scarlet robe Herod had put on Jesus, the soldier draped it around him once again. Jesus moaned when it touched his back, the weight of it stinging him badly, bringing tears to his eyes. They put a staff in his right hand, knelt in front of him, and mocked him, saying, "Hail, king of the Jews!"

They spit on him and then took the staff, hitting him repeatedly on his head. Jesus did nothing in retaliation, although at any moment he knew he could call on his Heavenly Father to put a stop to everything—but he did not. He tried to wipe his face of the blood and spit. He was finding it difficult to stand. His head exploded once more with pain. Dizzy and disoriented, he felt his knees buckle and he fell to the ground.

"Are they done yet?" Pilate asked his attendant for the third time.

285

"No sir, they are still meting out punishment."

"Still? It has been at least an hour. How much punishment can one man endure? Bring him to me—*Now!*"

When Pilate saw what they had done to what he considered an innocent man, he was appalled. He had seen the victims of many a scourging, but he had never seen anyone treated this badly. *When the Jews see him,* he reasoned, *surely they will think he has received his just punishment.*

Once more Pilate came out and said to the Jews, "Look, I am bringing him out to you, to let you know that I find no basis for a charge against him."

Jesus, guarded by two soldiers, came out wearing the crown of thorns and the scarlet robe Herod had placed on him. He could barely stand and the soldiers knew they were the ones holding him up.

Pilate pointed to Jesus and said to the people, "Here is the man!"

As soon as the chief priests and their officials saw him, they shouted, "Crucify him! Crucify him!"

Pilate was disgusted with these people. The man was almost dead! It was one thing to punish a criminal who deserved it, but to punish an innocent man did not sit well with him.

Pilate answered, "You take him and crucify him! As for me, I find no basis for a charge against him."

"We have a law," one of the elders shouted from the courtyard, "and according to that law he must die, because he claimed to be the Son of God."

When Pilate heard this, he was terrified, for earlier his wife had sent him a message that read: *"Do not have anything to do with that innocent man, for I have suffered a great deal today in a dream because of him."* He went back inside the palace and summoned Jesus. When the guards brought him in, Pilate asked, "Where do you hail from?"

Jesus stood with his head bowed and gave him no answer.

"Do you refuse to speak to me?" Pilate's eyes blazed with fury. "Don't you realize I have power either to free you or crucify you?"

Jesus lifted his head and answered haltingly, "You would... have no power over me ... if it were not given to you... from above. Therefore... the one who handed me over to you... is guilty of a greater sin."

Once again, Pilate tried to set Jesus free, but the Jews kept shouting, "If you let this man go, you are no friend of Caesar. Anyone who claims to be a king opposes Caesar."

That was all it took. Pilate could not have Caesar hear that he had let a usurper of the throne go free. He valued his position too much for that. He brought Jesus out once again and sat in his judge's seat. It was the day of Preparation of Passover Week, about the sixth hour.

"Here is your king!" Pilate said to the Jews.

"Take him away! Take him away! Crucify him!"

"Shall I crucify your king?" Pilate taunted.

"We have no king but Caesar," the crowd roared.

When Pilate saw that he was getting nowhere, he took water and washed his hands in front of the crowd.

"I am innocent of this man's blood," he said angrily. "It is your responsibility!"

And all the people answered, "Let his blood be on us and on our children!"

So Pilate handed Jesus over to them to be crucified.

CHAPTER
— 37 —

They made their way back to the upper room where they had celebrated the Passover. One by one, they turned up there, finding a place to sit and wait, ashamed and embarrassed that they had deserted the One they had believed in for so long. Peter and John were the last to arrive. Peter had spent the night mourning his denial of the Lord. At daybreak, he heard a commotion at Castle Antonia and went to investigate. He was stunned by what he saw—Jesus on display in the courtyard, his hands shackled and tied behind his back. He was barely recognizable and hardly able to stand. The people were shouting, "Crucify him! Crucify him!" Peter was horrified. These were the same people who not a week ago had been proclaiming Jesus King.

"No!" Peter strode through the crowd, begging to be heard. "No! He is the Messiah! You are crucifying your king!"

"Who said that?" Caiaphas scanned the crowd around and saw Peter pushing his way toward the front of the crowd. "Grab him and shut him up!" he yelled to the temple guards. As one, the temple guards rushed Peter and ushered him roughly out of Pilate's courts. John, who had not left Pilate's courtyard since Jesus' arrest, saw Peter struggling with the guards and hurried outside the gates to be with him. Together they made their way back to the upper room and recounted to all present what they had seen and heard.

"He's to be crucified at Golgotha immediately," John said wearily.

"Someone must tell Mary," Andrew said. He sighed and ran a hand through his hair. His brown eyes were bloodshot from a sleepless night accompanied by tears of sorrow and guilt.

Several heads nodded in agreement, but no one moved.

John sighed. "I'll tell her." He stood up as if to leave, then sat back down again. "What should I say?" He scanned the faces of his friends and saw nothing but guilt and shame on every one of them. They had no answers for him, for what does one say to a mother whose son is about to die?

He could not endure much more. They had taken off the scarlet robe and stripped him of the rest of his clothes. Save for a loincloth, he was completely naked. Now he knew what it was like to feel embarrassment and shame. Never in his life had he been so exposed and vulnerable. He had always felt in complete charge of his life. He knew he was one with the Father, and that unity kept him strong.

He learned that he was to be crucified with two other prisoners and they were all to carry their own crosses. Jesus was shocked when he saw the cross he was to carry, for he feared he would be unable to bear it—a crossbeam of wood at least six feet long and weighing around a hundred pounds. Would his already weak body make it through the city gates, up the long rocky path to Golgotha? He nodded at the other prisoners as the guards brought them out. It was obvious they had suffered from a flogging, but their wounds were not as bad as his.

A young soldier, about twenty years of age, stopped before him and hesitated. His face blanched at the sight of him. He paused to look at the other prisoners and then glanced back to Jesus. Jesus heard him vomiting a few moments later.

"What's the matter, Proctus? Can't take the blood?" A few soldiers laughed. The young man stiffened and glared them into silence.

"There is so much blood on him, I can't even tell if he has any skin left!" Proctus wiped his mouth with the back of his hand and spit on the ground. "Put his robe back on. I can't stand the sight of him."

Jesus groaned as the robe chafed against his wounds, but when they placed the cross on his shoulders, he crumpled beneath the heavy beam and fell to the ground in agony. Shards of wood lodged themselves in his back, making each movement excruciating.

The centurion in charge, Gaius, sat atop his horse watching Jesus stumble down the path toward the city gates. He frowned. Twice now, Jesus had stumbled and fallen, making their pace slow. He became concerned that his prisoner would not make the climb up the hill to Golgotha. Death before crucifixion would not be acceptable. Pilate would be furious. Crucifixions were Rome's way of keeping the people in line—a sign to everyone who was in charge.

He had to do something. His eyes widened and he sneered. The gods were favouring him today.

"You there!" Gaius pointed at a tall young man coming through the city gates. "What is your name?"

"Who me?" The young man's eyes darted toward the soldier, then scanned the prisoners. "S–S–Simon of Cyrene... sir."

"You will carry this man's cross!" Gaius knew the young man couldn't say no. To do so could forfeit his life.

Simon swallowed, the bile rising in his throat. The man whose cross he was to carry was a bloody pulp. *What has this man done to deserve such treatment?* he wondered.

The soldiers removed the heavy wooden beam from Jesus' shoulders and transferred it to Simon. Simon's knees bent beneath its weight but soon balanced it evenly on his shoulders. He looked down at the man who had crumpled to the ground. He didn't care what the man had done. Compassion overwhelmed him and he reached down to help him up.

When Jesus lifted his head up toward him, Simon gasped. *The teacher from Galilee!* He had heard him speak and seen the wonders he had performed. *How has he come to this?* Simon thought.

A large number of people followed them now, including women who mourned and wailed for him. Jesus turned toward them, "Daughters of Jerusalem, do not weep for me. Weep for yourselves and for your children. For the time will come when you will say, 'Blessed are the barren women, the wombs that never bore and the breasts that never nursed!' Then they will say to the mountains, 'Fall on us!' and to the hills, 'Cover us!' For if men do these things when the tree is green, what will happen when it is dry?" A few women ran forward and tried to wipe the blood from his face, but the soldiers pushed them away.

When they came to the place called the Skull (or Golgotha), the soldiers ordered Simon to drop the cross on the ground. He didn't know what to do, but fearing he would be pressed into service for something else he took one last look at Jesus and ran down the hill, back toward the city.

One soldier offered a cup of sour wine mixed with myrrh to each prisoner. The myrrh would deaden their senses and ease their pain—the only act of mercy the soldiers would show this day. When they came to Jesus, he felt as if a war was waging inside him. He had not had a drink since the night before, at the Passover meal. Now he was unbelievably thirsty. His throat was parched, his tongue engorged, his lips were dry, swollen, and cracked. But he refused to take a drink. *I must be fully aware of what I am doing. I must still be in control.* When the guard saw that Jesus would not take the drink, he shrugged and threw the cup away.

They stripped Jesus of his clothes again, except for the loincloth, and ordered him to lie down on the cross. The other two prisoners put up a fight and refused to cooperate. A scuffle ensued and it took several soldiers to force the men onto their crossbeams, where they tied their arms with leather straps. Jesus prayed for the two men as he watched the soldiers drive nails into their hands. Gut-wrenching screams filled the air. Jesus winced with each stroke of the hammer, knowing his turn was coming.

The soldiers turned toward him, expecting him to fight, but much to their surprise he willingly laid down on his cross and stretched out his arms. He winced as the shards of wood dug into his back, each movement horrendous. *It will not be long now,* he thought as the crown of thorns pressed further into his scalp.

After tying his arms to the crossbeam, the soldiers took a spike, and with one blow of the hammer drove it into one hand and then the other. The pain radiated up and down his arms and seemed to explode somewhere behind his eyes. Next, they hoisted him up, so that he was now hanging by his arms. It was agonizing. He could barely breathe. Left dangling by his arms, with no place to put his feet, he knew he would suffocate. Frantically, he tried to push himself up but could not find a foothold. "Father! Father!" he groaned. Finally, someone lifted his feet up and placed them on the ledge of another pole. Jesus gasped as he gulped in air. *What relief! Thank you, Abba!* However, relief was not in sight, for the soldier who had grabbed his feet was positioning them one on top of the other, so that another soldier could drive in the last spike. One more blow with the hammer and the spike went through both of his feet. The pain was indescribable, for it left his legs useless and now he felt like he would never breathe again. If he pushed up with his feet, excruciating pain flared up his legs. If he moved his arms, pain exploded down them and engulfed his chest. He realized quickly that he would suffocate to death, and so he stilled to wait that hour of his choosing. And so they crucified him, along with the criminals—one on his right, the other on his left.

"Father, forgive them, for they do not know what they are doing," Jesus cried.

As word spread about the crucifixions, people coming in and out of Jerusalem stopped and gathered to watch. When they realized that Jesus was being crucified, many were in shock. Some had believed he was the Messiah and wondered how such a thing could happen. Several became angry that he had deceived them and began mocking him. The chief priests and Caiaphas noticed this and, wanting to prove the justice in their decision to crucify Jesus, they encouraged the ridicule.

"He saved others!" Caiaphas shouted. "Let him save himself if he is the Christ of God, the Chosen One."

One of the thieves who hung there also hurled insults at him. "Aren't you the Christ? Save yourself and us!"

But the other thief rebuked him. "Don't you fear God, since you are under the same sentence? We are punished justly, for we are getting what our deeds deserve—but this man has done nothing wrong!" Wearily, he turned his head toward Jesus. "Jesus, remember me when you come into your kingdom."

What joy! On this cruel beam of oppression, Jesus rejoiced over the repentant thief beside him. He had not failed, for even at this late hour, one had turned to him. Jesus gathered his breath and said, "I tell you the truth, today you will be with me in paradise."

Gaius, the centurion, stood at the foot of Jesus' cross. He listened intently to the exchange between the two prisoners and felt his heart quicken. *What is it about this man?* There was a written notice placed above Jesus' head written in Aramaic, Latin and Greek, which said: "THIS IS THE KING OF THE JEWS." Without mocking in his voice, but with a sense of urgency, he said to Jesus, "If you are the King of the Jews like this sign says, save yourself."

Furious, Caiaphas went to Pilate to get him to change it so that it would say, "He said he was the King of the Jews," but Pilate refused.

When John arrived at his mother Salome's door in the early morning hours, he found Mary Magdalene, Joanna (the wife of Chuza), Miriam (the wife of Cleopas), Mary (Jesus' mother), and her sons. She knew right away that something had happened, because he avoided her eyes. Salome invited him in and he stood for a few moments in silence, not sure where or how to begin. When she could stand it no longer, Mary spoke. "John, what has happened to my son?"

Tears pooled in his eyes. *What should I say? Where do I start, to make it easier on her?* He swallowed and said, "He has been arrested."

"What?" Miriam cried. "The Lord has been arrested?"

John nodded. "There is more."

He took Mary's hand and said, "There was a trial, Aunt Mary—he has been sentenced to death."

Mary's knees buckled and John caught her in his arms. He could feel her sobbing, but no sound came out of her mouth. His heart wrenched at what he had yet to tell her.

"There is more."

"M–more?" Mary whimpered as she tried to steady herself.

He took her hand and rubbed it. "He is on his way to Golgotha—right now. If you wish to see him before… before he… you must come with me at once."

They arrived shortly before he was nailed to the cross. John purposely kept her at the back of the crowd until she adjusted to the sight of him. *I should not have brought her here,* he thought. *The Master will not want her to see him like this. What was I thinking? She should not be witnessing the brutal way in which her son will die.* To hear his screams, to see his suffering, and not be able to stop it… it tore at John's heart.

Grief consumed Mary. She wailed and pounded on her chest at the sight of her beloved son. In agony, she watched her child suffer. Her gut-wrenching sobs tore at the hearts of those around her. For it passed quickly, by word of mouth, that she was the mother of the one who claimed to be King of the Jews. Those who believed that Jesus was the Messiah stood by Mary's side and wept with her. Those who believed that Jesus was a fraud looked at her with pity, "For no matter what her son had done," they reasoned, "he was still her son."

"I must see him, John," Mary wept. "He needs to see me and know I'm here."

"Do you think it wise?" John asked, for he feared her reaction to him when she got closer. Simon, Joses, Jude, and James urged her to stay with them in the back of the crowd. They felt nothing but guilt and grief—guilt of their dismissal of Jesus during his ministry and grief over his impending death. They stood rooted to the ground, unable to move any further. But Mary was insistent, so John agreed to take her closer, along with Salome, Miriam, and Mary Magdalene. The four women, plus John, made their way to the front of the crowd.

"Make room! Make room!" John shouted as they pushed through the crowd.

And like the Red Sea, the mob parted for the mother of Jesus.

CHAPTER
— 38 —

He sensed her presence the moment she arrived. As he saw her approaching him, his heart overflowed with love. From his mother he had learned much. Both she and Joseph had been exemplary parents and the best of teachers. He heard her wails of grief and the sorrow of it consumed him. *I need someone to watch over her after I am gone,* he thought. She had her other children, of course, but they did not yet believe in him and she would need support from those who did. The apostles would also benefit greatly from her wisdom. For it was through Mary's teaching and guidance that he had developed into the man God had called him to be. His disciples needed her strength now and she needed theirs. He noticed that John had his arms around Mary and silently thanked the Father for the peace of knowing what to do.

Mary stepped closer to the cross. She glared defiantly at the guards, daring them to stop her. Gaius gave a slight nod to the guards surrounding Jesus and they let her approach. As she stood looking up at him, Jesus turned to her and said, "Dear woman, here is your son." He pointed his chin in John's direction. Acknowledging that she understood, she took John's hand in hers. Then he looked at John and said, "Here is your mother." John nodded to him and, weeping, he held fast to her. He knew the Lord had just bestowed on him a great honour and he determined that day to take her into his home and care for her always.

The hours dragged on—Mary knew that crucifixions could take as long as a week before the victims succumbed. However, as she kept her vigil she realized that the beating Jesus had endured at the hands of the soldiers would ironically be a blessing, for it would mean that he would die quickly.

The crowd started to thin after a while, until only his family, a few of his disciples, and those who had wanted him dead remained. The curious came for a short time, but soon became bored waiting for the victims to die. Some asked questions, some hurled insults, but most were respectful of Mary and came quietly—watched—then left. Jesus was exhausted and clearly nearing the end. He struggled for every breath. His swollen face, combined with congealing blood, gave his features a grotesque, distorted look.

Wearily, he looked with longing at the people before him. *Do they realize that I am taking their punishment for them? That the wrath of God intended for them at the end of this age is even now being poured out on me?*

Those weeping were his own. Oh, how he loved them and rejoiced that they had found the truth in him! However, those mocking and insulting him also made him weep, for he came for them as well and for them he would die.

Come to me! he prayed. *I love you greatly! Your yoke of rules and regulations to live by are too heavy a burden to bear. My yoke is easy and my burden is light. When will you see? When?* He moaned, not for the pain he was enduring but for what he knew awaited those who rejected him.

Come to me! You who are heavy laden with the cares of this world. This world will soon pass, and then where will you be? Come to me! I will give you rest.

Mary could see Jesus' lips moving but could not hear him. He was looking intently at the crowd of people gathered and she whispered to John, "He's exhausted. He has no energy left even to speak."

"Perhaps he is praying," John suggested, eager to alleviate her grief.

"Perhaps." She sniffed and wiped her tearstained face with the hem of her robe. "Look at his eyes, how passionate his look is."

To John, Jesus looked delirious. "He's in pain, Aunt Mary. His eyes are nearly swollen shut."

"In pain, yes," she said with a nod. "But not of a physical nature."

"Not of a physical nature? How can you say that?" Salome asked, perplexed at her sister's observation. "Look at him, Mary. He is in great pain."

"Of course he is in pain, Salome! That much is obvious. What I meant is that Jesus is experiencing more than physical pain. I know my son, Salome. He has always had a heart for God. He used to tell me God's heart weeps for the people He created to have fellowship with Him. He deeply felt the burden of Yahweh's love and felt the

Father's grief. Don't you remember what He said? He and the Father are one." Mary sighed. "He would often go into the hills to be alone in his grief, coming back with a new determination to bring the people back to God."

"Are you telling me that even now, Jesus is weeping for those who wanted him dead? The same people who only a week ago were declaring him the Messiah?" John frowned.

"He weeps for all people, John." She patted his hand. "The rich, the poor, the good, the bad. *We* are for whom he weeps. For we, as a people, have broken fellowship with our Heavenly Father. We were created for that purpose, you know."

"To have fellowship with God?" Mary Magdalene asked.

"Yes," Mary replied. "Look around you, Mary. Look at the people. They are from every nation. It is no coincidence that the sign above Jesus' head is in three different languages. The King of Kings loves them desperately and they do not know it. They are, as Jesus said, 'like lost sheep.'"

John looked at Jesus again and said, "Yes, but who will guide the sheep now, once the shepherd is gone?"

"That's strange," Mary Magdalene said sometime later. "Has anyone noticed it is getting darker? I fear it might storm."

Miriam huddled closer to the others. "It is getting colder, too, and a breeze is picking up. Are you sure you want to stay until the end, Mary?"

"How can I not stay, Miriam? Look at him! His agony is so great." She began to weep. "I cannot leave!"

"Of course you must stay… I don't know what I was thinking. I'm just concerned for you." Miriam drew Mary into her arms.

Mary patted Miriam's hand. "I understand. It is hard to know what to do or say at a time like this." She grasped Miriam's hand in hers as the five of them continued their vigil.

The end was upon him. Jesus had finally come to the part he had dreaded the most—coming face to face with the sins of the world. Of course, he knew how bad the sins of the people could be; he knew their hearts, for he had walked among them. However, he had never, in all his thirty-three years, given in to the temptation of sin. His final hour had arrived. He could feel his Father's presence. He knew they were one and that nothing could separate them. Oh, what a bittersweet joy he felt, knowing that his purpose had finally arrived and yet having to endure the stain of sin to fulfill that purpose. For this reason he had come—to bear every act of disobedience of evil, hatred, and lust. Every act of immorality, every transgression ever committed past or future by humankind, was poured out on the Son of Man in full force. Darkness was upon him and the land, for the light that had come into the world was about to be extinguished.

"*Eloi, Eloi, lama sabachthani?*" Jesus cried, startling those below him.

"Listen," Salome cried. "He's calling Elijah."

"No," said Mary, weeping for her son. "What he just said was, 'My God, My God, why have you forsaken me?'" Mary's eyes widened. "It is Psalm 22! Even now he is fulfilling prophecy!"

"I thirst," Jesus groaned.

A man ran, filled a sponge with wine vinegar, put it on a stick, and offered it to Jesus to drink.

"Now leave him alone. Let's see if Elijah comes to take him down," the man joked to those around him. However, not even the soldiers found it funny anymore.

But Jesus had thirsted for more than a drink. He thirsted to be in the presence of his Father and so, mustering what little strength he had left, he said loudly for all to hear: "Father, into your hands I commit my spirit. It… is… finished."

At that moment, the earth shook and the hill of Golgotha began to shake and split. As Mary tried to find safe ground, she looked up to see Jesus' body swaying on the cross. Without thinking, she ran forward and grabbed the bottom of the pole, for fear he would topple over the edge of the cliff.

"John!" she screamed, her face white with terror. "Help me! Please! I do not want to see his body crash to the ground. He has endured too much."

Even though he knew Jesus no longer lived, John ran forward to help her, for the desperation in Mary's voice and the look on her face broke his heart. However, before he even reached the cross the earthquake stopped as suddenly as it had started.

Those around the cross slowly rose from beneath it and backed away. Gaius and those with him who were guarding Jesus were terrified. Some of the soldiers were so afraid that they would not even approach the man from Galilee.

But Gaius stepped closer to the cross and, looking up at Jesus, boldly proclaimed, "Surely, he was the Son of God!"

"Joseph of Arimathea is here to see you, sire," Pilate's servant announced.

"Joseph of Arimathea? Who is he to me?" Pilate answered, irritated that these Jews had not stopped bothering him all week. Just moments before, they had been requesting that the legs of the prisoners be broken to speed up their deaths, because they did not want their bodies hanging on the hill during Passover. *Hypocrites!* Pilate muttered to himself.

"Sire, he sits on the council," the servant bowed. "He wishes to speak with you about Jesus of Nazareth."

"The King of the Jews?"

"Yes, sire—he wants his body."

"His body? He can't be dead yet!" Pilate muttered to himself. "Send someone to confirm this, and show this Jew in while we wait," he commanded, intrigued by the strange request from a member of the same council who had wanted Jesus dead.

"Why are you still here?" Pilate fumed when the servant didn't leave. Instead he remained with his head bowed.

"Sire… their laws… he cannot come into the palace. You must go outside to him." The servant stuttered, clearly afraid of the anger that was sure to follow. And follow it did, for Pilate had endured enough in the past few hours by the "wretched Jews," as he called them, to last a lifetime. As he made his way to Joseph, who was waiting in the outer court, he cursed and shouted at anyone in his way.

Joseph could hear him coming. He worried that Pilate in his anger would deny his request for Jesus' body.

"What do you want?" Pilate roared when he saw him. "And be quick about it!"

Joseph humbled himself, bowed before the Roman governor, and said, "Sire, I would like the body of Jesus of Nazareth."

"Why?"

"So that I may bury it."

"You wish the responsibility of burying the body of a man you wanted dead?" Pilate sneered.

"I did not agree with the council," Joseph explained. "Sadly, I was not vocal enough and any suggestions I made were disregarded. I did not wish to see the death of Jesus, but it has happened and I wish to honour him now by burying him in my own tomb."

"Are you telling me he is dead already?" Pilate asked, surprised.

"Yes, sire—he died right before the earthquake and at the moment the temple curtain was rent asunder."

Pilate became uneasy when he heard this.

"The temple curtain?" Pilate paused. He could feel the hairs on the back of his neck rising. "It is destroyed?" he asked.

Joseph nodded. "It was split right up the middle, sire."

Pilate could feel beads of sweat on his upper lip. He was anxious to have this whole matter over and done with. The gods may not have been pleased with his decision to crucify this man. His servant arrived and bowed in submission.

"Report." Pilate wiped his lip with the back of his hand.

"The King of the Jews is dead, sire."

Pilate shook with fear. "Take him! And do it quickly, before I change my mind!" he shouted and stomped back into the palace.

"What are they doing?" Miriam asked as she saw soldiers with clubs approach the prisoners on either side of Jesus.

"They are breaking their legs to speed up their deaths." John sighed, clearly worn out by the day's events. "They will suffocate and die quickly, as they will no longer be able to push themselves up."

The women moaned, sorry to see even men who had committed crimes endure such torture.

"At least they won't have to touch the Lord," Salome said and they all nodded in agreement, thankful that his body would not suffer any more atrocities. But without warning, one of the soldiers took a spear and stabbed Jesus in the side. They screamed in horror at the cruelty of the act and watched as blood mixed with water poured out the side of their Saviour. In stunned silence, they stood there, unsure of what to make of all they had witnessed.

Joseph of Arimathea soon arrived and handed a notice to Gaius, who gave the order to take the body of Jesus down and hand him over to Joseph for burial. Joseph walked over to Mary and, taking her hands in his, he kissed them and said, "Woman, I am sorry for your loss. I tried to save him, but my words were not heeded. Please let me have the honour of burying your son in my tomb, which has not been used, so that he might rest in peace this day."

Mary nodded her agreement, swallowing the lump in her throat that was making each moment difficult to breathe.

"Mary—Miriam, Mary Magdalene, and I will stay with Jesus to see where he is laid," Salome whispered in her sister's ear. "John, take her home now. She has endured enough."

John nodded and, with one last look at Jesus, Mary willingly went with her nephew back to where they were staying.

Nicodemus arrived as they were leaving. Ashamed that he had not come to Jesus' defence, he wanted to do something to atone for his cowardice, so he had brought seventy-five pounds of myrrh and aloes with him with which to prepare Jesus' body for burial. Joseph had purchased a new linen cloth in which to lay him and together they hastily wrapped Jesus' body with the spices, in strips of linen, in accordance with Jewish burial customs. Then they placed Jesus' body in the tomb and rolled a stone across it. Salome, Mary Magdalene, and Miriam saw where Jesus was laid and once the stone was secured they walked home and prepared their own spices and perfumes in which to anoint the body.

CHAPTER
— 39 —

They spent the Sabbath day together, anxious for it to end, that they might go and anoint Jesus' body. Mary spent most of the day sleeping and weeping. As she lay in her bed, she recalled every moment of his life, constantly replaying the scenes in her head: Jesus' birth, his first steps, and his first tooth. Jesus bringing her wild flowers, Jesus laughing, Jesus praying, Jesus healing people, on and on it went, moments now frozen in time. Mary sobbed uncontrollably and finally fell into an exhausted sleep.

As for the others gathered, their grief was also great. They had spent the last three years following the man they thought was the Messiah. They believed his Kingdom had arrived when he had entered Jerusalem the previous week. Never would they have expected such a dramatic turn of events.

Meanwhile, the Sanhedrin busily tried to ensure that nothing would stop them from retaining their power over the people. They approached Pilate and said, "Sire, we remember that while he was still alive that deceiver said, 'After three days I will rise again.' So give the order to make the tomb secure until the third day. Otherwise, his disciples may come and steal the body and tell the people that he has been raised from the dead."

Pilate laughed. "What are you so afraid of, you hypocrites? Losing your power, or knowing that you killed your Messiah?"

Ignoring the truthful sting of Pilates' words, they said, "This last deception will be worse than the first."

"Take a guard, then," Pilate answered. "Go—make the tomb as secure as you know how." He sneered. "But if he is your Messiah, not even you will be able to keep him in the ground."

So they went and made the tomb secure by putting a seal on the stone and posting a guard.

When the Sabbath was over, Mary Magdalene, Miriam, Salome, and Joanna arose before dawn and gathered spices with which to anoint Jesus' body. They walked outside the city gates toward the tomb.

"How will we roll the stone back?" Miriam asked. They stopped and looked at each other, not knowing what to do, for the stone was heavy and required more than one man to move it.

"I heard this morning that the chief priests have guards posted," Salome remembered.

"Guards?" the other women cried in unison.

"Whatever for?" Mary Magdalene asked.

"They believe that the followers of Jesus are going to steal his body," Salome said as she shook her head in disbelief.

"Steal his body! That is disgusting. Why would they think such a thing?" Joanna shuddered.

"I'm not sure—anyway, we'll tell the guards that we've come to anoint Jesus' body. They can roll the stone away."

"What if they won't roll it away?" Joanna asked.

"Of course they'll roll it away." Salome frowned. "They know our customs. We are his kinfolk. We did not get a chance before the Sabbath to anoint his body. Would they deny three women in mourning?"

"They might," Joanna said.

"If they do deny us, they'll have four weeping women on their hands, now, won't they?" Miriam said as they made their way closer to the tomb. "I know Cleopas would do anything to keep me from crying."

"Yes, but he loves you," Mary said. "I doubt we'll get any sympathy from these soldiers. They have been standing guard for three days. I imagine they'll be tired and angry that they've had to waste… their… do you feel that?" she said as the earth began to tremble beneath her feet.

"Earthquake!" the women screamed and fell to the ground as it shifted and moved beneath them.

"Well, this has certainly been a waste of time!" said the young soldier as he stirred the fire to keep warm.

The soldier with him nodded his agreement. "Six soldiers to guard a dead man? What was Pilate thinking?"

"He lets those Jews run all over him!" the first one snarled. "Two soldiers at the bottom of the hill, two at the top of the path, and us two here, plus a seal on the tomb. What are they so afraid of anyway?"

"Apparently, the chief priests think Jesus' followers will try to steal his body and claim he has risen from the dead."

"So why are we only here until this evening? Why only three days?" the first one asked.

"Who knows?" The other shrugged. "All I know is that there is no possible way anyone is going to get to this body." Chuckling, he added, "And if he does try to get out, we'll just push him right back in again!"

Their hoots of laughter were momentary, as the first tremble of the ground brought them up short.

"Earthquake!" they shouted in unison, trying to stay upright.

"Look!" the first soldier cried as he pointed to the tomb. The seal had broken and the huge stone was beginning to move. A bright, momentary flash blinded them and when their eyes adjusted an angel appeared before them, rolled back the stone, and sat on it. His appearance was like lightning and his clothes were white as snow. The guards, terrified at what they were witnessing, became like dead men and fell in a heap on the ground.

"It's over," Mary Magdalene said as the seizing of the ground came to a stop. They were lying side by side on the ground with their faces pressed into the dirt. Miriam lifted her head and looked around. Salome realized she had clutched a fistful of grass in her hand in a lame attempt to hold on. She slowly stood up and wiped her hands on her robe.

The others followed suit, dusted themselves off, and in silent agreement continued on the path to the tomb. As they drew closer, they saw two Roman soldiers lying on the ground.

"Are they dead?" Salome asked as they stepped closer to them.

"Perhaps they were hurt in the earthquake," Miriam suggested.

"They've not a mark on them," Mary Magdalene observed. Stepping closer, she boldly nudged one of the guards with her foot. The others gasped and jumped back, but the soldier did not move. "Well, they're not dead. I can see them breathing."

"What should we do?" Joanna asked, her blue eyes round with fear.

"We keep going." Mary Magdalene shrugged and began to walk bravely beyond the sleeping soldiers. The others quickly followed her and, as they approached the top of the hill, they found two more soldiers "asleep" on the ground.

"What is going on?" Miriam demanded. "Why are they all sleeping at the same time?"

No one knew the answer, and as they came closer to the tomb they saw two more soldiers sleeping. Sitting on the stone which had sealed the tomb, they encountered an angel of the Lord.

"Do not be afraid," the angel warned, "for I know you are looking for Jesus, who was crucified. He is not here, for he has risen, just as he said." He pointed to the tomb and motioned for them to go inside. "Come and see the place where he lay. Then go quickly and tell his disciples and Peter: 'He has risen from the dead and is going ahead of you into Galilee. There you will see him.' Now I have told you." Then he disappeared.

The women stood transfixed for but a moment before they made their way into the tomb.

"He is gone," whispered Mary Magdalene. She shook her head and fell to her knees. "He is really gone!"

Salome, Miriam, and Joanna fell beside her and began weeping. "Where could he be?" Salome asked. "Who could have taken him?"

"Why do you look for the living among the dead?" a voice asked.

The women screamed and jumped as two angels dressed in glistening white robes appeared before them. "He is not here. He has risen! Remember how he told you, while he was still with you in Galilee, 'The Son of Man must be delivered into the hands of sinful men, be crucified and on the third day be raised again'?"

"I remember," whispered Joanna, and as she said those words the angels left them.

Shocked, the women fled from the tomb. They raced back to Jerusalem intent on telling the disciples everything they had seen.

"Did we just have a dream? Was that real?" Salome cried as they raced back to the city. "Did we really see angels?"

"Is that something we would all dream at the same time?" Mary Magdalene gasped as she tried to catch her breath.

"What should we say? How should we tell the others?" Miriam asked. "Mary is going to be devastated—Jesus is missing!"

"Missing, Miriam? Did you not see the same angels we did? You should be thrilled, not sad. Jesus has risen!" Mary Magdalene said, her eyes shining with hope.

"But Mary, we did not see him. What if someone did steal his body, as the chief priests feared?"

They did not know what to think, and as they tried to process all they had seen and heard it was decided that Mary Magdalene would speak for them and tell the disciples everything.

"Remember, Mary," Joanna said as they approached the house where the disciples were staying, "talk to Peter. For he is the one the angels mentioned specifically."

"I will," she said as they knocked on the door and announced themselves. When they entered, the women darted across the room to Peter, who was talking to John.

"They have taken the Lord out of the tomb, and we don't know where they have put him!" Mary cried, falling to her knees beside the startled men.

"What?" Peter frowned. "What did you say?"

The women all started talking at once, making it impossible for Peter to understand them. Others in the room became aware of the women and their story and started questioning them as well. Frustrated that he could no longer hear Mary over the din of other voices, Peter stood up, his tall frame filling the room.

"Enough!" he shouted, waving his arms. "Calm down! One at a time!" When everyone quieted, he looked at Mary Magdalene and asked again, "What did you say?"

"They have taken the Lord out of the tomb, and we don't know where they have put him," she repeated loud enough for all to hear.

"Who has taken him out, Mary?" Peter asked. His usually pale face was beginning to turn red, an indication that he was very concerned.

"I—I don't know, Peter. That is—I mean to say—" Mary faltered, wringing her hands in despair.

"This is impossible!" John interrupted. "You've gone to the wrong tomb!"

The women's scathing looks silenced John. Peter, knowing better than to argue with women, opened the door, nodded at John, and said, "If he has risen, I want to know. If his body was stolen, I want to know. Either way, I'm going to find out."

"Stay here!" John said as the other apostles moved to go with Peter. "We can't all be running up there. We'll be back as soon as possible." He took off after Peter.

Both were running, but soon John outran Peter and reached the tomb first. He bent over and without going in looked inside at the strips of linen lying on the ground. When Peter arrived, he stepped boldly into the tomb. He saw the strips of linen exactly where Jesus' body had been, as well as the burial cloth that had been around Jesus' head. It lay folded up by itself, separate from the linen. He picked up the cloth and the linens to investigate them, half expecting Jesus to be hiding somewhere beneath them. Finally, after waiting what seemed an eternity, John also entered the tomb.

They stood in silence for some time, hoping that the two angels who had appeared to the women would also appear to them. Disappointed when nothing happened, they silently returned home.

After Peter and John had left to go to the tomb, Mary Magdalene started to follow them.

"Where are you going?" Miriam reached out and grabbed her arm, pulling her back from the door.

"Back to the tomb, of course."

"But John said to stay here."

"You can stay here if you like, Miriam," Mary said as tears started filling her eyes, "but I must find out what has happened to the Lord. I have to go back!"

Miriam nodded her understanding, released her grip, and said, "May you find your answers."

Peter and John were just coming out of the tomb when Mary arrived. They looked at her, their faces a mixture of hope and loss, for they really did not know whether or not someone had stolen the Lord's body.

"We are going back home," Peter mumbled. "Are you coming, Mary?"

She shook her head, suddenly aware that all the guards were gone. "I wish to be alone for a time," she said. They nodded and left.

As she stood watching them leave, she began to weep. As she wept, she bent over to look into the tomb and again saw two angels in white seated where Jesus' body had been, one at the head and the other at the foot.

"Woman, why are you crying?" they asked her.

"They have taken my Lord away," she cried, "and I don't know where they have put him."

"Woman." She turned around and saw Jesus standing there, but she did not recognize him. "Why are you crying?" he asked. "Who is it you are looking for?"

Thinking he was the gardener, she said, "Sir, if you have carried him away, tell me where you have put him, and I will get him."

Jesus smiled, and said, "Mary."

She turned toward him and cried out in Aramaic, "Rabboni!" She fell to the ground weeping with joy, reaching out to kiss his feet.

"Do not hold on to me," Jesus warned. "For I have not yet returned to the Father. Go instead to my brothers and tell them, 'I am returning to my Father and your Father, to my God and your God.'"

She whispered his name repeatedly as she lay prostrate on the ground, her happiness mingling with tears of relief. He was alive! The Lord was alive! She had seen him and knew it was true, so she went to the disciples with the news: "I have seen the Lord!" And she told them with great excitement the things he had said to her.

But no one believed her.

CHAPTER
— 40 —

I don't understand, Miriam," Mary said to her friend after discovering that she had also seen the Lord. "Jesus was my son. Why would he appear to you and Mary Magdalene but not to his own mother?"

"I don't know why, Mary, but I tell you—when we went back to the tomb to look for Mary Magdalene, we were on the road and suddenly Jesus was there! He told us to tell everyone to meet him in Galilee."

"Galilee? Why Galilee?"

"I don't know, Mary, but please come and join us for dinner. This is all very exciting! Your son is not dead, Mary. He is risen! Trust me. I would not lie to you."

Convinced that something exciting truly had happened, Mary joined the others for the evening meal. As the meal progressed, talk of the soldiers who had been guarding the tomb came up.

"I heard today that the Sanhedrin offered the guards a large sum of money," Philip declared, "telling them to say that we came during the night and stole Jesus away while they were asleep."

"Why would they make up a story like that?" Nathanael asked. "To admit to sleeping on the job could result in their executions."

Philip shrugged and said, "Obviously, they didn't think things through. But some of the soldiers took the money and are telling everyone that we did, in fact, steal Jesus' body."

"Some of the soldiers, Philip?" Mary asked, intrigued.

"Yes, there are some who apparently saw the same angels the women saw, and now they are believers as well."

A loud banging on the door, followed by muffled voices, caused everyone to jump. Although the door was locked, it did little to assuage the fear felt by every person in the room that the temple guards could be outside the door waiting to arrest them.

"Cleopas!" Miriam jumped up and flung the door open, startling Peter and the others.

"I thought it was your voice!" Miriam said as she hugged her husband. "I thought you would still be in Emmaus. Why have you both returned so soon?" She looked from her husband to Simon the Zealot, who accompanied him.

"We have seen the Lord!" Cleopas shouted as they came into the room. "Everyone, we have seen the Lord!"

"Tell us everything," Peter said, hope building in his heart.

"Well," Cleopas began, "we were traveling to Emmaus and we were talking with each other about everything that has happened. As we talked and discussed these things, Jesus himself came up and walked alongside us."

"But we were kept from recognizing him," Simon interjected.

"Yes, that's right. We didn't recognize him."

"Go on. Then what happened?" Peter asked.

"Well, he asked us what we were discussing and I asked him if he was only a visitor to Jerusalem, and didn't he know the things that had happened there these past days?" Cleopas continued.

"And he said, 'What things?'" Simon went on. "And we said, 'About Jesus of Nazareth.' Then we told him all about Jesus. We told him how the chief priests and our rulers crucified him and how we had hoped he was the one who was going to redeem Israel. We also told him that it had been three days since all this happened." Simon rambled on, not pausing to take a breath in his excitement to finish his story. "Then we told him about the women going to the tomb this morning to find that his body wasn't there and that they told us they had seen a vision of angels, who said Jesus was alive. Finally, we mentioned that some of our companions went to the tomb and found it just as the women had said, but him they did not see. And you'll never guess what he said to us!"

"What did he say?" Mary, Jesus' mother, asked.

"He told us we were foolish and—"

"Foolish?" Philip chuckled. "He said that?"

"Yes," Simon laughed, "because we were so slow in remembering all that the prophets predicted. He asked us, 'Did not the Christ have to suffer these things and then enter his glory?'"

"And then," Cleopas added, "beginning with Moses and all the Prophets, he explained to us what was all said in the Scriptures concerning himself."

"Yes." Simon nodded. "As we approached the village, Jesus acted as if he was going further. So we urged him strongly to stay with us, for it was nearly evening and the day was almost over."

"Keep in mind that we still didn't know it was him," Cleopas added.

"That's right!" Simon jumped in. "We still didn't have any idea who he was." Simon took a deep breath and continued, "So he came in to stay with us and when we were at the table he took some bread, gave thanks, broke it, and began to give it to us. Then all of a sudden our eyes were opened and we recognized him, and he disappeared from our sight!"

Everyone gasped and began to chatter. Some believed the report; others did not.

"It is true!" Cleopas shouted. "The Lord has risen and has appeared to Simon." He said this so that the other apostles would believe, for Simon was one of the Chosen Twelve.

While they were still talking about this, Jesus himself appeared among them and said to them, "Peace be with you."

Everyone was shocked and frightened, thinking they were seeing a ghost. He said to them, "Why are you troubled, and why do doubts rise in your minds?"

He walked around the room and said, "Look at my hands and my feet. It is I myself!" Spying his mother, he said, "Touch me and see—a ghost does not have flesh and bones, as you see I have." Overcome with joy, Mary wept as Jesus caressed her face. Smiling, he showed them his hands and feet, and while they still did not believe it because of joy and amazement he asked them, "Do you have anything here to eat?" So they gave him a piece of broiled fish, and he took it and ate it in their presence. Then he said to them, "This is what I told you while I was still with you: Everything must be fulfilled that is written about me in the Law of Moses, the Prophets, and the Psalms."

Then he opened their minds so they could understand the Scriptures. He told them, "This is what is written: The Christ will suffer and rise from the dead on the third day, and repentance and forgiveness of sins will be preached in his name to all nations, beginning at Jerusalem. You are witnesses of these things. I am going to send you what my Father has promised, but stay in the city until you have been clothed with power from on high."

Then he breathed on them and said, "Receive the Holy Spirit. If you forgive anyone his sins, they are forgiven. If you do not forgive them, they are not forgiven."

Then he disappeared.

Elated, the room erupted with shouts of joy and thanksgiving. So loud was their praise that they did not hear Thomas enter the room.

"What is going on?" Thomas shouted above the voices. He yelled again, "What is happening?" Still no one heard him. Finally, he screamed, "*Peace!*" The room quieted, all heads turning toward him with questioning gazes.

"What is going on here?" Thomas inquired. "No one heard me come in, no one heard me at all! I had to shout just to get you to quiet down. You can all be heard from the city gates! Have you lost your minds? Do we no longer fear the council?"

Everybody in the room seemed to have the same silly smile plastered on their faces and Thomas was just a little unnerved.

"We have seen the Lord!" Peter exclaimed as everyone started talking at once.

Besieged by the information coming at him, Thomas held up his hands to quiet everyone. Looking at Peter he said, "Perhaps you would like to speak for all, so that I may discern what has taken place here tonight." Peter nodded and began to recount the events of the day, beginning with Cleopas' and Simon's story, to Jesus' appearance moments before Thomas had walked in the door.

Thomas shook his head in confusion. "I know that you would not all lie to me, and I wish I had been here to see for myself. But unless I see the nail marks in his hands and put my finger where the nails were, and put my hand into his side, I will not believe it."

"Thomas!" Mary cried. "I am his mother. I would not lie to you. We have seen the Lord!"

Thomas took her hands and said, "Woman… I mean you no disrespect… but you have been in great pain these last days. It would not be unusual for you to suppose you had seen your son, simply because you want to believe he has risen."

"No!" Mary shook her head. "You are wrong, Thomas." The other disciples came to her defence, but Thomas refused to believe, as he thought the same thing about them.

"You are all in mourning," he said. "You're imagining things." And he refused to believe.

One week later, the disciples were in the house again, and Thomas was with them. Though the doors were locked, Jesus came and stood among them and said, "Peace be with you!"

As before, everyone was taken aback by his sudden appearance, none more so than Thomas. Jesus looked compassionately at him and, laughing, he said to him, "Put your finger here—see my hands." He grasped Thomas' hand and placed it on the scars left by the nails.

"Reach out your hand and put it into my side." Likewise, he placed Thomas' hands on his side where he had been run through with a spear.

"Stop doubting and believe," Jesus said, his eyes shining with love.

In shock, Thomas fell trembling to his knees and said to him, "My Lord and my God!"

"Because you have seen me, you have believed. Blessed are those who have not seen and yet have believed."

Everybody rejoiced that Thomas finally believed Jesus had risen. Now that every one of the Apostles believed, they decided to travel to Galilee, as the Lord had commanded them through Mary Magdalene. Not knowing what to expect but knowing they were no longer alone, they set off on their journey.

CHAPTER
— 41 —

Since most of the disciples came from Galilee, many of them returned to their homes to visit their families and neighbours and to tell them of the events in Jerusalem. Mary returned to Nazareth with Simon and Joses, while her sons James and Jude continued to Capernaum to stay with Peter and Andrew. Mary's daughters were distraught when they learned of Jesus' death, and perplexed when their mother and brothers kept insisting that he had risen from the dead. It would be some weeks before they, too, would believe that their eldest brother was, in fact, the Messiah.

Mary was thrilled to see her grandchildren again and surprised at how they had grown. Three boys and two girls! Oh, how she had missed them. There was much catching up to do and she and her daughters, Anna and Ruth, spent many hours together baking bread, washing clothes, and doing whatever other chores needed to be done.

"So what will you do now, Ima? Stay at home and live with us?" Anna asked one day. They were in the courtyard, grinding grain and preparing for the evening meal.

Mary shook her head and replied, "No. When Jesus was dying, he looked at me standing with John and said that I was now his mother and John was my son. John means to take care of me, so I suppose I will go with him."

"But why should John do that?" Ruth asked, hurt that Jesus had thought they could not care for their own mother. "You have your own sons and daughters to care for you."

"It's not like that, dear one," Mary said. "The disciples need guidance now, and I suppose Jesus thought my experience and wisdom would be of some help to them. For I am sure their journey ahead will be as wrought with perils and joys as Jesus' was. For they are young and impulsive," she remarked, recalling Peter and how he would often speak before thinking. She smiled in amusement as she thought of how James and John loved to laugh and play practical jokes on the others. But they would also often argue over petty things. "Don't worry, my daughters. I will be spending enough time with you that you will never miss me for very long. Now let's get this grain made into bread, or we'll have none for supper!"

Meanwhile, Peter was glad to be home with his wife Perpetua, in Capernaum. He was still feeling somewhat guilty since denying the Lord before his crucifixion. Perpetua tried to tell him that he should not fret over something like that, since the Lord was alive, but Peter could not shake the feeling of shame over how he had openly denied his Saviour.

"Everyone was frightened, Peter," Perpetua said as she gently caressed his face. "They all fled. Do you think they feel good about what they did?"

"Not everyone denied him out loud, Pet. Yes, they deserted him. We all deserted him when he needed us the most. But I... I denied even knowing him! And he knew I would do it! I will never forget his look when that rooster crowed. It cut right through me."

Perpetua hugged her husband and said, "I am sorry for what you are going through. I think, however, that the Lord would not be so hard on you. Why don't you go fishing tonight? It will take your mind off things for a while."

Peter nodded and said, "You are a good and wise woman." He kissed her. "I'll do just that." He could hear the water lapping at the boats and his heart stirred to be at sea. He stepped outside the house and headed toward the Sea of Galilee. *How fortunate we are,* he thought, *to live so close to the sea.* He took a deep breath and released his tension. *Yes, fishing will be good,* he thought.

Thomas, Nathanael, James, and John were sitting on the beach with the others when they spotted Peter heading toward his boat.

"Peter!" James yelled. "Where are you going?"

"I'm going out to fish," he said as he checked his nets.

"We'll go with you," James responded. John put the fire out and they all headed over to the boat.

They spent the night casting the nets but caught nothing. Discouraged, they decided to head back to shore.

While they were still a ways out, someone yelled to them from shore. "Friends, haven't you any fish?"

"No," they answered.

The stranger pointed at the water. "Throw your net on the right side of the boat and you will find some."

When they did, they were unable to haul the net in because of the large number of fish.

Then John said to Peter, "It is the Lord!"

As soon as Peter heard him say that, he wrapped his outer garment around himself—for he had taken it off—and jumped into the water. The other disciples followed in the boat, towing the net full of fish. When they landed, they saw a fire of burning coals with fish on it, and some bread.

Jesus said to them, "Bring some of the fish you caught."

So Peter climbed aboard and helped the others drag the net ashore. It was full of large fish, 153 of them, but even with so many the net was not torn. Jesus said to them, "Come and have breakfast."

They came quietly and reverently. None of the disciples dared ask, "Who are you?" They knew it was the Lord.

When the fish was cooked, Jesus took the bread and gave it to them, and did the same with the fish. Everyone was silent while they ate, enjoying the food and just being in the presence of the Lord again.

When they had finished eating, Jesus motioned for Peter to walk with him along the beach.

"Simon son of Jonah, do you truly love me more than these?" He waved to those remaining by the fire.

"Yes, Lord," he said. "You know I love you."

Jesus nodded and said, "Feed my lambs."

Peter knew that Jesus often referred to the lost as his "sheep," or "lambs," so he acknowledged his understanding with a nod.

A moment passed and Jesus said, "Simon son of Jonah, do you truly love me?"

Peter frowned and answered, "Yes, Lord, you know I love you." He felt confused that Jesus would need to ask him a second time.

Jesus said, "Take care of my sheep." They walked in silence for a while, then Jesus asked a third time, "Simon son of Jonah, do you love me?"

Peter was hurt then, and in anguish he cried, "Lord, you know all things! You know I love you!"

Jesus repeated, "Feed my sheep." Then Jesus turned and put his hands on Peter's shoulders. Looking directly into his eyes, he said, "I tell you the truth, when you were younger, you dressed yourself and went where you wanted. But when you are old, you will stretch out your hands and someone else will dress you and lead you where you do not want to go." Jesus said this to indicate the kind of death by which Peter would glorify God.

Then Jesus said to him the same thing he had said three years before: "Follow me!"

Peter smiled through watery eyes. He had denied Jesus three times and declared his devotion for Jesus three times. He felt a heavy burden lift from his shoulders and affectionately squeezed the Lord's arm in thanks. He was forgiven and he was overcome by the love that flowed out from His Saviour toward him.

Peter turned and saw John following them. As he watched John approach, Peter asked, "Lord, what about him?"

Jesus answered, "If I want him to remain alive until I return, what is that to you? You must follow me."

Later that day, Jesus met the eleven disciples at a mountain he had told them to go to and said to them, "All authority in heaven and on earth has been given to me. Therefore, go and make disciples of all nations, baptizing them in the name of the Father and of the Son and of the Holy Spirit, and teaching them to obey everything I have commanded you. And surely I am with you always, to the very end of the age."

———

"After that, John came and took me back to Jerusalem to live with him, because everyone was going back there. Jesus did not want the disciples to leave the city until we had all been empowered by His Holy Spirit to carry out His great commission," Mary said to those around her, as she waited for the ship to dock.

"He appeared to us over a period of forty days. He often ate with us. It was dreamlike." She tried to explain, "He was supposed to be dead, but he was alive. It was… it was… remarkable." She could not describe the feeling she'd had whenever he appeared.

"On one occasion, while he was eating with us, he commanded us not to leave Jerusalem, but to wait for the gift our Heavenly Father promised, which we had heard Jesus speak about. For John baptized with water, he said, but in a few days you will be baptized with the Holy Spirit."

"This Spirit… would it empower you to take over the Roman Empire?" Julius asked, wondering about the fate of his fellow citizens, for during the journey he had come to believe that Jesus was indeed the Son of God.

"Well, when we met together, we asked him if he was going to restore the kingdom of Israel. He said that it was not for us to know the times or dates the Father has set by his own authority. But he did tell us we would receive power when the Holy Spirit came upon us and that we would be his witnesses in Jerusalem, in all Judea and Samaria, and to the ends of the earth.

"Then, he took the eleven Apostles out to the vicinity of Bethany and he lifted up his hands and blessed them. While he was blessing them, he was taken up before their eyes, and a cloud hid him from their sight." She laughed. "They must have looked awfully strange to anyone passing by."

"Why do you say that?" someone asked.

"Because, according to John, they just stood there looking up into the heavens—not sure if he was coming back, not sure if they should leave. In fact, they really didn't want to leave, because now he was gone and it was kind of frightening to be on their own."

"So what did they do, Mary?" Luke asked.

"While they were looking up into the sky, two men dressed in white stood before them. And they said, 'Men of Galilee, why do you stand here looking into the sky? This same Jesus, who has been taken from you into heaven, will come back in the same way you have seen him go into heaven.'"

"He's coming back?" Julius cried.

Mary laughed and said, "Yes! He is coming back! Which is why I urge each one of you to repent, turn from your sins all of you, and be baptized in the name of Jesus. For we do not know the day or the hour of his return and there is no other name under heaven, no other god, no other way, in which to be saved."

Moved by all they had heard, several men came forward wanting to be baptized, so Luke agreed to take them down to the beach when they disembarked to do that very thing. But some stood back, still not convinced that Jesus was the only way.

Luke noticed them and said, "Men, what you have heard from this woman is true. She benefits in no way by revealing to you that she is a Christian, for you all know what is happening to us in Rome. We risk our very lives by talking to you. God has used her in a mighty way and she has revealed His Son to you. Jesus died for you—as his mother said. He sacrificed himself to save you from the fires of hell. He took your punishment! No one deserves the gift of salvation Jesus offers us, but in his loving mercy, our Father wants us to take it, to come back into fellowship with Him. Our Heavenly Father loves us with a consuming passion! So much so, He sent His only Son to take upon himself the sins of the world, so that whoever believes in Him might have eternal life and not perish. Jesus has made the way possible for you to approach his Heavenly Father. Do not reject Him, for today is the day of your salvation!"

Mary rejoiced as more people recognized Jesus as their Messiah and committed their lives to following him. It was a wonderful thing to behold. Luke sent a runner to John, telling him to come quickly to the Port of Ephesus, to help baptize new believers. John was at first surprised by the message and then excited, as he quickly made his way to the pier where the ship had docked. Together, he and Luke baptized over a hundred people that day. Mary was overjoyed, and as each one gave their life to God they would go to her and receive a special blessing, an encouraging word, or a hug. There was much rejoicing, and the new disciples added to the number of the Church in Ephesus.

As the day wore on, however, Mary started to weaken. It seemed as if she had been saving her strength until they reached Ephesus. She could no longer hide her pain from those surrounding her and, although she never complained, everyone knew she was struggling.

It was late in the day when Luke and John finished ministering to the people. John became alarmed at the deathly pallor on Mary's face. Luke noticed it as well, so they said their goodbyes and quickly took her home.

That night, after Mary had retired to bed, John asked Luke how she was faring.

"She has a very strong will," Luke said. "But I'm afraid a strong will is not going to overcome her obvious physical ailments."

"She has lost a great deal of weight since I saw her last. I know she's in pain. I see her grimace and struggle from time to time," John commented.

"I agree with you. At times, she can barely move. I've noticed the weight loss as well. I've also observed that her breathing is extremely laboured." Luke paused and said, "I do not know what is causing it, as she will not confide in me, nor will she let me examine her. I think her days may be coming to an end."

"I will take good care of her, Luke. Do not worry. She is more than just my aunt, you know—she is like my mother as well. Her last days will be good ones."

"I know, Brother… I know." Luke had grown quite attached to Mary, as had all the disciples. She was their last link to the Lord. When they looked at her, they saw Jesus, and the two men felt they were losing a part of themselves.

When they said goodbye the next day, Mary knew she would not see Luke again. Luke sensed it, too. "Mary, will I see you again?"

She smiled at him and, remembering the comforting words Jesus had offered her that Passover night so long ago, she said, "In the coming Kingdom, we will spend much time together."

Luke kissed the top of her head and, hugging her close, he whispered, "I'll be seeing you then."

Six weeks later, she was gone. John held her in his arms and wept. As he had watched her struggle to breathe, grief overcame him and many times he was tempted to heal her, a gift he and the other Apostles had received from the Lord on Pentecost, when the Holy Spirit had come upon them. However, he knew that would be using the power bestowed on him for selfish reasons. With great sadness, he watched her slip away. However, before she passed, Mary reminded him, "John, I will see you again."

Eyes tearing, he kissed her forehead. "Yes, in the coming Kingdom we will spend much time together."

She rubbed his hand in comfort, closed her eyes and, with a faint whisper, said, "I'll be seeing you then."

EPILOGUE

When Luke heard from John that Mary had died, he returned as quickly as he could. He arrived to find a large crowd gathered outside John's home. Hundreds of others who had known her came during the week to mourn her passing.

Of the Chosen Twelve, three remained and came together to remember the woman who had been such an inspiration to them. They were Matthias—elected to replace Judas after he had hung himself—Thomas, and James the Younger, the rest having been martyred for their faith.

James, Mary's nephew and John's brother, had been the first to suffer martyrdom. He was beheaded around 44 A.D. Peter was crucified in 67 A.D., during Nero's reign. He was hung upside down on a cross at his own insistence, as he felt himself unworthy to die in the same manner as his Lord. His brother Andrew was martyred two years later, also suffering crucifixion. Philip, Nathanael, Jude, and Simon the Zealot were all crucified. Matthew was tortured to death in Ethiopia by the people to whom he was witnessing.

As Luke pondered the fates of his fallen brothers in Christ, he wondered how his own life would end. He knew that whatever the Lord called him to do, he would do it willingly. That much he had learned from Mary—obedience and trust—something she had shown since the first angel appeared to her.

As Luke rounded the corner from the house, he took a well-worn path that led him outside the city. As he drew closer to Mary's tomb, he noticed how quiet everything was, with the occasional cooing of a dove floating to him on the wind. The path led him directly into a little grove that housed a garden of fresh blossoms, which added sweetness to the air. He found John sitting on a familiar bench outside the tomb.

"Well, here we are again, my brother." John motioned for Luke to join him on the bench.

As Luke approached, he recognized it immediately. "Whose idea was this?" he asked as he sat beside John.

"Mine. She would like knowing her bench was close by, don't you think?"

Luke studied John for a moment. He grinned. "I never would have guessed you could be so sentimental."

John shrugged. "It's a nice place to come to pray and meditate. Why not have someplace comfortable to sit?"

"Why not, indeed?" They sat in silence, remembering the sight of Mary on her bench. She had always had a knack for being on it at just the right time, for someone would inevitably arrive and she would be the first one to greet them.

"Why do I feel like I should have a bowl in my lap?" Luke said suddenly.

John chuckled. "I have some peas that need shelling, if you're up to it."

Luke grinned and shook his head. "I think my days of women's work have finally come to an end, my friend. It's time I moved on."

Again they fell silent, lost in their memories of all those who had gone before them.

"I wanted to see you before I left, John. I'm on my way to Greece… the Lord has shown me that I will not return."

John nodded, his heart sinking at what might await his friend. Luke reached into his robe, pulled out several scrolls, and handed them to John.

"What's this?" John asked.

"Do you remember my friend Theophilus?"

"I believe so—a Roman officer, isn't he?"

"And a believer as well. Many years ago, I wanted to start a written account of Jesus' life. I went and talked to Mary and she shared some remarkable stories with me and with Matthew about the Lord's birth and his childhood. This is my half of that record. You knew Jesus personally, John. I never met him. I hope what I have written here will bring glory to his name. I am sending it to Theophilus, in the hopes that he and others will know the exact truth about what they have been taught. I want to make sure that the gospel message it holds is accurate. Will you read it for me, before I send it off?"

John looked at the letter in his hand and smiled. "The Gospel According to Luke. I'm sure it will be just fine."